LESS THAN

A.D. LONG

ZADA PRESS

FIRST EDITION

Identifiers: ISBN 978-1-7390718-0-6 (EPUB) | ISBN 978-1-7390718-1-3 (paperback) | ISBN 978-1-7390718-3-7 (audiobook)

This novel is entirely a work of fiction. The names, characters and incidents portrayed in it are the work of the author's imagination. Any resemblance to actual persons, living or dead, events or localities is entirely coincidental.

Excerpts from *In the Realm of Hungry Ghosts: Close Encounters with Addiction* reprinted with permission from Dr. Gabor Maté.

Cover illustration © 2023 Michael Bernier @michaelbernierart

Edited by Heather Sangster, Strong Finish Editorial Design

ZADA PRESS
www.zadapress.ca

To Josh, my partner in everything. Without you, none of this would've been possible.

And to my dad who, unlike so many, made it through.

PROLOGUE

"I TOLD YOU NOT TO CALL ME."

The voice on the other end of the phone is barely louder than a whisper.

He lets his head fall forward, tears stinging behind his exhausted eyes. "I know. I'm sorry, okay? Please. I don't want to make you uncomfortable, but I don't have anybody else." He wipes his nose, adding a wet line to the crusted trails on the arm of the sweatshirt he's been wearing for more than a week.

"Right."

"Look, I don't know what you want me to say, other than I'm sorry. I know I fucked up. And I only called because I'm desperate." Picking at an old scab, he waits until he can no longer stand the silence. "I get it. You hate me. You're pissed at me. I mean, considering what you've been told, I don't blame you. But I'm not what you think I am. I've made mistakes—a lot of fucking mistakes—but that doesn't make me a monster. I've never done—would never do—anything to hurt you. You have to know that." He swallows against the lump in his throat. "Whatever you think of me—not all this shit you're being fed, but what you actually think of me—just know it can't be any worse than what I already think of myself."

A long minute passes, each second marked by the thrum of his heartbeat pounding in his head. Finally, a loud sigh.

"What do you expect me to do?"

"Come meet me. I want to see you. Just a few minutes so I can explain what actually happened."

"So, you called because you miss me?"

"Well, yeah. Obviously I do." His ears burn hot. "And I think you deserve to know the truth." If only it was that simple. He takes a deep breath. "But also, I could really use some help. Things aren't lining up like I hoped they would. I just need a hand to get my feet under me." He squeezes his eyes shut, ashamed at what he's said and what he has left to say. "But, please... Please, just don't tell anyone, okay? I'm counting on you, so, please, don't let me down."

PART I

People jeopardize their lives for the sake of making the moment livable. Nothing sways them from the habit—not illness, not the sacrifice of love and relationship, not the loss of all earthly goods, not the crushing of their dignity, not the fear of dying. The drive is that relentless.

DR. GABOR MATÉ, *IN THE REALM OF HUNGRY GHOSTS: CLOSE ENCOUNTERS WITH ADDICTION*

1

THE SUN BEGINS TO ILLUMINATE THE SHADOWS, EXPOSING WHAT went on under the cover of dark; the same will go on again tonight, and again the next, night after night after night. While the city stirs to life—graffitied rollers opening, shops reappearing, legitimacy restored—the unwanted remain tucked away in cracks and crevices, disinclined to start the day, a day that will have nothing more to offer them than had the previous, or that before it. The rumble of delivery trucks and the slamming of dumpster lids are unrelenting alarm clocks, reminding the uninvited that checkout is at sunrise; time to move on.

However, the wake-up call isn't necessary for everyone this morning. The wild-eyed man with the untamed beard isn't sleeping.

He unfolds himself—daylight relieving him from the burden of the night watch—stuffing the tattered blanket into his backpack, unbothered by the stink of his worn clothing. The weather is starting to turn, early summer giving way to warmer temperatures, but he's far too preoccupied to notice it's already fifteen degrees, or to consider removing a layer of clothing. He's rarely warm these days anyway, down nearly ten kilos, and it's easier to wear his clothes than to carry them. Besides, the last of the junk will be slipping from his bloodstream at any moment.

By the time the sun crests the North Shore Mountains, coming to settle high in the clear sky, the jitters are coming on strong. He staggers down East Waterfront aimlessly; luxurious lofts overlook their tent-dwelling neighbours, the *haves* involuntarily coexisting with the *have-nots.*

"So, are you like a cop or what?"

He turns around out of curiosity; not because he thinks the woman with the smoker's voice is talking to him, but because the mention of cops is enough to increase any drifter's heart rate, especially one who's living a double life. Standing face to face with an unusually tall woman, her scabbed face covered in a thick layer of foundation, he frowns in confusion.

"So, are you?" she asks again. "Actually, let me guess—you can't say, right?"

Having no idea what she's talking about, he looks over his shoulder, sure she must be speaking to someone else. She says nothing more, just stares at him with an unnerving intensity. His body is begging for a fix and he's getting more agitated by the second. Emotionless tears spill from his watery eyes. Swiping them away, he turns around, shaking his head, hoping that'll help organize his thoughts. He searches his mind, confirms he doesn't know her. He doesn't know much of anyone around here, quite on purpose. And since his deprived mind can't come up with any logical reason why this woman—wearing the skin-tight uniform of a sex worker—would be striking up a conversation with someone she thinks is a cop, he concludes that he must be hallucinating. He must've imagined her voice; maybe she isn't there at all. He does see things sometimes, especially when he waits too long between fixes.

He pulls his ball cap farther over his eyes and keeps walking. Chewing on what's left of his thumbnail, he tries to formulate a plan. He's spent every unremembered day on the streets doing what he can to avoid falling into the black hole of withdrawal, and today will be no different. Except that today is the day he's been dreading: having drained his bank account, he's down to the few bucks in his pocket, and last night he snorted the last of his supply.

"You know, on second thought, you're too skittish to be a cop."

He looks nervously over his shoulder, surprised to see a body to account for the voice he keeps hearing. Picking up his pace, he is acutely aware of the spike heels of her thigh-high boots scraping on the sidewalk behind him. His nose drips like a faucet, the throbbing in his head intensifying with each step. He's just trying to think— trying to make a plan—but he can barely hear his own thoughts over the rush of blood in his head, not to mention the sound of her stilettos scuffing against the pavement as she hurries after him. He can't remember the last time he ate, every precious dollar having been consumed up his nose, and after a month of sleeping in grungy alleyways, he's exhausted. He just needs a minute of goddamn silence so he can think. Stopping abruptly, the woman slams into him, knocking him to the ground.

"Oh shit," she says, her eyes wide. "Sorry. Jesus. Didn't realize you'd stopped. Not too steady for such a big guy, are ya?" She tugs at her bottom lip, a failed attempt at concealing a smirk.

"It's fine," he mutters. Shrugging off his backpack, he drags himself over to lean against a boarded-up doorway. He rests his head back, closing his eyes and hugging his bag to his chest. He swallows hard against a wave of nausea, trying to ignore the repulsive smell of piss that lingers in every street and alley in the Downtown Eastside.

He starts to chew on his thumbnail again but stops, hearing his mom tell him to keep his disgusting hands out of his mouth. He can't remember the last time he had a decent shower, let alone properly washed the grime out from under his fingernails. It's a bad habit, one he's had as long as he can remember—one of the many things about him that gets on his mother's nerves. She tried all the conventional methods in her fight against the filthy habit: bitter nail polish, rubbing his fingers in hot sauce, even painting them bright red, thinking that might embarrass him into quitting. When nothing else worked, she started smacking him upside the head anytime she caught him doing it, though all that did was make him more discreet. When she was within arm's reach, he relieved the urge by compulsively tapping his fingers, another habit she found irritating, and also tried to erase with force. Eventually, she gave up all together—the nail-biting easier to ignore than the incessant tapping—but she's never stopped reminding him how vile it is. "If you want to have disgusting nails, that's your problem," she said. "But just know that no girl is ever going to let you touch her with hands like that."

"You don't talk much, do ya?" He jumps at the voice, surprised to find the strange woman still standing there. "If I can't know whether or not you're a cop, can I at least know your name?"

Squeezing his eyes shut, he hopes she'll take the hint and leave him alone. He doesn't know what she wants, but he isn't interested. He's managed to survive street life on his own this long, and he's not about to start making small talk now. "Evann. And I'm not a cop," he says, afraid to open his eyes. "Now you know, so will you leave me alone? Please." He can feel her presence in front of him now—blocking the sun and casting a shadow over him—and he's quite sure if he opens his eyes, he'll be looking straight up her crotch-length skirt.

"Huh. Pretty sure I had a stepbrother named Evan. He's dead, though. Or maybe he's not the dead one. I dunno. Guess it doesn't matter either way. But you—Mr. I'm-Not-a-Cop—you don't fit in here."

He frowns. Of course he doesn't fit in here. Nobody fits in here, which is precisely why they're here at all. Skid row is full of society's misfits. The only thing they all have in common is that in some way or another, none of them belong anywhere else.

"What's that supposed to mean?" he asks.

"It means you don't look like the rest of us. You're skinny, but not too skinny. You got those fancy clothes—I mean, they look like they could use a good wash, but they aren't handin' out clothes like that over at the Sally Ann. Tells me you got money—or at least you *had* money."

So that's it, he thinks. *She's looking for money.*

"I really hope this doesn't come across as rude, but I'm not interested in whatever, uh"—he considers his choice of words carefully—"whatever services you're offering."

She lets out an obnoxious cackle and sits beside him. He scoots away, his eyes watering from the overwhelming smell of perfume and stale cigarettes.

"You're a real prick, you know that? You don't know nothin' about me and you just assume I'm a whore. Fuck, a girl can't even dress up nice without people thinkin' she's a hooker."

"My mistake," he says without really meaning it. In his other life, a girl getting dressed up meant she put on a dress that sat above the knee—not above the cheeks—and a pair of dangly earrings, not a crop top that showed her stretch-marked belly overhanging a perilously tight miniskirt.

"Just so we're clear, I'm not a hooker... Well, not officially," she says. "I turn tricks once in a while if I really need the cash, but that don't make me a hooker."

He grins, feeling the warm sun against his face. *So, you're pretty much a hooker then.*

"Yeah. Got it. Sorry if I offended you," he says. "But listen, I'm really not feeling too hot right now, so I'd rather be left alone."

"You're getting sick, eh? How long since your last fix?"

He opens his eyes into a squint, the bright sunlight too much for his pounding headache. "What makes you say that?"

She laughs again, the jarring sound reverberating in his pounding head. "Not my first rodeo. I know sick when I see it, and you, my friend, are dope sick. I mean, just look at you. You look like shit."

"Yeah, thanks," he says sarcastically.

"So you want some junk or not? I can get you pretty much anything, just tell me what you want."

"I don't need a dealer," he says. "That's not the problem. I'm out of money."

"Hmm. Yeah, that's an issue. Not gonna get far without cash."

He opens one eye just enough to see her perched beside him. She rubs her chin as though trying to solve a difficult problem, not understanding that even if she did manage to think up some magical solution, nothing will undo the two years he's spent ruining his life.

"Shit. Yeah, that sucks, dude," she finally decides. "I mean, I don't wanna scare you or anything, but it looks like you're new to this game, and what you're going through now is nothin'. Only thing worse than being dope sick is being dope sick out here. And you're just getting started, by the looks of it."

He doesn't respond. They sit in silence until a shopping cart, overflowing with plastic bags crammed full of bottles and cans, rattles to a stop in front of them. A shrivelled old man leers down at them. "Hey, baby girl. You're looking sexy this morning," he says, swaying side to side as if at the whim of the breeze.

"Fuck off, Bear," she says, lighting a cigarette. "You know I don't do that shit no more."

"Real shame," Bear says, running his hand over his matted hair. "You probably already know this, brother, but she gives wicked—"

"I said get the fuck outta here." She jumps to her feet, sending Bear staggering back to his cart, a nervous smile exposing his toothless gums.

"Easy there, baby girl. I'm not looking for no trouble." Bear teeters slowly down the sidewalk. The makeshift walker and the crippled man support each other as they clatter away—the cart on three wheels, the man on one good leg, the other dragging limply behind him.

Anywhere else, a self-proclaimed non-hooker dressed an awful lot like a hooker screaming profanities while towering over a hunchbacked man of about sixty-five might've drawn a crowd; out here, it hardly warrants a glance. He watches the woman stomp after Bear, waving her cigarette around wildly. He leans forward into his backpack, relieved she's finally gone.

———

Doing a mental inventory of the items he still has in his possession, he considers what he can sell. He doesn't have much—mostly unwashed clothes and art supplies—but he does have a dead iPhone with a cracked screen, an old film camera, and a gold chain. He'll only be able to get pennies on the dollar for even the most valuable items, but without a better plan, he doesn't have much choice. Swallowing against the lump in his throat, he considers what it would mean to sell the necklace. It was a gift from his dad, and although he's done a lot of shameful things in pursuit of his next high, to sell the chain would constitute a new low.

Holding his hands over his ears, he starts to rock, unable to tolerate the sirens, the rattling buggies and carts, the incessant shouts and chatter of all these people—people with whom he simultaneously has nothing, yet everything in common. It's all too much. Too loud. Too raw. Too vivid a reminder of every wrong turn he's taken to land himself living among the destitute.

"Look what I've got." The singsong tone might have sounded playful if not for the harsh rasp of her voice. "Bear owed me a favour, so it's your lucky day," she says, nudging him with the toe of her boot.

"Can you please just leave me alone?"

"What? One minute you tell me you're hurtin', the next you don't want what I got?"

Evann tosses his bag aside, dragging himself to his feet. Anxious to get away from this crazy woman who's making his headache worse, he's about to walk away when he sees what she's waving in front of him.

"Where'd you get those?" he asks, fighting the urge to lunge for the baggie of pills dangling from her hand.

"I told you. Bear owed me a favour."

"I thought you said you weren't a hooker." He immediately regrets saying it, deciding right then and there—with snot dripping into his beard and an excruciating wave of nausea pounding his stomach from the inside out—that there's nothing he won't do to get his hands on those pills.

"I'm not. Fuck, man. What's wrong with you?" She starts to leave. "Besides," she calls over her shoulder, "Bear couldn't get it up even if I was willing."

He watches himself lunge forward, grabbing her arm with a firm intensity. "Look, I'm sorry," he says, loosening his grip. "I—please. I need those. Please, just tell me what you want for them."

2

INVISIBLE KEYS SLOT FLAWLESSLY INTO THEIR RECEPTOR LOCKS, serendipitous pairs releasing the anaesthetic spoils of Evann's perpetual pursuit. It's like reuniting with a long-lost friend. He hovers just beyond himself, not entirely awake, but also not sleeping, his eyes lazily tracking the movements around him. It's in this state that he feels most at peace, the space where he is conscious but lacking awareness, lacking attention, his thoughts allowed to wander innocuously, their sharp edges dulled.

"How did you manage to get these?" he asks in a drowsy slur, his mouth finding it difficult to shape fleeting thoughts into comprehensible words. He feels as though melted chocolate is flowing through him, every cell saturated with the satisfying and delicious warmth of the dense liquid. He allows himself to be pulled under its spell.

The woman, whom he now knows as Crystal, lets her head roll to the side. She blinks at him, her eyelids slow and heavy, but doesn't answer.

He nudges her, but she makes no effort to move, letting her eyes drift closed. His foot has gone numb under the weight of her head, but he doesn't mind. It's been almost two years since he's been able to get his hands on OxyContin, and he's going to enjoy the rush while it lasts. Having snorted one and swallowed the other, everything is finally set right in Evann's world.

Pills have become a delicacy. On pills, he can function; he can walk in a straight line, he can get himself washed and fed and looking presentable. But the thing with pills is that the game is rigged. The goalpost moves further and further down the field, demanding more, stronger, riskier substances to get the same effects. They're also expensive, and by the time Evann realized there was no winner in this game, no point at which enough would indeed be enough—once he started to understand the tightening grip of physiological and psychological dependence—it was too late. Sick minds, damaged minds, the minds of unlovable little boys in fully grown bodies have a funny way of shielding themselves from reality, and it wasn't long before the walls of logic fell, and heroin seemed a perfectly acceptable alternative to pills.

Ironically, the illegal stuff—the stuff that could put him away for years, could kill him, could destroy his life—is the easiest to get. Healthcare bigwigs decided that prescription drug abuse was a crisis to be managed and had started to crack down on the doctors prescribing them. Apparently, he wasn't the only one who took a liking to the long-lasting embrace of OxyContin because the drug company was forced to reformulate the pills to be abuse-deterrent. The garbage being prescribed these days can't be crushed or melted. No good for snorting. No good for smoking. No good for shooting. No good for selling. No buyers: no suppliers. Every dealer on every corner has a steady supply of rocks and powders—heroin, cocaine, meth—but Crystal has managed to find the lucrative wonder drug, a drug so hard to come by that Evann had accepted he'd never experience its warm embrace again. It's the drug—that for him—started it all.

He looks down at this woman, a perfect stranger only an hour earlier, through blurred eyes. Studying her features, he wonders who she is, and why she's being kind to him. Beneath her heavy makeup, he sees a youthful face—covered in scabs and scars, but unwrinkled. She probably isn't much older than he is, but she looks a whole lot worse. Lying awkwardly on the sidewalk, her track-marked arm twitches, her eyes rolling open and closed discordantly as though she's a defective baby doll. Maybe she's genuinely willing to help him out, no strings attached. She could just be another lost soul looking for companionship.

It's a decision he suspects he'll regret, but she's caught him in a moment of desperation—a moment when he has nothing left to lose, when she has exactly what he wants—so he's decided to trust her.

She blinks sleepily. "How'd you—" she starts, licking her lips with a dry tongue, "how'd you end up down here?"

Shrugging, Evann considers the question. These days, he hardly has the wherewithal to find a private place to take a piss, let alone for quiet contemplation. That's a privilege reserved for the living, and he can't really be considered among the living anymore. Yet somehow, he's not quite dead either. He's caught somewhere in the space between, like a daisy at the end of summer after the bees take their bounty, the petals slowly wilting and falling to the ground, one by one.

"I dunno. Started with pills, upgraded to heroin when I ran outta money," he says.

She lets out a soft snort. "Right, just like that, huh?" Her bony arm strains against the weight of her hand, its fingers refusing to cooperate as she tries to snap them. Instead, her hand hangs open as she drifts off, swaying gently in midair as if it too has forgotten what it set out to accomplish.

He'd given her the simple answer, in part because the whole truth is something even he can't fully understand. He tiptoes into dangerous territory—lets his mind wander toward the past. He tries to think back to why he started—tries to pinpoint what exactly it was that made him feel so hopeless, so fragile, so willing to risk it all—but he can't quite put his finger on any one event. The more he lets himself think about it, the less he understands what it was he'd been so desperate to escape. And the less he understands, the stupider he feels. Compared to the path it has led down—sleepless nights and hunger pangs, sweat-stained clothes and ravenous cravings, an empty bank account and abandoned dreams—it's hard to imagine anything in his former life being worse than it is now.

"I actually started with oxy," he says, unsure if she's even listening. "Stole it from my mom. At first, I didn't realize I was getting hooked. I just felt better when I took it, and like shit when I didn't, so I kept taking it." The words come slowly, but it's a relief to finally say them. "If they hadn't stopped making it—like, the good stuff, I mean—I probably would've been fine. Well, maybe not fine. I guess I woulda run outta money eventually. But life was sweet on pills. It's the junk that ruined everything."

He sinks deeper into the sidewalk, his head lolling back against the wall, oblivious to the sharp bricks poking at his skull. From his daze, he revives the memory of a night not so long ago. He floats beyond it, unbothered, like an impartial witness, an outsider watching an unknown man pull the thread that will unravel his life. As the man leans over the coffee table, he watches, begging to feel the rush he's been craving since that first time the powder entered his nostril, flooded into his capillaries, rode the speedway to his brain, and bathed him in the most pleasurable relief he'd ever experienced. The feeling is just out of reach as he watches from above, the man's skin flushed, his entire being wrapped in a warmth more comforting than any hug. Evann had spent more than a year chasing what that first OxyContin had given him, but that night, as he leaned over that coffee table, the thrum of the bass reverberating through his body, all his worries—everything that was wrong in his world, everything that was wrong in his head—had faded away like fireworks in the night sky. And as his peers counted down, welcoming the year 2015, unbeknownst to him, he entered into a union with a lover who knows nothing of give and has an insatiable appetite for take.

His arm dangles in front of him, reaching for that powder, that feeling. Her raspy voice pulls him from his reverie.

"What are you running from?" she asks.

The edges around the memory begin to dissolve. He frowns, willing his mind to stay with it, willing his imagination to let him feel that feeling. She swats at him with a limp hand.

"What are you running from?"

The crease in his forehead deepens. "Huh?" he asks, sure he misunderstood her slurred speech.

"Come on. We're all running from something. Why else would we poison ourselves with this shit?" He strains to understand, her voice fading until he can barely make out each word. "So what about you? What are you running from?"

He doesn't know what to say. He's never considered it. Crystal snores quietly in his lap.

A lifetime ago, when he was a small boy, he sat in his Gram's garden, listening to her hum softly while she snipped dead blooms off her rose bushes. He worried the plants would be hurt by the cut of her shears, but she just chuckled, her face lighting up in a wrinkled smile. "No, sweetie," she said, her dirty hands cupping his flushed cheeks. "We remove the dead bits because it creates space for new life to grow."

Perhaps that's his problem, all these years later: He grew up knowing that he couldn't be himself, because being himself wasn't good enough. Over time, the diseased and useless bits had become indistinguishable from those with potential, and it was just easier to spray the entire garden with poison than it was to prune it. Turns out, self-hatred is a powerful venom—probably even more so than the shit he snorts up his nose these days.

He pulls himself back to the present, scrambling to avoid falling any further into the cruel darkness of his past, but his eyelids are so heavy, and he can feel himself slipping. The images from that desperate day are dull and distorted, locked away deep within the vault of his weak mind, but the feelings are vivid; the heaviness in his chest, the pounding in his head, the reckless desire to be free, unable to bear another moment in the turmoil. Evann struggles for distance —feels himself being sucked into the past.

———————

It might've been easier if he'd simply pushed aside his cowardice and killed himself, but being that he was too pathetic to do even that, he took the easy road, though it wasn't that calculated in the moment, and it certainly hadn't turned out to be painless.

About to leave home, to move to a new city, to step out of his life as a boy and into his life as a man, he hadn't known. Hadn't known what he was doing, hadn't known what it would cost him, hadn't known it would be the decision that severed his life into before and after. He hadn't considered the consequences, and he hadn't cared. He was young enough and dumb enough to believe it wouldn't happen to him—whatever "it" was. The horror stories he heard in high school assemblies, the mugshots of scabbed addicts with no teeth, the commercials and campaigns telling him it would only take one time—he hadn't thought about any of it. Even if he had, he was too desperate to give a shit. Too desperate to quiet his anxieties. Too desperate for a moment of reprieve from the filthy words—some his own, most those of others—that had been poisoning his mind:

What're you going to do with an arts degree?

You've never finished anything, and this won't be any different.

Are you sure you're good enough?

Why not do something worthwhile with your life?

It was easy to get that first fix. Probably a bit too easy. Avoiding the reflection of his tear-streaked face, he went into his parents' bathroom and pulled out an old bottle of OxyContin. It wasn't the first time he'd reached into that cabinet, abundant with a variety of medications for an endless list of insecurities and ailments: diet pills to counteract the munchies, Ativan to take the edge off, Gravol to fall asleep. Tiny consumable bandages to temporarily mask the symptoms of living, to provide some perceived sense of betterment, insomuch as a strip of duct tape could repair a torn hull. But the oxy was different: twenty minutes after swallowing that pill, it swallowed him. He stared up at the ceiling while it washed over him, absolute euphoria enveloping him before dissipating into an all-encompassing numbness, the intoxicating nothingness exactly what he hadn't known he'd been craving. What a relief it was. It was the first time in his life he felt nothing. No pain. No guilt. No shame. No hatred—not for himself, and not for the family he'd had the misfortune of being born into.

He's been chasing that feeling ever since.

———

Crystal's head hangs heavy atop his numb thighs. He shifts his hips, the best and worst of it behind him. "So?" she asks without opening her eyes.

He shrugs. "I was stressed. About to start university, wasn't sleeping, always felt anxious, and it was too much. My head was always fucking throbbing. Nothing was helping—not pot, not drinking, not drawing—so I figured I'd take a painkiller."

She raises her pencil-thin eyebrows, swallowing slowly against a pasty-dry mouth. "Yeah, but that doesn't answer my question."

He considers it again, struggles to gather what feels so abstract into something tangible, something explainable. In the two years since, his obsession has taken his past, his present, and his future; his dreams and desires; his safety and security. He's down to the clothes on his back, the last of his possessions carelessly stuffed into a ratty old backpack. He's tried pills and powders, prescription and illicit, uppers and downers, all in the fruitless pursuit of the euphoric numbness of that first time using. And the worst thing is, if he's being honest with himself, he'd willingly given it all—and he'd do it again—because without the smack, nothing feels right; but on it, there's nothing in the world worth worrying about.

"Myself," Evann finally answers. "I guess I'm running from myself."

3

Apprehensively, he follows Crystal, wondering if she has more junk stashed in her purse and hoping she's still feeling generous enough to share. Somehow, he doesn't remember seeing the handbag before she ran off to chase Bear. He must've been really out of it when they met because it's hard to miss—more a sack than a purse—and it reminds him of a spawned-out fish, most of its shimmering green sequins missing. He follows the bag, drawn to its sparkle, drawn to the mystery of what lies hidden inside. His mom used to carry an obnoxiously large purse too, but for all its potential, he never found anything more exciting in it than discarded receipts, spare change, and the house keys that always found their way back to the bag's deepest depths. It drove him nuts to stand there while she scrounged around, often ending up with the contents dumped out on the front porch, looking for those damn keys. Such an unnecessary problem, with such an easy solution. But the chasm between his tendency to apply logic and her tendency to apply emotion is just one of the many reasons he and his mother have always been an ill-matched pairing.

Evann allows his imagination to run wild, dreaming of baggie after baggie of pills filling the bottom of Crystal's purse; after all, she probably doesn't have house keys, so what else would she reasonably keep in a bag that big? He doesn't want to push his luck, so he keeps his mouth shut. He has a few hours yet before he'll really start clucking for a fix.

"So, you gonna tell me your story or what?" she asks, turning to look over her shoulder. She walks surprisingly fast for someone navigating uneven pavement on three-inch spikes. "Actually, hold that thought. I gotta piss. Keep walking that way, I'll catch up." She disappears into a stairwell.

She catches up with him a block down Alexander Street. "Where were we?" she asks as she passes him, not waiting for him to answer. "Oh yeah, you were just about to tell me your life story."

Rolling his eyes, he quickens his pace, hoping if he can get close enough, he might be able to peek inside her bag.

"I'm being serious! I know you got somethin' juicy. Why else would a good-looking guy like you end up in the festering asshole of the country?"

"I already told you. I moved here for university. Got hooked on pills, then heroin. Ran out of money. The end."

She spins around and marches back toward him. His eyes widen at the sight of her dilated pupils and frizzy black hair. She has the unhinged look of a captured animal.

"Let me get this straight," she says, poking him with a sharp red claw. "You come to me, hit me up for free pills, follow me around all day, and I don't get to know anything about you?" That's not how he remembers the day going, but he's well-versed in when not to argue with a woman with a hot temper, so he lets her finish her rant. "I mean, Jesus. I don't even know your fucking name."

He recoils, realizing he should've listened to his gut, never should've trusted this crazy stranger. "What? Yes you do. Evann? Remember?"

"Oh! That's right. Evann," she says, slapping her thigh. "Can't believe I forgot. I'm usually pretty good with names and faces. Sorta have to be when you're working the streets—not that I do that anymore. Anyway, I'm just gonna call you Evvy, kay? Definitely won't forget Evvy."

His cheeks blush beneath his thick beard. "Uh, no. Please don't call me that."

She shakes her head dismissively. "You got it, Evvy."

"I'm being serious. Please don't call me that. Ev is fine, but not Evvy."

Shrugging her shoulders, she turns on her heel, once again taking off down the sidewalk.

"Look, I don't know what you want me to say. I'm a private person," he says to the back of her head.

Stopping, she spins around again. "Let me tell you something, *Ev*. Being a loner will get you killed down here. You might think it's the junk you have to worry about, but it's not. It's being alone."

But speaking of junk... he thinks, taking a step back. He knows he should split while he has the chance, but he's like a magpie, drawn to the hidden treasures within Crystal's mysterious bag.

"You know what happens when a wolf gets separated from its pack? It dies. We're no different. You try to do this alone, you're gonna end up dead." She turns and stomps away.

He tags behind her wordlessly like a reprimanded child, watching the hypnotic swing of her bag. He's knocked from his trance by an unexpected blow. Keeled over, hands on his knees, he struggles to catch his breath. "Jesus Christ. What was that for?" he croaks, bringing his hands up to protect himself as she pulls her arm back, ready to swing the purse again.

"For starin' at my ass." She smiles, a slash of red lipstick smeared across her yellowed teeth.

He gasps for air, sputtering between breaths. "What the fuck are you talking about? No. I wasn't."

The smile dissolves from her face, replaced with a pouty frown. "Well, why not? Am I not good enough for you? Not pretty enough? Don't I got an ass worth checkin' out?"

"Are—are you being serious?"

"Nah, I'm just fuckin' with ya. Come on, let's go."

He shakes his head in disbelief. "Listen. You said earlier you might be able to help me out..." He can't bring himself to ask outright.

With the wave of a hand, she's marching on again. "Yeah, yeah. We'll see. Depends how good you are," she says, winking over her shoulder. "So let's hear it. We all got a sob story. What's yours? You an orphan? Kidnapped by a Russian spy? Get hooked on pills after falling off your horsey?"

He rubs at his stomach, a tender bump forming over his ribs. "No, I didn't fall off my horsey," he says mockingly. "I already told you. I dropped out of university. Got a bit too into the drug scene, I guess."

———

He was four weeks shy of his eighteenth birthday when he left home to start the visual arts program, and every moment of anxiety he had in the lead-up had been warranted; his every fear did, in fact, become his reality, and despite stressing about it for months, he found himself grossly underprepared for the transition. Not only was he immature and naive, but he also hadn't expected to feel handcuffed by the structure of the program. Prior to starting university, he drew whatever inspired him; he drew because it was something he was good at, something he enjoyed. He picked up a pencil and without strain, without effort, a beautiful image appeared, as though his movements were guided by something beyond his awareness. His work was never so much a process of conjuring an image as it was about allowing something to be expressed *through* him. But the curriculum didn't provide the time or space he required for that kind of authentic expression. To make things worse, he fell behind in the academic courses, struggling to learn the concepts, to memorize the theories and histories, and unwilling to buy the idea that anything he was being force-fed in lectures would improve his ability to draw. The subjects and mediums were indiscriminately assigned; every student

—whether illustrator or photographer, aspiring filmmaker or animator —was forced to set aside their craft in order to check items off some arbitrary list created by uninspired professors who were obviously more interested in flaunting their own talents than fostering those of their students. It was the antithesis of art as far as he was concerned, and while his peers settled in, he developed a crippling creative stutter.

Taking drugs turned out to be a widely accessible and socially acceptable way to spark creativity. By the time he turned eighteen, he was making his way through the long list of pills and potions the city kids were selling. Smoking weed helped tamp down his self-criticism, but that alone made him too hungry, too sleepy, and too placid. Most of his classmates used shrooms and Molly on the weekends, but all he managed to create while tripping were the stereotypical abstract patterns, minus the bright colours, which—as a realist pencil illustrator—didn't exactly fit into his portfolio. He rationed his beloved OxyContin as best he could, since, of everything on the menu, narcotics were the trickiest to get. But it turned out Adderall was a decent go-between. A quick online search provided a list of complaints, and after repeating them verbatim to the inept doctor at the walk-in clinic, he was handed a prescription for study buddies. Although the Adderall did make his anxiety a bit worse, it suppressed the munchies, improved his motivation, and helped him stay focused. He worked feverishly until his work was done, then popped a couple of Gravol, had a few drinks, or took a sleeping pill to come down.

He eventually fell into line, churning out assignments with the help of a revolving cocktail of weed, alcohol, Adderall, and anything else he could get his hands on. In high school, he was an art nerd; at this school, so was everyone else, the difference being they were considered "creative" and "imaginative" rather than "losers" and "freaks." To his surprise, he started to enjoy the social aspects of university life; stoned Evann was a lot more talkative and outgoing than sober Evann. He felt a pleasant weightlessness when he used. Everything was a bit easier—as if his mind and body floated buoyantly in a warm sea. Maybe he could've continued on that way. Maybe he even would've completed his degree, proven his mom wrong, and shown the value of his work. He should've known the dangers of floating out beyond the horizon, but he remained ignorantly unaware that he was gradually drifting toward a ruthless whirlpool. Even as he was being pulled closer, bobbing just at the edge of the vortex, he refused to see his accelerating drug use as a problem. Turns out that denial is a powerful weapon of self-destruction.

———

"Hmm," Crystal says with a snort, "I can relate to that. Not the university shit—I didn't even finish high school—but it's easy to get sucked in. 'Specially down here with nothin' better to do. What'd you study?"

"Visual arts."

"Yeah, I don't know what that means."

"I was an illustrator."

"Was?"

"Well, yeah, technically. I haven't picked up a pencil in months."

"How come?"

"Uh, spending my days worrying about where I'll find my next fix hasn't exactly been inspiring."

"So, like, you moved here and went to some fancy school just to learn how to draw? Wait, no—sorry—'illustrate.' I mean, I didn't know that was even a thing. I've been hustling out here since that bitch foster mom kicked me out in, like, grade nine. Meanwhile, you rich kids are going around getting degrees in arts and crafts? That's fucked."

"You sound like my mom."

"At least you have a mom."

Easy for you to say, he thinks. *You don't know her.*

They walk silently for what feels like hours before finally reaching their destination—the place Crystal has insisted on dragging him to. After a moment of hesitation, he ducks through a gap in the chain-link, following her along a graffitied wall. "I don't think we're supposed to be in here," he says, looking around.

He feels the vibration deep within his chest for several seconds before he sees its source.

"Hurry up," she says, starting to run.

He struggles to keep up, his heavy pack swaying back and forth as he runs along the tracks, the light in the distance growing larger and larger as he and the train hurry toward each other. She makes a sudden left, and he follows her into the narrow space between two dilapidated buildings.

Shoulder to shoulder they sit, watching as the freight trains rumble by, the shrill blast of their horns reverberating off the walls around them. It's terrifying and thrilling.

"Do you ever think about what will happen when the big one comes?"

She turns her head to face him. Even in the dim light of dusk, he can see confusion in her glassy brown eyes.

"You know—the big earthquake? The one they keep talking about? Doesn't the feeling of the trains going by remind you of an earthquake?"

Shaking her head, she reclines back on her elbows.

As information whorls around his head, facts and statistics and likelihoods jostling for his attention, he finds himself getting irritated. If she understood how serious an event it would be, surely she wouldn't be so nonchalant about it. "But, like, you do understand there's a pretty good chance there will be a megaquake in our life-time, don't you? Like a ten percent chance. Even a magnitude 7, which actually isn't that significant—"

"Dude. Are you really still talking?"

Evann feels his ears grow hot. He's thankful she doesn't open her eyes, doesn't see his shame burning red on his fair skin.

"You worry too much. You know that?"

He shrugs. There's something in the tone of her voice that stings. They barely know each other, so he shouldn't care, but her comment makes him feel small, reminds him of something his mother would say. He's always struggled with anxiety—even as a little kid, long before he had the language to call it that. His mom, who was impatient with him even on a good day, had never taken much interest in helping him manage his worry. He tries to ignore the familiar feeling of shame churning in his stomach. If he can just get his hands on another pill, or even a bit of down, he won't have to feel like this.

Evann hugs his knees to his chest, flooded with memories.

———

He must've been getting ready for preschool because he remembers his mom struggling to fasten the buckle on Nicole's baby carrier, his *Thomas the Train* lunchbox sitting on the counter.

"Mommy, I don't feel good," he said. It didn't matter what he said, or how he said it, she had little tolerance for his voice, which she found to be whiny and irritating.

"What do you mean?" she asked, rolling her eyes.

"It feels like there's something fizzy in my tummy," he said, fingers in his mouth.

"It's in your head, Evann. We're going to be late." She reached past him to grab the diaper bag, not noticing—or perhaps not caring—that it hit him as she swung it over her shoulder. "Jesus Christ, there's always something wrong with that kid," she muttered. Under her breath, but within earshot of impressionable ears. He didn't move, his mom's words stinging like a slap.

There's something wrong with him.

There's something wrong with me.

"Go get your shoes on. And for the last time, get your goddamn fingers out of your mouth!"

———

A tiny seed took root in the boy's psyche, growing into a vine that's crept its way into Evann's chest, down into his belly, up into his mind. It continues to smother him with its greedy tendrils. His breath catches as he feels it squeeze at his heart. He hadn't known it as anxiety then, but it's a feeling he knows all too well—as if an entire pouch of Pop Rocks is about to explode in his stomach. And it, like so many other feelings, is one he's eager to mute with whatever he can get his hands on.

4

IF HE WASN'T SO GREEDY, HE'D BE FEELING GOOD RIGHT NOW, not staring down the barrel of another comedown. He should've known better. Should've known not to take both pills Crystal gave him at once, but he was desperate to be set right, worried she might change her mind and ask for the second one back. He wasn't thinking straight, but then, it was his own stupidity that landed him in this situation in the first place—deprived enough to take what he could get—and he should know better. How many times had his parents told him to take responsibility for his behaviour? How many times was it drilled into his head that actions have consequences? Yet still, he's incapable of doing the right thing. He chews at his cuticle in an attempt to soothe himself. It won't work. He knows it won't; the only thing that can reliably calm his anxious mind is using, and with zero dollars to his name, getting another fix is easier said than done.

"Man, if I didn't know any better, I'd bet you were strung out on meth," Crystal says, watching his foot vibrate. "What's your issue? You got ADD or somethin'?"

He stares straight ahead, chewing intently on his nail, his teeth scraping back and forth, searching for the tiniest ridge to bite onto, wondering how is it that time—a concept so concrete, so universally accepted, so objectively measurable—can warp and bend and expand and contract into so many iterations.

Sixty minutes.

Three thousand six hundred seconds.

Three million six hundred thousand milliseconds.

An hour is an hour, but not all hours are equal—not in the life of an addict.

An hour on the nod passes in the blink of an eye; yet in an hour spent jonesing, time stands still, every millisecond a micro tear, threatening to rip him into pieces.

How many hours had he spent believing his own self-absorbed lies? How long had he been stupid enough to buy into the narrative that using drugs was inconsequential, that it was just something kids *do* in university? How many hours have passed since his life unravelled?

When exactly was that?

Was it back when he was buying pilfered Percocet from a clean-cut design student on campus? When he was using uppers to stay awake and downers to go to sleep? Did he cross the line when he snorted powder for the first time? Or had the line simply disappeared altogether, up his nose, along with his dreams, his ambitions, his money, his talent?

How many of the hours since has he spent void of consciousness? How many have been spent suffering, gritting his teeth through every excruciating minute between fixes? How many torturous milliseconds will he have to endure this time?

———

As always, the Downtown Eastside is abuzz—deals being made, tricks being turned—an all-day every day, all-night every night party where no one is having fun anymore and an invisible surprise in the gift bags might kill them. He knows it. They all do. But fear alone isn't enough to slay the monster in his mind. Maybe if he wasn't so preoccupied snorting a steady supply of drugs up his nose, he might've seen what was coming, and perhaps he wouldn't be out here relying on some girl he doesn't even know, terrified to buy drugs he can't even afford.

By the start of his second year of university, he wasn't using to feel more creative, or more focused, or more calm, or more social; by then, he was using because he had to if he was going to get out of bed in the morning, to go to class, to fall asleep at night, to function. He didn't realize how quickly he was depleting his bank account, how drastically his grades were plummeting. He felt blindsided when an academic adviser explained his options—which felt a lot like an ultimatum—after midterms.

"Evann, you're young," the woman said. Something about her oversized glasses, undersized nose, and straight brown hair reminded him of a mouse. "You're what? Twenty?"

"Nineteen."

"Oh, that's right. Well, university can be a big step up from high school, especially for someone your age. Sometimes people just need more time before they're ready. They regroup and come back when they're better prepared to meet the demands of the program."

Evann sat silently. He wasn't totally oblivious to his runaway habit, and it was true that he was using a bit more than he had the previous semester, but he'd hardly touched heroin since New Year's —not since discovering that crushing and snorting Percocet intensified their high. Add in an Adderall or two and he could find inspiration anywhere he looked. He was surprised to be having this conversation. His creative block was a thing of the past; he could easily pump out half a dozen assignments in a single sleepless night.

The adviser turned her screen, his latest submissions marred with criticism from his professors.

"Flat and uninspired," one read. The piece was a rough sketch at best. It looked as if an amateur had traced it and added some clumsy shading. It wasn't a finished piece, and it certainly didn't showcase Evann's talent. He felt a hot wave creeping up his neck. *Did I actu-*

ally submit that? I don't even remember drawing it. The adviser continued to scroll through his portfolio, pausing to read the next comment. "C minus. Not on par with what's expected at this level, Mr. Cartwright."

The final exhibit in the lineup was far and away the most disgraceful. "Incomplete. I'd remind you that this course is titled Drawing Collage, and that the course syllabus is very clear. My expectations were outlined in the assignment description. I'm not able to accept your submission. Make an appointment during office hours if you'd like to discuss a possible opportunity for resubmission."

He let his head drop forward. *Fuck.* There was nothing more to say, no explanation he could offer, no words to express the humiliation he felt, his ears burning. He couldn't very well tell this stranger that, although she'd caught him off guard, he wasn't all that surprised. Of course it would be only a matter of time before he was knocked from his pedestal. Evann's life had been one long game of lava tag: he could hop from the platform to the slide, the monkey bars to the walkway, but sooner or later, he'd slip up and his foot would touch the gravel.

"So, what are the options?" he asked.

"If you want to continue on, we'll have to put you on academic probation, in which case I'll have to insist you drop all your electives this semester to focus on your core course requirements." She leaned toward him, tucking her hair behind her ears. *Not a mouse,* Evann suddenly realized. *She looks like Arthur! That's who she reminds me of!* He suppressed a smile, then scolded himself for making light of the situation. He ran his hand through his hair, pinching the back of his neck hard, the punishment soothing in its familiarity.

The aardvarkian adviser continued, "Hopefully with a decrease in workload, your performance would improve enough that we could reconsider your probation for the fall semester. But honestly, Evann, based on the quality of work you've submitted so far this semester— and I'm talking about in every class, not just what we've looked at today—not to mention the number of classes you've missed, I don't think you're going to be able to improve your grades enough to enter third year in good standing." He felt her eyes on him, but he couldn't bring himself to look up from his lap, too embarrassed to meet her gaze. "At this point, I really think your best option is to apply for a late withdrawal. It won't impact your GPA, and you can take some time to recalibrate. You'll be able to pick up where you left off when you're ready to take this seriously."

———

"All right, Tigger, quit bouncing like that. You're stressin' me out. Here," Crystal says, motioning for him to come closer. She reaches into her bag and pulls out a tiny clear pouch. Its contents remind him of the baby teeth he used to tuck under his pillow, wrapped in toilet paper and waiting for the tooth fairy.

"What am I supposed to do with that?" he asks innocently.

She studies him for a moment before bursting into laughter, mascara-stained tears streaking her cheeks. "Fuck me, Ev. You're hilarious," she says, punching his arm playfully.

He laughs along awkwardly, his arm aching, too embarrassed to admit he wasn't kidding. Other than powdered heroin, he's only ever taken pills. In fact, he was only introduced to heroin by happenstance, having no idea what he was agreeing to when he was offered his first line. He hadn't bothered to ask, more worried about fitting in than what he was snorting off a stranger's coffee table.

It was only later, when he went in search of another dance with his new mistress, that he asked her name. It was only then that he was formally introduced to his China White.

5

EVANN STARES INTENTLY AS THE OFF-WHITE PEBBLES MELT IN the foil, transforming into a muddy-brown paste. After Crystal pushed the baggie into his hand, he'd held on to it while they walked back toward skid row, trying to guess what it was and what he was meant to do with it. Eventually, when he could no longer stand it— the tiny pouch sticky in his hand as his palms began to sweat with anticipation—he'd made his confession: he'd never tried chasing, never tried crack, and had no idea how to turn the gerbil food in the baggie into the vapour he's seen other junkies inhale.

Crystal takes the first hit, teaching Evann how to heat the rocks to just the right temperature, telling him when to gently suck back on the glass straw to allow the vapour to fill his lungs. It's harder than it looks, and after singeing the skin on both thumbs, it's clear he's too shaky to master the dexterity of holding the foil steadily over the flame. She smiles as she does it for him, coaching him not to burn the rest of his fingers on the hot pipe.

Within seconds of inhaling, every one of Evann's senses is heightened. A bitter taste coats his tongue, his nostrils filling with the smell of burning tires. Red and blue lights strobe in a vibrant, distorted pattern, illuminating Crystal's pockmarked face, the moon of his pupil eclipsing each smoky iris, his eyes unable to organize the blurred shapes into fine focus. The sounds of the world around him fall away, replaced with a reverberating frequency inside his head, as if his skull is a tower, his brain the bell, the clapper striking again and again and again. He's suddenly overcome with agitation, an uncontrollable rush of energy lifting him to his feet.

Never has he looked upon these streets with such intensity, such exhilaration, such curiosity. Everything he passes—the tarpaulin structures and overflowing trash cans, the tattered clothes and destitute faces, even the ceaseless bell ringing in his head—is irrefutably beautiful. Graffiti-covered walls become magnificent murals. The underweight prostitute—her stockings torn, skin scabbed, ill-fitting skirt hiked high—becomes an irresistible temptress. In the way heroin is the key to freeing his mind, crack is the key that opens his heart. The exultancy of the high is unlike anything he's ever experienced.

And the crash is just as intense.

What was beautiful minutes before becomes terrifying, the chaos and cacophony of the night assaulting Evann's disorganized thoughts. He is frozen in place, his stance widened, arms reaching, trying to steady himself on the unreliable surface of the earth beneath his feet. The ringing in his ears is replaced with the rhythmic thumping of blood forcing its way into his head, each hastened heartbeat slamming against the inside of his skull. Crystal grabs his outstretched arm. Evann flinches, but he doesn't pull away, unable to conjure any fight.

He's frozen.
Paralyzed.
Vulnerable.
Terrified.
And then, sad.
Heartbreakingly, profoundly, overwhelmingly sad.

Am I dying?

"Hopefully. Everyone will be better off without you anyway."
Why does it feel like my heart is about to explode?
"That's what unlovable hearts feel like, Evann."
I don't want to hurt my family.
"Don't worry about that. Your parents won't miss a useless son
—not when they've got a perfect daughter. Besides, you've
done nothing but disappoint them."
That's not true!
"Isn't it...?"

He's no longer able to distinguish fact from fiction, internal from external, hearing from thinking. He's become a spectator in his own mind, defenceless against the vulgar dialogue. There's nowhere to hide, nowhere to escape the assault of thoughts he knows to be true but is too weak to face—implanted beliefs that have festered since childhood, reinforced over and over and over again. Within the span of thirty minutes, Evann oscillates dramatically, as though he started off running, uninhibited, full tilt straight toward the open door of nirvana, only to reach the end of a cable—a bungee—the tension holding tight for a fraction of a second before violently thrusting him backwards, past the point at which he started, into the deepest depths of despair. It's a place so dark and so hopeless that he hangs, suspended in time, unable to discern living from dying.

Crystal gently guides him to a quiet spot on the sidewalk where they sit side by side, Evann shaking uncontrollably, tears streaming into his overgrown beard, his head jerking left and right as he struggles to make sense of his surroundings. The tightness in his chest is unrelenting. A pool of sweat gathers at the base of his spine.

A slight man shuffles along the sidewalk, coming to crouch in front of him. The man's black eyes are piercing, a long braid draped over his bony shoulder. He gently grasps either side of Evann's damp face, holding him with the tenderness afforded to a child waking from a night terror. His toothless grin comes into Evann's narrow field of vision.

"Hey, pal. Look at me, okay? Look right in my eyes. You're just overamping, brother. It'll wear off pretty quick, okay? You're safe, all right? You're gonna be okay." The man slowly eases himself to the sidewalk, his right leg—femur twisted and joint fixed at the knee— remaining suspended at an awkward angle. The ghostly figures lurking the street stare curiously at the mismatched trio.

———

As a child, there was an entire year in which, several times a week, Evann woke to find himself in the strangest of circumstances. Once, he was having a dream, and in the dream he was shouting at the dog, scolding her for peeing in the house. He'd seen it all with such vivid detail: There she was, a small puppy, her dark eyes staring at him apologetically while she relieved herself right beside his toy shelf. He felt the panic in his chest, not worried the carpet would be soiled, but that her smelly pee might splash into the bin and onto his Lego. "Stop that!" he screamed in vain. She didn't stop. Instead, she turned to him and shouted back, his mother's voice coming from the dog's mouth. He was shaken awake to find himself standing in his open closet—his PJs around his ankles—the unmistakable sound of liquid splashing onto the carpet and his feet soaked in a warm puddle of his own pee.

Another time, he was an ancient archaeologist, trekking through the desert in search of dinosaur bones. The hot sun was beating on his neck, cool sweat dripping between his shoulder blades. He'd just settled in, carefully laying out his tools, about to set to work brushing away the sand, when an enormous Pterodactyl swooped at him, its sharp beak opening in an ear-splitting screech. Terrified, he tried to run, his effort futile, each step causing his feet to sink deeper into the loose sand. He screamed as the desert swallowed him—screamed until he could no longer distinguish the Pterodactyl's screeching from his own—until suddenly the ground beneath him gave way and he fell—down, down, down. Just when he thought he might fall forever, he plunged into a pool of icy water. Kicking with all his might, he tried to get to the surface, his screams silenced by the water filling his lungs. He woke up in a cold bath, with a hand clamped over his mouth, his mom violently shaking him by the shoulders.

No one ever got to the bottom of what caused him to sleepwalk or to have night terrors, not that there had been much effort. An astute doctor might've noticed a pattern, might've asked why he only had them while his dad was away at work. Instead, the child psychologist reassured his parents he'd grow out of it eventually. For their part, his parents did notice enough of a pattern to force him into what were cleverly marketed as "Pull-Ups" after the peeing-in-the-closet incident was closely followed by the peeing-in-the-Christmas-cactus incident—though that one did become his mom's favourite tale to tell. Rarely was there a family gathering where she didn't revive his embarrassment in her obnoxious reminder that the plant had flowered for the first time in years after his special watering. The Pull-Ups had been short-lived; no nine-year-old could be tricked into seeing the marketing as anything more than a euphemistic front for a big-kid diaper. And besides that, in both the peeing-in-the-dishwasher and then the peeing-in-the-dog's-water-dish incidents, his untethered body was smart enough to understand that taking off Pull-Ups was no different than taking off any other underpants.

Fortunately, the doctor was right, and in the same sudden and unexplained manner that it had started, it stopped. The night terrors morphed into nightmares, which continue to haunt him as an adult, but now any time he jolts awake—his pulse racing, his breath ragged, sweat saturating his hair—he finds himself in the same place he'd gone to sleep, wearing dry pants. It's been over a decade since he was last trapped in a night terror, but this comedown feels just like it. He's exhausted by the time he stirs from the waking nightmare.

———

He finds himself sandwiched between an off-duty hooker and an unfamiliar old man—yet another piece of nonsensical information for his muddled brain to untangle. Maybe he's still caught in a nightmare. Maybe he will never fully wake up. Everything is happening so slow, but it also feels so fast. He shakes his head, trying to make sense of it all. Maybe he'll be stuck on the edge of reality forever, never able to escape from the fringes.

"There you go, my man. Better, eh?" The man smiles, despite his obvious discomfort. "All right. I better get goin' again. Can't sit too long or the leg'll seize right up."

By the time Evann can get the message from his brain to his body to utter a thank you, the man is gone, hobbling down the sidewalk.

Looking straight ahead, he quietly addresses Crystal. "I'm really sorry. I don't know what happened there." Shame envelops him. His voice cracks. "I really appreciate what you did for me, you know...that you stayed with me."

She takes a deep breath, exhales loudly. "Fuck, man. That was my bad. Maybe a bit too much for your first time. Why don't we go back to my place," she says. "You can sleep it off there."

6

THE LAST THING HE REMEMBERS IS TAKING THE HANDFUL OF pills Crystal gave him.

Three days later, he wakes up to a gentle tickle on his bare ribs. Groaning, he rolls to his side, his hand grazing over something soft, something warm. Something alive. His eyelids hang heavy, the task of lifting them momentarily insurmountable. Fighting to overcome their weight, he watches through crusted lashes as a fuzzy smudge squirms its way under the covers. For a moment, he's frozen, his delirious mind struggling to make sense of the unfamiliar surroundings. The air is thick with the musty smell of stale cigarettes. Mould spots the cracked plaster walls of the tiny room, and a floral sheet hanging over the window blows in the hot breeze. His back aches, bedsprings jabbing into his flank, his skin itchy against the filthy cotton sheet, and it feels like there are sharp claws scampering through his leg hair.

In an instant, he's up, wide awake, tangled in the sheet, and fighting to get away from whatever it is that's in the bed with him. He swings wildly, his elbow slamming into a tall dresser, its overflowing drawers haphazardly hanging from its cracked frame. A jolt of pain shoots through his elbow, rendering his hand useless.

"Good morning, Sleeping Beauty." He spins around to find Crystal, crouched against the door, holding a lighter to a glass pipe. "It looks like you got your beauty rest," she says, raising her eyebrows suggestively.

His head spins as he struggles to make sense of the situation. He doesn't know where he is, and he can't figure out how he ended up in a room with a girl he doesn't really know, wearing nothing but a pair of week-old boxers. Something drops to the floor in front of him, scurries away. As his eyes adjust to the dim light, he sees cockroaches skittering along the walls, suspended from the ceiling. From the corner of his eye, he sees something small and brown run along the bare mattress before disappearing under the bed.

"Jesus Christ! What the fuck was that?" Nothing is safe—the walls, the floors, the bed—every surface is crawling. He shudders. Whatever she gave him must've been crazy strong because there's no way this place is real.

"Settle down. It's just a little mouse. He don't bite." Smoke swirls around her face as she gently sucks on the pipe. "Besides," she says, drawing a long breath, "consider yourself lucky. Couple months ago a rat —a real big motherfucker too—fell into the tub while I was takin' a shower. Scared the shit outta both of us. The fuckin' thing was the size of a house cat, and too fat to get out, so there I was screamin' my fuckin' head off and this thing's tryna scratch its way over the edge of the tub or whatever." Her eyes are glossy, her movements spastic as she tips her head back to cough out a laugh. "The fuckin' scumbags that own this place still haven't fixed the ceiling, but one of the guys put cardboard over the hole, so at least I don't gotta worry about it rainin' rodents no more."

"What the fuck is this place?" Wide-eyed, he scans the room, taking in the water stains on the ceiling, the sticky, peeled linoleum beneath his bare feet. A boxy old TV teeters precariously on a stack of milk crates. There's hardly space to turn around in the cramped room, every surface covered in stuff. Next to the bed, beside a half-eaten burger, sits a Gatorade bottle full of frothy amber liquid. Rusty water drips from the sink in the corner. Between the slamming and banging and shouting of the neighbours, he hears liquid rushing through a pipe above them, bringing with it the pungent smell of sewage. Evann gags.

"Welcome to the Hilton, my friend."

"This is where you live?" he asks, searching for something clean to hold over his nose.

"Yeah. Why? You don't approve of the decor, rich boy?" she asks, sweeping her arm grandly around the room. "Only the finest for the scum of the city."

"I don't get it. Is this, like, a shelter?"

"Fuck no! This is mine. Well, I mean—I don't own it or nothin', but it's where I live. Costs me $400 a month to stay in this shit hole. But it's all I can afford, so whatcha gonna do?" Evann watches her jaw move back and forth. She stops grinding just long enough for another sentence to come spilling out from between her blistered lips. "Better than sleeping rough. Least I don't gotta squat behind a dumpster no more."

He pulls on his clothes as he looks around, bewildered. The hot air is stagnant—oppressive—and his unwashed clothes stick to his dewy skin. The sour smell of his sweat is enough to make his eyes water, but Crystal doesn't seem bothered. He has never been in such a repulsive place in his entire life. In fact, he's used campground outhouses that smelled better than this place does.

"How long was I out? And what the fuck did you give me?"

"Couple days I guess." She shrugs. "I dunno. A bit of this, a bit of that. Seems like you needed the sleep, though. Why—you don't remember?"

His heart flutters in his chest. Remember what? What happened that was worth remembering? He has no recollection, no memory—not of eating or drinking or doing anything to meet his basic needs. Obviously he must've gone to the bathroom at some point—by the looks of it, in a bottle—but he can't recall when or how, and he can't bring himself to think about the fact that she probably had to help him.

"Anyway, we gotta talk. You can't just keep freeloading off me. We gotta sort out a deal," she says. She picks mindlessly at a scab on her shin, unbothered or unaware that it's started to bleed, a thin line slowly crawling down her leg.

"Yeah, I know. But I told you I don't have any money."

"Okay, so I got an idea," she says. After several attempts, she manages to get to her feet. "My boyfriend was over, and he gave me some cash—"

"What? Your *boyfriend*? You have a boyfriend? And he was here? While I was here? Jesus Christ, Crystal. Are you trying to get me killed?"

She rolls her eyes. "Don't be so fuckin' dramatic, all right? My man's not like that. He don't care who I hang out with. Prolly a good thing you don't remember him bein' here, though," she says with a wink. "But don't worry. We stayed on the floor." He watches her rifle through the open dresser, discarding clothes and makeup and shoes at her feet, her frenetic movements oversized in the small space.

He massages the back of his neck, achy from God-knows-how-long spent passed out face down on the stained mattress. His head is throbbing. With a sudden realization, a knot forms in his stomach.

"Where's my chain?" he asks, frantically feeling for it around his neck.

"What chain?"

"My necklace. The gold necklace I was wearing. Where is it?"

"Dude, I don't got no idea what you're talking about, but you better watch your tone, all right? I didn't take nothin'. You musta lost it or somethin'."

"Fuck," he says, shaking out the crumpled sheet. "Fuck!" Down on his hands and knees, he peers under the bed. A floppy condom is plastered to the floor, a handful of used rigs scattered about—some capped, most not. There is no way he's reaching his hand under there. He sits on the edge of the bed, holding his head in his hands. "Fuck, fuck, fuck."

"Okay, so about the cash. I was thinkin', I can front you till you get your cheque on Wednesday, but I'm gonna have to charge interest or whatever."

He squints up at her. "Cheque?"

"Yes, cheque. It's Mardi Gras this week, so once you get your cheque, you just pay me back what you owe." She wipes the blood from her leg, licking it off her fingers. "Plus a little extra for the loan. So I figure you give me, say, $250 and we call it even."

"I literally have no idea what you're talking about? There's no cheque. And what the fuck does Mardi Gras have to do with anything?"

She stares at him through dilated pupils. "Ha! You're fuckin' with me again."

Evann shakes his head unknowingly.

"Mardi Gras? Wely?"

He says nothing.

"How long you been living down here and you don't know what fuckin' Mardi Gras is?" Evann shrugs and she returns to tearing a hairbrush through her dark hair, the splayed bristles only serving to make it even frizzier. "What the fuck, man? Are you tellin' me you're not on assistance, and you just spent like, what—a month—sleeping rough? By yourself? How the fuck have you been surviving?"

He honestly doesn't know. He'd had no other choice, had figured it would be like camping to sleep out under the stars. Only the stars were streetlights.

———

Once it was apparent there was no point in trying to salvage his academic year, Evann spent a few months keeping his shameful secret to himself. At first, he carried on with his normal schedule, waking up to his alarm and heading off to "school," but as his dependence on sleeping pills intensified, it became more and more difficult to carry on with the act. Fortunately, his roommate—a rather aloof and antisocial character—didn't seem to notice when he started spending most days isolated in his bedroom, so it wasn't until finals that everything really started to unravel. With no school, no job, and nothing much better to do, his "recreational" spending increased substantially. Unable to cover the summer rent without a roommate, he had no choice but to move out of his place. Reaching out to The Bank of Mom and Dad wasn't an option. Not only had they made it perfectly clear there would be no more handouts once the money in his education fund was gone, but he also wasn't about to explain how he'd spent enough money to cover four years in less than two. The coffers had run dry.

Seeing his savings dwindling rapidly, Evann broke his lease, pared his life down to two boxes and a forty-litre backpack, and moved into a friend's place. Once upon a time, he was stupid enough to think that he and Dani might end up together. Things with her felt comfortable and effortless, but when she introduced him to Amy, he was thankful for his cowardice—thankful not to face the embarrassment of her rejection.

Living on Dani's couch, he only managed to secure one freelance design gig—which, in the end, he overpromised and underdelivered. With not much better to do, he sunk deeper into his addiction. He spent a month bumming around in unwashed sweatpants, snorting lines with the bathroom tap running, and passing out in front of the TV, fading in and out of reruns of *The Big Bang Theory*. Had he not overheard Dani and Amy talking about how weird he was acting, he might still be living on her couch, but he was smart enough to know he'd overstayed his welcome, so he invented a story about going to stay with his parents for the rest of the summer. With nowhere else to go, Evann left his boxes behind and moved out.

———

"So can this Dani chick help you out? You still got stuff at her place?"

"No, I can't do that," he says. When he stopped sleeping at her place, he had the sense to leave some of his valuables behind. Going back for his MacBook and his camera equipment now would mean answering questions about where he'd been, what he'd been up to, and why, all of the sudden, he wanted his stuff back. If she laid eyes on him, she'd know he wasn't okay, and she'd worry about him—maybe even try to get in contact with his parents. Admitting one lie would risk revealing the entire truth of his humiliating situation.

"And you can't just call your parents?"

He laughs. "Absolutely not. They don't even know I dropped out. They'd fucking kill me if they found out."

"Okay, so make something up about you needing cash for books or some shit."

"No," he says firmly. The band around his head tightens, making it harder and harder to think straight. "Look, that's not an option. They didn't want to pay for my school in the first place, and I barely even talk to them. There's no way they're going to give me more money."

"You've got no money left in the bank?"

He rolls his eyes. Grabbing his bag, he begins to dig through it, laying out its contents for her to see. "Dirty clothes, more dirty clothes, underwear—dirty too, by the way. An old film camera that's probably not worth shit, my art stuff. When I say I'm broke, I mean it." He opens his wallet, shaking it upside down to prove his point. "Bank card for an account with like five bucks in it, credit card, student card, bus pass, BC ID, McDonald's coffee card. That's everything I have."

"Wait—what?" Crystal asks, a sly smile creeping across her face.

7

CRYSTAL LEANS INTO HIM, RESTING HER HAND ON HIS ARM. HIS skin burns beneath her touch, a wave of nausea surging up into his throat. She must notice the shift in his posture, the way his shoulders tense, the way he holds his breath, his gaze shifting back and forth from her hand to his sketchbook, because she quickly pulls it away, moving her attention to a scab on her ankle. They've spent the better part of a week going up and down in her dank little bedroom, but this is the first time she's touched him. She claims to have a boyfriend, and Evann thinks he's been pretty clear he's not interested in anything more than having someone to hang out with.

They've settled into a nice routine since she introduced him to the magic of the cash advance. He's paid off his debt, and thanks to his newest muse—speedballs—for the first time in several months, he has the urge to draw. With the blend of upper and downer—cocaine and heroin—he's found the perfect synergy. First, he goes up, and for ten frenzied minutes he draws, a flood of creative energy tumbling out of him, slowed only by the speed of his hand, never quite able to keep up. Trading his pencil for a Sharpie, he's covered the mould stains and punched-in drywall with an elaborate underwater scene of two orcas swimming through a bed of kelp. Crystal, with her preference for uppers, passes the time colouring in the mural while he spends the next few hours nodding in and out of reality, sometimes falling into a fitful sleep, sometimes slurring answers to her incessant questions.

He inches away from her, propping himself in the corner. Uncapping the marker, he lazily adds to the seascape, the pen strokes sweeping slowly across the wall. They've covered the basics, but her appetite to know everything about him and his situation is insatiable. She—who spent her early years bounced between aunties and uncles and grandmas and grandpas before being dropped into a system where there was no more stability, and a whole lot less people who looked like her—couldn't seem to wrap her head around how Evann could grow up in middle-class suburbia with a mom and dad, a sister and even a dog, yet still end up in a piss-stink alleyway snorting himself into a stupor.

"Man, I woulda killed for your life when I was a kid," she says, not for the first time. "Livin' at the same place all the time, mom there to cook me breakfast and shit insteada only gettin' to see her in some social services office, her twitchin' like she couldn't wait to get outta there. Fuck. You don't know how good you had it."

There's nothing to argue. He lets his head droop forward. *Jesus Christ, Evann. Don't you dare cry. Don't be such a fucking baby*, he thinks. It's true. He grew up privileged and he knows it, in no small part thanks to his parents' constant reminders. Nothing in his life has been bad enough to justify complaining; his childhood was a cakewalk compared to Crystal's. Every hardship has been of his own making. His mom was always telling him how lucky he was, reminding him that she had the power to make his life a whole lot harder. He still hears her voice sometimes, a devil on his shoulder regurgitating a lifetime of threats:

I brought you into this world—I can take you out.

Don't you know how fortunate you are?

Don't be an ungrateful little prick—there are kids starving in Africa.

Don't you know how lucky you are just to have a roof over your head?

I wouldn't have to spank you if you would just behave—if you'd just listen. Are you really so stupid that you still can't understand that?

How many times do I have to wash your mouth out with soap? Should I use Tabasco sauce instead? Do I need to get the wooden spoon?

He doesn't know how to explain to Crystal—who was dealt an undeniably shit hand—that there's more to a happy childhood than a big house and trips to Disneyland. What he's thinking—but doesn't dare say—is that for him, maybe a mom like hers—one who cared enough *not* to stick around—would've been a blessing. Instead, his mom was there, but she wasn't *there*—at least not for him. When she wasn't irritated by him, she seemed to find his tics amusing, mocking him relentlessly for what she thought of as his "neurotic tendencies," purposely creating chaos as he fought to create order. Almost as if he was birthed by the wrong woman, his insecure and clingy nature such a stark contrast to her don't-give-a-damn demeanour. Sometimes for no reason at all, he felt like he was caught in a snowstorm, icy flakes stinging his bare cheeks, snow blowing in his eyes. When he got caught in one of those internal storms—like his head was a shaken snow globe—he wasn't able to see the way forward, hadn't been sure it would ever end. She had neither the time, nor the energy, nor the desire to consider that maybe he wasn't whining just for the sake of whining, to consider that her irritating child was frantically grasping for anything that would allow him to gain a stable footing because he didn't know how else to manage the storm of thoughts in his little head.

But when he reached for her, desperate to have her wrap her arms around him, to wipe away his tears, to tell him everything would be okay, she pushed him away, told him to stop crawling all over her, to grow up and quit his whining. To this day, his mother doesn't seem to understand her firstborn, and he doubts she ever will—doubts she's even tried to.

The anxiety never went away. If anything, it only got worse as she pushed him further and further away, but he figured out how to deal with it; not by expressing himself better, but by withdrawing into himself—retreating from the things that shook his snow globe.

When he was five or six, his Auntie Barb gave him the most amazing kit of art supplies: pencil crayons, markers, pastels, and watercolour paints. His mom was polite in front of the rest of the family, wearing a duplicitous smile that stretched a bit too wide as she reminded Evann to say thank you, the subtle inflection in her voice betraying her true feelings, as it so often did around her sister-in-law. Before letting him take the kit to his room, she removed the paints, but not before making one final threat about what would happen if she found so much as a smudge of colour on her carpet. But Evann didn't care. He was well aware of the rules, well aware that fun things like Silly Putty and Play-Doh were off-limits in *her* house. He wasn't all that interested in painting anyway; something in the simplicity of needing nothing but a pen or pencil and a piece of paper captured his attention. It didn't require permission, was something he could do without the help of an adult, and as long as he was careful, he didn't have to worry about staining her carpet. Auntie Barb's gift not only sparked his love for art—it offered him a safe escape. He spent hours drawing and colouring alone at the little desk in his bedroom, allowing himself to be consumed by his imagination. There, whatever he thought, whatever he wondered, whatever he imagined, it was all okay. He was in control. Through his small hands escaped the expression of a lost soul struggling to otherwise connect with the hostile world into which he'd been born. Before the dope, it had been the only safe space to hide, a place where he could pretend to be anything or anyone. Nothing seemed to shake his snow globe as long as he was drawing.

Through art, Evann had been able to convey what he didn't know how to communicate with words. It fed his innate craving for acceptance and understanding. In the imagined worlds he drew, things were different—peaceful. In those worlds, his mom didn't get a headache when he was around, she didn't roll her eyes or pinch the bridge of her nose when he needed her. Where he escaped, he was exactly who his mommy needed him to be—silent and self-sufficient —and that meant he was lovable.

He shakes the filthy thoughts from his mind. There's nothing wrong with his mom. He's the one with the problem. There are limits on unconditional love. He was too clingy, too whiny, too needy; and then too quiet, too in his head, too weird. She did her best. Were he worthy, she would love him just as she loves his sister. She's more than capable of loving—it's him that makes it nearly impossible.

The pen has fallen from his hand, the black ink bleeding into the yellowed mattress. His chest aches, his head throbs. He can feel the junk starting to dissipate, leaving him in the company of his ugly self. Picking up his sketchbook, hoping to cram the painful emotions back into their little box, he flips through old sketches, trying to clear his head, trying to find the escape hatch in his mind, the place he used to sneak off to when he was drawing. But Crystal won't give it up, won't stop asking her prying questions, cocking her head awkwardly to stare at him through her beady eyes, as though if she stares hard enough, she might be able to see right in. She isn't leaving any stone unturned, asking him about his sister, her dance, the times he went fishing with his dad, university, the last time he went home—all the things she didn't get to experience in her own childhood. He rubs at his temple, answering her in as few words as possible.

"Do you ever do portraits?" she asks, unexpectedly veering the conversation in a new direction.

"I used to, yeah. Mostly just famous people. And animals. I used to draw a lot of animals."

"I want you to draw me like one of your French girls."

He looks over, surprised at the comment and alarmed to see her perched like a bird, her face inches from his own. Unable to back up any farther, he silently begs the paper-thin wall to give way.

"You get it?" she asks.

Of course he gets it. He—along with every other boy from their generation—had nearly worn out the second VHS in that boxset rewatching the part with Rose's tits. At twelve years old, he would've killed to draw a naked girl, but here in the room of a prostitute covered in track marks, with thoughts of his childhood banging around in his scrambled brain, he can't think of much worse than her lying naked on the bare mattress. He draws his lips into a thin smile, suddenly wishing she'd just continued on with her interrogation. He nods, holding his breath against the smell of burnt rubber escaping between her chapped lips.

"Well? Will you?" she asks, her face moving even closer. He turns his head to the side, feeling an urgent need to create space between them. His heart thumps against his breastbone.

"Can you please back up a bit?"

"Why?" She rests back, her long legs folded beneath her, a teasing pout on her face.

"I just like my personal space." A bead of sweat trickles down his chest.

"Oh! I get it," she says, nodding as though everything suddenly makes sense. "You're gay. That's why you haven't made a move."

His face flushes. "No, Crystal. I'm not." There are at least a dozen reasons he hasn't made a move on her—none of them being that he's not into women.

"Then what's wrong with you?" She sticks her bottom lip out even farther.

The question strikes a nerve. It's one he asks himself more often than he's prepared to admit.

"Look, it's nothing personal. I, uh—I need to take a piss," he says, sliding off the bed, careful not to touch her, and even more careful not to meet her glassy eyes.

By the time he returns from the bathroom—where he had no choice but to piss in the sink, the toilet a revolting cauldron filled to the brim with discarded needles and other people's shit—she's snapped out of it, a fresh track in the crook of her elbow. He holds on to the door frame for support, his legs feeling like limp noodles. The thought of the metal tip sinking into her scarred skin makes him feel nauseous and relieved all at once: he can't truly be an addict if he still can't stand the thought of needles.

Right?

8

THE METAL BACKSTOP PRESSES DIAMONDS INTO WHAT LITTLE flesh they have left on their backs. Across the field lies a lifeless man. As the paramedics work on him, squeezing air into his lungs, injecting him with dose after dose of Narcan, Evann wonders who the man is. Had he once hoped to make something more of his life? Had he too looked up one day, surprised to find himself living among the dead? Does he have a family? People who love him? If these are his final moments, will anyone even miss him? Or will he be another corpse left unclaimed in the morgue?

"You ever think about quitting?" he asks, hardly able to muster a whisper. He can't pull his eyes from the violence of the scene in front of him. Of course, the paramedics are trying to save the man's life—but at what cost? His withered frame collapses farther into the dirt with each chest compression.

Crystal coughs out a harsh laugh, lighting another cigarette. She turns toward him, exhaling smoke directly into his face. He stifles a cough, blinking away tears. "Listen, I know you're new here, but let me tell you something. People have been dying down here forever.

This bullshit," she says with a careless wave of her hand, "it's nothing new."

He's still trying to understand how things work around here. There's a strange sense of community among *them*—this eclectic patchwork of people—and in a lot of ways, they have each other's backs. These people, who have so little—support, family, hope—are fighting their own battles, enduring unimaginable suffering, and yet, are still capable of such generosity; he's experienced it first-hand. But as he watches people walk by, hardly giving the dying man a passing glance, he wonders how both can be true—the same people willing to share what little they have can also be so self-serving, so crass. Sure, Crystal is a bit unhinged, but she's been there for Evann when no one else has; yet she too appears to be entirely unbothered by what they're watching. "But doesn't it scare you? That any of us could be next?"

"I use 'cause it's the only thing that keeps me even a little sane in this crazy fuckin' place. This place where a little girl's mom can go missing, can stop showin' up for her visits, can fall off the face of the fuckin' earth, and nobody cares 'cause they all just think she's a worthless lowlife junkie. You have any idea what it's like to be told that your mom's not coming 'cause she don't love you as much as she loves using? To grow up believin' that, only to find out she didn't stop coming 'cause she didn't love you. She stopped coming 'cause nobody loved her. 'Cause maybe if someone had loved her, had asked about her, had looked out for her, she might've kept coming to those visits, instead of ending up in a pile of pig shit." She takes a long drag off her cigarette, her free hand restlessly picking at the scabbed skin of her legs. "So, yeah, I think about dying, but only when I'm wishing for it. The rest of the time, I thank God for the creation of drugs. Some of us just aren't destined for anything better than what we got, so at least we got dope to get us through the days when dying would be easier than living."

He sits in silence, unsure of what to say. For him, it's become less about what he feels while using and more about what he doesn't. It's not about getting high—it never has been. It's not really about getting anything. If anything, it's more about getting away. When he uses, it's like being in an impenetrable bubble, where the world can carry on and he doesn't have to be in it; where emotions can float around in his mind and soul, and he can watch them as they pass by.

Seeing a person lying on the ground—first responders working to bring them back to life—is still new to him, but it's become a daily occurrence around here. People like Crystal, the ones who have been out here long enough to have watched their friends die—from heroin, from HIV, from a general lack of giving-a-shit by anyone with any power to do anything about it—have grown numb to this sight, feigning indifference to the life of one man, not because they don't care, but because every death is a reminder that they could be next, a reminder of everyone they've lost, of all those yet to go.

He's starting to understand. Here sit two people who, on the surface, should have nothing in common—not gender, nor class, nor circumstance—yet have landed in the same place. He doesn't know what it means to be abandoned, but he knows what it is to be an outsider. He doesn't know what it's like to grow up in the legacy of a murdered prostitute, but he knows the pain of needing to lurk in the shadows to survive. He doesn't know the terror of having a stranger's hands around his throat, but he knows the slap of a backhand, the hurt of rejection, the heartbreak of being cast aside. For all their differences, they have a lot in common. He takes hold of her hand, gives it a gentle squeeze as he forces himself to meet her eye.

The lifeless man is loaded onto a stretcher; whether headed for the emergency room or the morgue, Evann can't tell. He looks around. Skid row is a graveyard. Barely breathing corpses littering stairwells and storefronts; zombies staggering through the streets; demons belligerently screaming at garbage cans and passersby; mummies slumping to the side, oblivious to the painful cellulitis festering beneath the filthy bandages wrapping their limbs; dishevelled goblins tiptoeing on bare feet. Those who don't make it are simply gone—some remembered, some memorialized on concrete walls and plywood windows, many altogether lost, laying unclaimed, accumulating in Vancouver's morgues.

For those dying on the streets, death isn't as much an event as it is a process. Once discarded there—by family, friends, society—they wither away day after day. The unlucky ones will be revived—once, twice, perhaps a dozen times; allowed to suffer another day. But the harsh reality is that breathing only equates to *alive*, not to *living*. Breathing or not, many of these people have been dead for a lot longer than it would take the Narcan to pull them back to life. Crystal doesn't use to keep living. She uses to keep dying.

Evann can't help but wonder if there's really any difference.

He feels himself start to spin, starting to think and feel and notice. As the dope slithers out of his system, the dam opens, unleashing unacknowledged thoughts in a torrent that threatens to drown him. If he doesn't fix soon, his mind will take off on him, and there's no saying what it will have in store for him this time.

———

Minutes later, he tenderly caresses the pipe with his cracked lips, inviting the dragon into his body, allowing it to consume his awareness—to feed off his hurt. As he nods off, a distant corner of his mind ignores the understanding that he might be next, an understanding that his parents could join the thousands of others who have lost a child. It doesn't make him particularly sad, nor is he particularly keen to die. As the dope hits his system, he feels rather indifferent. Indifferent to living. Indifferent to dying. Indifferent to the intensifying possibility of leaving his family behind.

Maybe it would be a relief to have him gone—out of the way. Surely his parents would rather he die anonymously on some side street than have to face the reality of what he's made of his life. But, even if this fix is his last, his shame won't die with his body. There's nothing heroic in having a child die of an overdose.

Through the haze, he considers how much easier it would be for his family—his mom, in particular—if he'd been considerate enough to die of cancer or in some sort of accident. That way, his family could cast aside all his flaws and immortalize him as brave and kind and caring and hardworking. They could exaggerate the good times, and disregard the bad because at least then, their child would've died of something worthy and acceptable. No one wants to talk about fighting demons—not like they commend fighting cancer. There are no "Fuck Addiction" bracelets, no "Run for the Cure," no parents proudly standing on podiums to share the story of how their child battled bravely against drugs or alcohol. Surely when his time comes, they'll think up a creative euphemism. Perhaps "he passed in a tragic accident" would be a suitable alternative to "he died alone in an alleyway."

Evann folds into himself, his torso collapsing forward over his crossed legs. His face hovers above the ground, the muscles in his back half-heartedly resisting the stretch, his brain ignoring a muffled complaint against the contorted posture. He quietly counts the hot tears as they drip onto the dry earth, losing track somewhere around twelve. Dark thoughts swirl like a menacing tornado as he prays for the down to flip the switch between here and gone, between panicked and numb. His last thought is spent hoping that Crystal doesn't notice his tears; he doesn't want her to see how weak he really is.

And then he's gone.

9

THEY PLAN TO MEET WITH A FRIEND OF HERS, THEN GO THEIR separate ways.

His luck has run out. Apparently, overnight visitors are strictly forbidden at the SRO, so it's time to check out of the Hilton. Crystal says her "useless fuckin' junkie neighbour" keeps threatening to report her, and if that happens, they'll both be out on their asses. He senses it's just an excuse to get rid of him, because the story about her boyfriend has suddenly changed too. Evann's never even met the guy and isn't sure he actually exists, but according to Crystal, he has a bit of a jealous streak. She says he isn't too happy about them shacking up, even though Evann sleeps all night while she's out working and she hardly sleeps at all. It's not as if they're sharing a bed.

Of course he's disappointed, but he doesn't argue; it's obvious he's once again overstayed his welcome. She's taught him a lot about street life—where to line up for food, which alleys to avoid, who sells the clean down—so he knows more than he did the first time he had to sleep rough, and he made it through that okay. He tells himself not to worry, resting his hand over his savings—all that remains from the advance off his credit card—stashed in a sock and tucked in his boxers. Things have been awkward between them since she tried to make another move on him, so even before she gave him the official boot, he'd been planning to move out; Crystal has just given him the push he needed. It's bad enough she doesn't seem to understand the concept of no means no, but he can only stand to see her balloon tits hanging over her bruised ribs so many times. It took some prodding, but she finally admitted that, yes, she is in fact a sex worker and, yes, the bruises are from johns getting a little rough. The whole idea of her selling herself, enduring fear and shame and beatings just to support her habit, makes him sick to his stomach. But she says it's not a big deal, that it's all she's ever known.

Evann follows half a block behind her, not having the energy to keep up with her frantic pace, carrying his entire life on his back. She's uncharacteristically quiet today, especially when he tries to ask about who they're heading to meet. All she'll say is that it's someone she thinks might be able to help him out—with what, he can't imagine. His gut tells him there's something off about the whole thing, but he pushes it aside. He tries to convince himself that the knot in his stomach is the feeling of relief. It'll be nice to be out on his own again, not to have to rely on anyone else, to have only himself to worry about. Crystal promises they'll still have each other's backs, but he doesn't expect to see her again. A part of him has been waiting for her to betray him, just like everybody he gets close to does. Dani turned out to be a lesbian, crushing any hope of their imagined life together. His best—and honestly only—childhood friend, Sam, ran off to travel the world after graduation, leaving Evann behind. Even his baby sister—his first true friend—had grown up and become too preoccupied with her own life to give a shit about him.

How pathetic is he? A drug-fuelled bond with a woman he knows has been using him for his money has become his most coveted relationship. The only relationship he still has, really. He doesn't trust his parents, his sister barely even talks to him, and Sam has probably found new, better friends and forgotten all about him. He slowly shuffles after Crystal, feeling sorry for himself.

He thinks back to the good times he had squishing into Sam's old treehouse taking bong hits. The two were inseparable, spending the summer before grade eleven getting high in that treehouse, glassy-eyed and giggling, making trips to the house to restock on snacks from the pantry. At a time when even drawing couldn't offer a total escape —doubt and self-criticism having crept into every aspect of his life— getting stoned allowed Evann a temporary reprieve from the relentless weight of his anxiety. For a while, pot had been enough. When he felt anxious or unsettled, bored or uninspired, he went for a walk and smoked a joint. His parents were either too stupid or too disinterested to question why their otherwise lazy teenager was suddenly interested in walking the dog, or why he was constantly dousing himself in drugstore body spray. His teachers were more astute, so as the summer came to a close, he started drinking instead.

It was easier to hide, not having to worry about his teachers noticing his glassy eyes and the telltale smell, and booze was actually a lot easier to get his hands on. His parents had a full bar; a quick top-up with water, and they were none the wiser that their sixteen-year-old was skimming off the sambuca. What he couldn't skim, he could buy. There was always cash around the house, and his parents either didn't notice—or didn't care—how much he was spending. A part of him hoped they'd ask—what he needed the cash for, where he was going, who he'd be with—but they never did. By fourteen, he was towering over his peers. By sixteen, he had the full beard of a man twice his age, and the deep voice to match it. He could walk into the liquor store and buy booze without a second look.

As soon as he had something his classmates wanted, the high school pecking order shifted. The same kids who'd been either tormenting or ignoring Evann since kindergarten were suddenly seeking him out every Friday, turning the tide for the kid who—for years—had been mockingly called Eve Ann. His new "friends" stuck around just long enough to make it through the final years of high school with a reliable boot. Most of them never repaid their debt, but he didn't care—it was an insignificant price to pay to finally feel accepted.

———

The back of his shirt is soaked through by the time they stop walking. Evann tries to act calm, but his stomach is in his throat. He drops his bag on the sidewalk, collapsing beside it. Exhausted and overheating, he greedily drinks the bottle of Gatorade that Crystal pulls from her magical purse. Catching his breath, he looks up at an unfamiliar house, a neglected old heritage home. In its prime, it would've been quite stunning, but in its present state—peeling fish-scale shingles and stained-glass windows backed by plywood—Evann's anxiety increases just thinking about the haunted figures that might be lurking inside. His shoulders ache from carrying his belongings, and he says a silent thank you to whoever decided to make Canadian bills out of plastic because, stashed against his balls, there's no way his stockpile has stayed dry in the late-summer heat. He watches Crystal take a bump, dipping her delicate long finger into the fine powder, careful not to spill a granule as she brings it to her nostril. For a second, he considers joining her but thinks better of it, reminding himself what had happened the one and only time he used a straight upper. He doesn't know what he's about to walk into, so as much as he's jonesing, he can sense he needs to be at least semi-coherent for this introduction.

"Are you—" his voice is high and squeaky. He stops to clear his throat, cursing his body for betraying his fear, as if the profuse sweating isn't obvious enough. He feels his red cheeks flush even brighter. "Are you sure it's a good idea for me to go in?"

She turns to face him. Something in her expression—the way her lips tighten slightly, the intensity with which she looks directly into his eyes—makes the hairs on the back of his neck stand up. "Yeah, no. I think it'd be better if you waited outside. Okay? I'll run in and see if he's even in there. Just wait here." She straightens her skirt, tugging it high over her hips before raking her fingers through her hair, a futile attempt to tame the wild frizz that's only been made worse by the humidity. "How do I look?" she asks, smiling wide so that he can check she doesn't have lipstick smudged on her teeth. She pushes her tongue forward to fill the fresh gap in her bottom teeth, the result of a fight over a lucrative corner.

"Fine," he says. She lifts her eyebrows expectantly. "Great," he says. "You look great."

Smiling, she tosses her hair over her shoulder. "Perfect. Just wait here. I got some business to take care of. It might be a while, okay? But don't worry."

———

Too scared to nod off, he only allows himself to snort a perc: just enough to keep him right, and nowhere near enough to tame the anxious energy coursing through his body. He watches the house, thinking back to all the times he stood by the front window waiting for his mom to get home, listening to the seconds tick by, counting every minute she was late as further evidence that something terrible had happened. The more time that passed, the more convinced he'd been that she was never coming home. It didn't matter how many times she casually wandered in—twenty, thirty, forty minutes late— and told him to quit being such a worrywart, he got worked up every time.

As he got older, his fears only became more elaborate: Maybe she was killed in a car crash. Maybe she decided she couldn't stand his whining anymore and had gone away like she sometimes threatened to do. Maybe she was shopping and the evil men from the TV crashed a plane into Walmart. He started to pay careful attention, trying to find a pattern. She was happy when he cleaned his room, put away his toys, and made his bed, so if he did those things, that must mean she'd come home on time. She wasn't happy when she got home to find him crying in the front window, so he started pretending to be reading while he waited, one eye on the clock as he watched the driveway. He held back his tears, tried to be on his best behaviour, helped take care of his sister—all so she would be proud of him; all so she would come back; all so nothing bad would happen to her. It didn't change anything; no matter what he tried, she was almost never on time. At least when he was good, he wouldn't have to spend the ten minutes it took his mom to drop off the babysitter anticipating a smack with the wooden spoon.

———

By the time the front door creaks open—a figure inching out through the narrow opening before scurrying down the creaky steps—Evann has chewed every biteable bit from every one of his fingernails. His body aches and his ass is numb from sitting perched on the concrete curb, waiting for something—anything—to happen. Under the dim glow of the streetlight, he can't make out the stocky shadow crossing the street toward him.

"You Evann?"

A knot forms in Evann's stomach. The voice is familiar. He files through his mind, trying to place the distinctive hoarse voice, but as the man moves under the streetlight, Evann immediately knows. He's met this guy before—several times, in fact—and their business relationship didn't end particularly well.

Before he hit the streets, back when he was a university student with a casual habit, he was introduced to a mean motherfucker who called himself Spider, presumably because of the tattoo adorning his face. Maybe the nickname had come first—Evann had never dared ask—but either way, the tattoo looked like it crawled out of his left eye, ugly and intimidating on his temple. Even though he was terrified of the dealer, the stuff Spider sold was legit, and Evann was the over-cautious type back then. Of course he was smart enough to understand that the "pure heroin" Spider supplied was cut with at least a little baby powder, some baking soda, and a sprinkle of cocaine here and there, but Evann trusted that the one thing he didn't cut into his mix was fentanyl, and that was all he really cared about. He'd relied on this guy for months, and Spider never sold him bunk.

Back then, the writing was on the wall. He'd gone from using only on the weekends, to only on the weekends plus every few nights before bed, to every day of the week, to at least twice every day. Back then, he was delusional enough to think that quitting would be a simple matter of willpower. So, in the dark alley behind a Chinese takeout place, he handed over the cash for just enough junk to keep him from being sick through the night, and he made the mistake of asking Spider not to sell to him anymore.

"I'm going to get myself turned around," he explained to the man.

Spider raised an eyebrow, the tattoo becoming an unrecognizable smear, a smug, half-toothed smile creeping across his ugly face.

"Ha!" he said. Not laughed. Said—as if Evann's comment had been too stupid to warrant a real laugh.

Without warning, Spider shoved him hard. He stumbled back against a piss-covered wall. "Fuck you, kid. That ain't how it works around here. I'm not your fuckin' mommy."

Evann put up his hands pathetically, muttered an apology, and skittered away. Stuffing the little pouch of smack in his pocket, he hoped the man didn't notice his trembling hands. The encounter left him jumpy, and by the time he burst through the door of his apartment—sliding the chain lock into place and latching the deadbolt behind him—he'd abandoned his childish sobriety pledge.

Evann's heart thumps in his throat as he looks down at that distinctive tattoo, praying that—unlike Spider—he has a face worth forgetting.

10

Perched in a darkened doorway, Evann sits, terrified, his dilated pupils—vigilant and indiscriminate—sending every moving shadow to be processed by his incoherent mind. Paranoia consumes him. With each sound, his stomach lurches into his throat, his heart thumps violently against his breastbone. The joints of his right hand ache, his fist clenching around the pocket knife. He releases his white-knuckle grip for only a second, just long enough to bring the junk to his nostril, allowing himself just enough to keep from bottoming out. The fingers on his left hand are bleeding stubs, each nail bed ravaged by his restless jaw.

Hour after sleepless hour, he tries to make sense of everything that has transpired in the past twenty-four hours. The day started off innocently enough—Crystal breaking the news that he could no longer stay with her—yet somehow ended with Evann pinned against a dumpster, a cool blade pressed against his throat. He replays the events over in his mind.

After strutting across the street, Crystal carefully made her way across the rotting porch—an impressive sight given her impossibly high heels—then disappeared into the house. She hadn't resurfaced. According to Spider, she was taking care of some business inside, and she'd catch up with him later. It wasn't what he and Crystal had discussed, but he knew how flakey she could be. He started to leave when Spider stopped him.

"Whoa, whoa, whoa. What's the rush, my man?"

A feeling of dread flooded over him. He was really hurting for a fix, and the longer he spent face to face with Spider, the more paranoid he got. Spider didn't seem upset, didn't seem to be carrying a grudge, but Evann wasn't keen on sticking around long enough to confirm. He should've insisted that Crystal tell him who they were meeting. He never would've agreed had he known.

"So, that Crystal chick tells me you might be interested in makin' some"—Spider cupped his palm beneath his chin, his fingers rubbing the stubble on his cheeks as he considered his choice of words—"some connections."

Evann held up his hands and started to back away. He didn't understand what Spider was proposing, but he did understand that this guy was a hardcore dealer and that getting involved with him would be a bad idea.

"Uh, I'm not sure what Crystal told you, man, but I'm not looking for any trouble."

"When'd I say anything about trouble?" Spider looked up at him, giving him a lopsided expression that read sneer more than smile. "That ain't what this is about," he said, stuffing his hands in the pockets of his shin-length cargo shorts. "All's I'm tryin' to do is offer you an opportunity. You're a big guy, which is probably why you're not dead yet, but you're not foolin' nobody. You don't know shit about what it takes to survive out here. I mean—look at you. You look like you're about ready to shit yourself just standin' here talkin' to me, and I'm one of the good guys." Evann's heart pounded as he forced himself to meet Spider's gaze—forced himself to search for a hint of recognition in those black eyes. "So lemme tell you what. You seem like a nice enough kid. Im'a take you under my wing."

Evann tried to make sense of it, his brain slow to comprehend the proposal. Before he could respond, Spider continued, "Nobody fucks around with me. People know you're one of my associates, nobody's gonna fuck around with you either. You see what I'm sayin'?"

Fear and confusion consumed him. Evann struggled to think straight, willed himself to snap out of it, begged his deprived brain to function for just a few minutes. He wished he could all at once be more stoned, yet more sober, either of which might've helped him make sense of what was being said. His mind raced. If he couldn't even understand what he was getting at, maybe Spider was right— maybe Evann did need protection if he had any hope of surviving street life.

"I don't get it. You're offering to protect me?" He regretted the words as soon as he heard them out loud, realizing they made him sound like a naive moron—which is of course true, but not the impression he was hoping to convey.

Spider arched his eyebrow and glared at Evann through hooded eyes. "Nothin's free, kid. If there's one lesson you better learn—and right quick—it's that nothin' 'round here is free. Ever. You hear me?"

Evann nodded.

"The deal is, you help me out with some deliveries, and I'll make sure people don't fuck with you. Plus, I'll give you special pricing on your purchases."

Run. Jesus Christ. Get out of here, you fucking idiot! Evann staggered side to side, the ground unsteady beneath his feet. "You want me to deal?"

"No, no, no," Spider said. "Just make the odd delivery. You know, you scratch my back, I scratch yours kinda thing."

What's the difference?

Seeming to hear his thoughts, Spider responded. "It's just, like...

my 'business,' we'll call it, has grown. I got people textin' me from all over the city, but I don't got enough time to go all over the damn place. So basically like, you need dope, you come to me. In exchange, you hop on the bus and head up to—I dunno, say East Van or whatever—drop off the junk, then bring back the cash. Easy."

Deep within Evann's gut, alarm bells sounded. At any other point in his life, he might've seen the offer for what it was: a scheme to take advantage of a vulnerable kid with no street smarts. And he was just that: vulnerable, stupid, and desperate. But something in Spider's tone made him think it wasn't so much an offer as an expectation. He nodded along as if it made perfect sense—as if they weren't talking about him transporting illegal substances around the city for a notoriously dangerous gangster. "Isn't it risky, though?" he asked in a rhetorical attempt to silence the *dude, no...this is a terrible idea* in his head.

"Nah, don't worry about it. You won't carry much dope. The cops ain't gonna go through all the paperwork to arrest you for havin' a couple grams on ya. Don't even gotta give 'em your real name if you don't wanna."

There were a million reasons he should've said no, but it had only taken one reason to say yes: what Spider was offering him wasn't just a job, or protection, or a discount on drugs. Spider was offering him an opportunity to belong, so in the handshake of the addicted, they sealed the deal by chasing vapour off a piece of tinfoil.

Evann headed back toward skid row under the cover of darkness, his head full yet his mind blissfully vacant. He was feeling good— great even—as he staggered along. He let his guard down, losing himself in the heavy weightlessness of the down, imagining himself floating on a river of warm syrup. He didn't notice the car slowing to a creep beside him, didn't react until two men—one with a baseball bat, the other with a hunting knife—jumped out. He tried to run, but his leaden legs betrayed him, and before he could comprehend what was happening, he was pinned to a dumpster.

They didn't say a word—didn't need to—as he stood frozen in place. While one held a knife to his throat—his breath hot against Evann's face, putrid with the smell of rotting teeth—the other reached down to unbuckle his belt. His baggy pants fell from his bony hips, landing in a heap around his ankles. For several terrifying moments, he considered what they might do to him, involuntarily clenching so hard his glutes burned hot, sweat soaking through the underwear gathered in his asscrack. The one without the knife looked directly into Evann's eyes as he reached his enormous hand under the band of his briefs. Evann swallowed hard against the blade, squeezed his eyes shut, fighting back tears and begging his bladder not to betray his terror. Spider's words echoed in his mind. *Nobody's gonna fuck with you.* Not an hour earlier, he'd knowingly made a deal with the devil for that very reason. It was a cruel reminder of just how vulnerable he was, how stupid.

The man's hands were rough, deliberate. It took Evann a second to realize that the groping was calculated. His attackers seemed to know exactly what they were searching for, and exactly where to find it. Evann's eyes flew open as the sock containing the last of his savings was peeled off his damp skin. As his waistband snapped, he lifted his gaze, just in time to see an enormous fist flying at his face. Giving him one final shove, the larger of the two men sneered at him, speaking words Evann was unable to hear over the ringing in his head.

When he came to, his head was throbbing. Pulling up his pants, he looked around, surprised to see that his backpack had been left behind, the baggie of down in his pocket left untouched. It was his fault; he was the one stupid enough to let his guard down, to be out wandering the worst neighbourhood in the city alone after dark. But he'd done exactly what Crystal had suggested; he'd stashed his money just like she told him to, on his person, rather than stuffing it in the bottom of his bag like he used to, and these guys still found it.

She was right. Spider was right. Without street smarts, he was destined to die—if not at his own hand, if not from the shit he was using, then certainly at the hand of any number of desperate people willing to do anything to survive.

Now, hours later, jonesing for a proper fix but too scared to let his guard down again, aching to move but paralyzed by fear, he thinks about something else Spider said: "Between you and me, brother, stay away from that girl. She's trouble."

11

IN THE BATHROOM OF A DINGY COMMUNITY CENTRE, EVANN sees his reflection for the first time since the attack. Hidden beneath his beard, purple and yellow bruises paint his pale skin. Staring at his reflection, he scrubs at his face, wondering how he's become the man staring back at him. After a hot shower, he sits in the cafeteria-style hall, slowly pecking at his food. Each bite serves as a reminder of everything that's gone wrong, the tender ache of his jaw joining his hollow stomach in protest, his guts reluctant to accept the first proper meal in weeks, though he no longer keeps track. It's become the norm. His days pass unremembered, uncounted, illegitimate, inconsequential, except for the brief moments when he drifts back to consciousness at some unanticipated time of day, in some unfamiliar and unexpected place, realizing—sometimes with relief, though lately more often with dread—that he's lived to die another day.

By the time he's managed to pick through two-thirds of the food, his abdomen is visibly distended, his swollen jaw is throbbing, and his cellphone has just enough battery life to power on. There was a time, in what now feels like a different life, when Evann didn't go anywhere without his iPhone, idle hands kept busy scrolling through social media. But like most things—school, drawing, keeping up with the latest episode of *Game of Thrones*—having a line to the outside world is no longer a priority. He often forgets it's there, crammed into the bottom of his backpack. It's impossible to keep charged, one more thing to risk being stolen, and he honestly doesn't trust himself to have it on hand, afraid he'll make a regrettable call or send a self-destructive text while he's out of it.

Evann maintains just enough contact with his family to avoid suspicion. It's unlikely they've noticed the increasing irregularity of his communication, and even if they have, they haven't cared enough to say anything. For now, he doubts they have any idea their supposed son-the-aspiring-visual-arts-major has deteriorated into their son-the-homeless-heroin-addict.

It didn't take him leaving home to feel like an outsider, certainly didn't take him becoming an addict; he's always existed on the outer fringe of an inner circle, occupying the space of the son but never quite knowing how to fill that role, never knowing how to be—who to be—because being himself has never been enough. All his life he's had an intuitive sense of being unwelcome, unwanted, out of place; a sense that perhaps their lives would be easier without him. He also understands the contradiction between how he feels and how important it is that he continue to fill that role—if only for the illusion—so he takes a deep breath and steels himself before unlocking his phone.

He opens an email from his dad, a tech-illiterate roughneck who can't be bothered to learn how to send a text or how to sign into Messenger. He still uses his original email address, bruce_is@yahoo.com, from the 1990s:

Hey Bud,
I guess you must be wrapped up for the summer by now.
How did finals go? Me and Dale found an incredible little
fishing spot up on the Stamp River. A real honey hole! We'll
have to check it out next time you're home.
Dad

He slumps forward on the table, a wave of sadness filling the hollow space in his chest. Maybe it's the sleepless nights, or the inadequate dope, or the unrelenting fear that's making him so emotional; maybe he's just lonely. Tears burn behind his eyes as he thinks back on the fishing trips he and his dad used to take together. Those weekends away are some of his happiest memories, the only times he felt a true sense of belonging—the only time he understood how to fit in to his role as the son. It wasn't that they had a ton in common. Unlike his mom and sister, who talked about anything and everything, he and his dad often spent their days in silence, wading through the cold water together, rhythmically casting their fly lines. His pulse quickens just thinking about the excitement of having a fish on. In the evenings, they'd stared into the fire—listening to the crackling of the logs and the river breaking around the rocky rapids—while they ate grilled steelhead. Sometimes they'd talk—about Evann's art or where they should go on their next fishing trip—but mostly they just enjoyed one another's company. For a moment, Evann allows himself to dream of a life in which he walked a different path—one in which art and fishing remained his obsessions. One in which he hadn't alienated himself from his only remaining ally, hadn't stepped outside of the bounds of their mutual understanding, hadn't been stupid enough to believe that Bruce might actually choose his son over his wife. Fighting back tears, he opens a message from his mom:

Hey Ev,
Super exciting news!!!
Nicole is going to be the principal in Swan Lake! You have no idea how excited she is!!!
Ms. Shelley says there have been scouts from the Royal Winnipeg Ballet asking about her!
October 9 & 10... Same weekend as Thanksgiving.
Make sure you make it to at least one of her shows.
Let me know which date so I can get an extra ticket.
Mom

Below it, sent ten days later, is another message:

Hi,
Still waiting on your dates.
I know you're busy with school and everything, but it's
important that you support your sister.
Mom

The last message is dated August 7. *Shit! What is it now? The 25th?*
He types a hasty response:

Hey Mom,
Sorry I didn't get back to you right away, I've been working
a ton.
You know I wouldn't miss an opportunity for turkey!
I'll definitely be there for October 10.
Give Nicole a hug for me. That's incredible news!
Love you.

Evann scrolls mindlessly through his Facebook feed, passing serial status updates about Nicole's "dance career." He flips through the photos of Sam's extended gap year: surfing in Nicaragua, standing in front of an enormous waterfall, a stunningly beautiful sunset from a terrace in Greece. He hits Like on every photo rather than letting himself wonder how different life might've been if he'd gone travelling with his best friend instead of going to university. As he swipes to close the app, an ad catches his attention:

NEED HELP FINDING A PLACE TO SLEEP TONIGHT? CALL THE SHELTER AND STREET HELPLINE. JUST DIAL 2-1-1.

He'd been too stubborn to admit that being mugged scared him shitless, but now he's too tired to keep up the act. Since that night, he's been wandering the streets in affluent Point Grey during the night and sleeping in Victory Square during the day, terrified to let his guard down while the rest of the world sleeps. He calls 2-1-1 and gets a list of local shelters. There's a tight band squeezing his head by the time he finishes calling the half-dozen places within walking distance.

"Sorry, no spots left for tonight."

"We don't do holds over the phone. It's first come first serve."

"Unfortunately, we can only accommodate men twenty-five and older."

"We're actually a youth shelter, so we only allow teens under nineteen."

"Beds are always opening up, so try again tomorrow."

"Availability changes daily, so please call back. It's best to call between 9 and 9:30 a.m."

Evann holds his head in his hands. Grabbing a handful of hair, he pulls, the discomfort a welcome distraction from the mocking voice in his head. *You can't do anything right. You're getting exactly what you deserve. You're just a worthless junkie.* Hot tears gather behind his exhausted eyelids. *Don't you dare cry, you fucking baby. If you want something to cry about, I'll give you something to cry about.* He jams his palms into his eye sockets.

Pushing back his chair, he shoves his leftover food across the table. The untouched soup sloshes onto the tray. He should know better than to waste good food; he spent an hour digging through trash bins to collect enough cans for the two bucks this meal cost. His cheeks tingle. For most of his life, his little tantrum would've earned him a smack across the face. *Grow the fuck up, Evann. It's time you start acting your age.*

He shakes his head, trying to quiet the familiar voice. Only an idiot would assume the city is full of shelters—that he could just wander in and get a bed whenever he got tired of passing out on park benches. He'd convinced himself that it was better to go it alone—that if he didn't bother anyone, no one would bother him. But now he knows better, understands the dangers that lurk in every dark alley, sees that behind every pair of glossy eyes is a deranged mind.

He considers texting Crystal but thinks better of it. Spider's warning has been on replay since the attack, consuming the brief moments of clarity between fixes, feeding the gremlin in his mind telling him to trust no one, to push people away, to shrink into himself —out of sight, out of mind. He wants to believe she has his back, that the timing of the robbery was an unfortunate coincidence, that cornering him into a relationship with Spider was an attempt at kindness. But that gremlin fills his head with nasty thoughts and cruel words, hateful sentiments. *She set you up. She saw how weak you are, how vulnerable.*

Maybe she *did* set him up. That would make the most sense; she knows him well enough to know he wouldn't defend himself, wouldn't cause a scene, wouldn't retaliate. *You didn't think she was actually your friend, did you? Jesus. You really are a degenerate loser.* He knows it to be true: he *is* a defenceless pushover, so preoccupied that it's likely he did walk straight into a trap. But no. She cares about him. Doesn't she? She helped him when no one else would. Evann tugs at his hair again. Maybe it was Spider who set him up. He was the one who watched him stagger away. He was the one who insisted they take another hit when Evann was already struggling to see from beneath his heavy eyelids. But would Spider have known where he had his money stashed? Did Crystal tip him off? Or does everyone around here keep their valuables next to their balls? Maybe neither of them had anything to do with it. Maybe he's being paranoid. Maybe he's worrying too much. He always worries too much. Between Spider and Crystal, his gut and his gremlin, Evann doesn't know who or what to trust. He can't even trust himself. How could he? Every decision he's made has led him down this path of self-destruction, straight into that alley, straight into the hands of his attackers.

He, like so many others, has become a sycophant shell, possessed by a one-track mind, a mind driven by a parasitic program that repeatedly tricks its host into believing that the very thing that will kill them is instead that which will provide salvation. In the pursuit of salvation, nothing is off limits, and he understands that now in a way he hadn't—couldn't have—before. On the streets, there are those who do the taking, and those who are taken from.

Oh Evann, you stupid boy. He hears his mother's voice. *You didn't actually think you could play with fire and not get burned, did you?*

12

Evann is starting to get desperate, no longer sure how many hours have passed since his last fix, only knowing that each one has been more agonizing than the last. Having run out of fingernails to ravage, he picks at the dry skin along his hairline, trying to distract himself from the gnawing pain eating through his stomach. Now and then he stops to wipe away the incessant stream of snot leaking from his nose. It's in these brief and unwelcome periods of lucidity when— in spite of his watering eyes—he sees clearly. He sees himself, and he sees what he's become: an untallied addition to the others. Another anonymous young man with vacant eyes and a haunted face, wandering the streets of the Downtown Eastside in search of his poison.

Last night, staring into the shadows, he promised himself today would be the day that he wouldn't cave to the craving, not because China White has loosened her deadly grip on him, but because he's simply too tired to carry on. Tired of the chase. Tired of having to watch his back. Tired of being let down. But too much of a coward to take the only sure way out.

The street life isn't easy. The party is long over, and he's trapped in a perpetual walk-of-shame, repeated each morning when the sun rises to illuminate his pathetic existence for all to see. He spends his days roaming aimlessly, not knowing where he'll get his next meal, his next fix, his next dollar—not knowing who to trust or who he can rely on. His withering muscles ache under the weight of carrying what little he has left. A once expensive and stylish wardrobe has been reduced to a handful of items, musty and weathered, which now billow around his thinning frame. He lives in constant fear: afraid his next fix will be his last, while worrying that it won't be.

As the coastal fog begins to dissipate, the North Shore Mountains become a surreal backdrop to the industrious city. It's an unseasonably cold day, but the peculiarity of the weather is lost on Evann, who is in far too much pain to notice the cool breeze. Not so long ago he might've stopped, pulled out his sketchbook, and captured the way the late-August sun burns behind the clouds. He might've noticed the way its light casts an ominous glow over the city, might've marvelled at the juxtaposition between past, present, and future, beautifully intermingling. Maybe he'd have found comfort in the permanence of the landscape grounding the ever-changing cityscape, the Coastal Mountains reliably still against the dynamic skyline. But today, he staggers forward, each step an onerous effort to escape his nefarious compulsion, the setting nothing more than a blank screen against which he fixates on the battle between body and mind.

Headed for the heart of Gastown, he resists the pull back toward skid row. He has no plan and no idea how he's going to get clean, motivated only by the fact that he's flat broke, out of dope, and still shaking from having a gangster's hand down his pants. He can't remember the last time he let himself rest, and can't bear the thought of yet another terrifying night wandering the streets. The darkness behind his eyelids has become a canvas on which his every failure, every painful memory, is displayed with unrelenting consistency. He can hardly bear to blink, afraid of what lies just beyond his consciousness. Every time he does start to fall asleep, the image of a hand coming at his face causes him to jerk awake. But it isn't the enormous fist of his attacker that he sees, it's his mother's: slender and perfectly manicured. Evann stretches his aching jaw, pushing away an old memory that keeps creeping into his consciousness.

———

He was the first kid in kindergarten to lose a tooth, though he never told anyone the truth of why. They were driving home from school, and as they went over a bump, his snack dropped into his lap.

"What do you think you're doing?" his mom asked as he rolled down the window.

Before he had a chance to explain, she reached back to smack him. Luckily, Nicole's car seat was strapped directly behind her in his old spot, so now it was harder for her to give him a good slap while keeping her eyes on the road. He saw it coming anyway and tucked his legs up so she couldn't reach him. His cheeks flushed, a bit scared of what might happen, but he clung to the lessons he'd learned in the CARE program. He was thankful Trusty had visited his class that morning, had taught them all about their bodies and how to stay safe. She reached around and swiped at him again.

"Mommy, no! Trusty says you can't touch me like that." He stared at her defiantly in the rear-view. He saw her smirk back at him but she said nothing.

When they got home, she calmly told him to go colour while she put Nicole down for a nap. He'd spread out all his crayons by the time she came up to his room a few minutes later. As soon as he saw the look on her face, he knew he'd made a mistake.

He knew that look—jaw clenched, a fury burning in her eyes— and he knew what it would mean. "Let's just get one thing clear, young man. I couldn't care less what that fucking dodo bird says." She held out the CARE handout from his backpack, made a scene of tearing it in half before letting it fall to the floor. "I am your mother. I *own* you. So don't you ever, *ever*, tell me what I can and cannot do again. Do you understand me?"

Trusty's advice swirled in his mind. He forced himself to meet her icy stare. "No, Mommy. You're not allowed to hit me. Trusty said so. My body is mine, and he said that if I don't like you touching me like that, you have to stop."

She stepped forward, vibrating as she reached out and grabbed him by the cheeks. Her sharp nails dug into his skin as she squeezed. "Oh really. And what did your friend Trusty say would happen if I did it anyway?" she asked through clenched teeth.

Evann struggled to answer, her grip tight on his face. "He said I have to tell someone and you'll be in big trouble," he whispered.

"You know what, Evann. You go ahead. Tell someone. In fact—" She turned and stomped down the stairs. For a second, he considered running—or even hiding—but he'd tried that before and it had only made her more mad.

She returned, tossing the cordless phone at him. He flinched as it hit him. "Go ahead. Call whoever you want. I don't give a shit. I'll even get you the number for Child Protection if you want. Just be prepared for what will happen when you do." He stared at the phone in his lap. "Look at me," she said through gritted teeth. "You may think you've got this all figured out, but you don't. If they come, it won't be to take *me* away, it'll be to take *you*, and it won't be long before they see what a spoiled little liar you are. Don't think for a second there's anyone who's going to want you. And if you think your life is hard now, you can't even imagine how much worse it's about to get."

Evann chewed at his thumbnail, fighting back tears. He should've known not to talk back, should've known it would never work, but Trusty had made it sound so easy.

"Do you understand me?"

He nodded, fighting back tears.

"Now what do you say?"

"I'm sorry, Mommy."

"That's what I thought." She waved him over for a hug. He didn't really want one, but he let his head rest against her chest, knowing better than to deny her. She pulled him into an uncomfortable embrace, squeezing until he started to squirm. "I'm not going to tell you again: I brought you into this world, and I can sure as shit take you out of it"—her voice a low growl in his ear—"and don't you fucking forget it." She released him, shoving him hard. He didn't see it coming, didn't have time to catch himself or to put up his hands before his teeth connected with the wooden bedpost. He landed on the floor with a loud thud. Down the hall, Nicole started screaming.

"Perfect," his mom muttered. "Just fucking perfect. I guess your shitty little attitude wasn't enough? You had to wake your sister too?" His door slammed shut. As she stormed down the hall, swearing under her breath, Evann retreated under his blankets, trying to catch his breath.

That night at dinner, he did his best to eat his grilled cheese with only his back teeth, but every bite seemed to make his wiggly front tooth more wiggly, and his fat lip more sore. She set down her wineglass and grabbed his chin, assessing his swollen mouth. "Hmm," she said casually, turning his head side to side, "looks like that fall off the swing set left quite a mark."

———

Up ahead stands the famous steam clock. Staggering through what he'd once considered to be one of the most beautiful spots in the city, today he only sees the ugliness—the clock a temperamental beast, the cobblestoned streets disorienting, littered with spent cigarette butts, gum carelessly discarded and stepped in. No longer does the leaching efflorescence provide charm or character. Instead, he sees neglect, sees how pathetic and dilapidated the historical square is. He stumbles toward the clock, exhaustion and agitation simultaneously gripping him. His legs shake beneath him as he staggers forward, trying to find somewhere to sit. There's an open space on a nearby bench, beside a young woman in an expensive-looking pantsuit who talks loudly into her Blackberry, the phone pinned between her ear and shoulder, a coffee in one hand, a bagel in the other. She looks up at him as he makes his way over, meeting his gaze momentarily, her face mirroring the exact disgust he feels whenever he sees himself. Putting her coffee down on the open bench beside her, she pulls her purse close to her side. He lowers his gaze and shuffles away, his stomach twisting against the understanding that his presence is making her uncomfortable—that his presence makes most of *them* uncomfortable. He longs for the ease of being unseen.

He used to wander these streets—coffee in hand, sketchbook under his arm, not so different from that woman—seeking inspiration. People had also looked through him then, but it was different. They'd overlooked him, not to pretend they didn't see him, but because he was so ordinarily normal that he blended into the surroundings—just another clean-cut white man, another anonymous face in a crowd. It must be the untamed beard, the sour smell of infrequently washed skin, the downcast gaze of a man decomposing from the inside out, that now makes him an invisible spectacle. He can feel their judgmental stares. They come from every direction. When he does dare look up, those who stare are the first to avert their eyes—to pretend they don't see him—anxious to avoid any interaction, meaningful or otherwise. He suspects they're probably afraid he'll ask for money, or food. Perhaps they're afraid he's one of the aggressive ones—the dangerous panhandlers, the deranged street people—they talk about on the news. As long as they don't see people like him, don't acknowledge their existence, they can avoid an awkward exchange. It saves them having to lie, having to admit they aren't willing to spare their meaningless nickels and dimes for a destitute man fighting for survival. Maybe they tell themselves that life wouldn't be so hard if *they* made better choices; that *those* people only want money to buy more drugs; that it's morally irresponsible; that handing over their hard-earned money would amount not to charity, but to enabling. Perhaps they feel a moment of pity before continuing down the street, sipping their six-dollar lattes. No one sees Evann as Evann anymore. He's tumbled down the rungs of society. No one knows his story and none of them give a shit—not about him and not about any of the other people dying on the sidewalks beneath their feet.

And it's that, that feeling of utter worthlessness, the looks of disgust, the poorly veiled judgment from strangers, the labels—junkie, free loader, transient, less than—that will send Evann back to the darkness of the alleyways. It isn't just the physical symptoms of coming down that make it damn near impossible to get himself turned around; it's the torment of knowing that other people see in him everything he hates in himself. Abhorrence is burning him from the inside out, and the only salve he's ever found to soothe that pain is dope.

He was once the one looking down at the filthy street people, he was the one shrugging his shoulders, he was the one with a grimacing smile, he was the one pretending he didn't hear their requests for spare change. But a flower doesn't bloom in an instant; unwatched, the progression seems sharp and unexpected. As it turns out, his spiral into addiction wasn't all that different; there had been a thousand tiny steps along the way, but one day he woke, surprised to find himself on the other side.

A whistle sounds, steam shooting from the top of the clock. Evann startles, not realizing he's been standing here, absently staring at it for nearly fifteen minutes. He returns to himself, the frenetic energy of the square disorienting. Tourists and businesspeople jostle past him. He struggles to make sense of the situation, trying to remember where he is, how he got here, why he'd decided to leave the anonymity of skid row. He looks around, imagining that while he was lost in his thoughts, impatient tourists were weaving around him. He eyes the nearby pedestrians suspiciously, wondering who had done their best to crop the zombie man from their picture and who had purposely snapped a photo of him to show their friends—living proof of the "problem population" in Vancouver.

He knows that unless he can get himself turned around, he's going to die, but knowing isn't enough. In a war of another kind, he might've bit down on a cyanide capsule. Quick and painless, merciful. He considers what it might be like to have an easy way out. Instead, in the battle against his demons, he's left to kill himself slowly, using a poison of a different kind.

Evann is jarred from his trance by the long blare of a car horn, unaware that he's wandered into the street. Convulsive cramps rip through his abdomen. Panicking, he scans his surroundings, acutely aware that if he doesn't find a toilet immediately, he's going to shit himself right here in the middle of the street. He begs his legs to start running, but he can barely muster an off-kilter trot, his pack lurching side to side with each agonizing step. He curls into himself as he staggers along the sidewalk, legs wobbly and unreliable, his arms wrapped around his roiling stomach, ass cheeks burning with the exertion of squeezing them together. *Jesus Christ, it's too far*, he realizes. There is no way any one of the shops along Water Street is going to let someone like him walk in, let alone use the toilet. Soon after he shifted from *one of us* to *one of them*, Evann learned that humanity is never prioritized over profit. Where to use the bathroom has become a daily consideration, but he usually isn't trying to find a toilet when his bowels have suddenly decided to liquefy. His eyes dart left and right, frantically trying to find somewhere—anywhere other than his goddamn pants—to take a shit. He just needs to make it to Waterfront Station, but right now two blocks feels impossibly far.

What the fuck is wrong with you? You're almost twenty years old and you're still shitting your pants—and in public, of all places. Not much has changed, I see.

Evann spins around, confirming his fear. He's clucking hard, unable to ascertain seen from envisioned, heard from imagined—his suffering vivid, his judgment clouded. His weak mind likes to play tricks on him—the border around reality fluid, the absolute blending inseparably with deluded apparitions—his mother's voice on standby, ready to invade his thoughts, ready to remind him of everything he isn't. Ready to remind him that he's amounted to exactly what he's worth.

He weaves around oblivious tourists, his pupils pinpoint, hair damp, sweat streaming down his forehead. He knows he won't make it. To the right, a passthrough leads away from the shops and opens into a vacant parking lot. He yanks at his belt as he rounds the corner, tears streaming down his face as he leans over and retches, acidic bile burning his throat, hot shame spilling out of him. Gagging against the acrid smell filling his nostrils, he begs his mind to take him away—to take him somewhere else, anywhere else—the humiliation too much to bear.

13

SURROUNDED BY PILES OF HIS OWN WASTE, HER VOICE continues to taunt him.

Jesus Christ. You're a disgusting animal. Have you lost all self-respect?

He swings helplessly from past to present, wishing to be anywhere but here, desperate to stay anywhere but there. The sour stink of vomit threatens to rip him back to an unhappy day headed to the Happiest Place on Earth. It didn't start out unhappy; in fact, it had every reason to be a particularly wonderful day. Yet it wouldn't be among his earliest memories if not for the lasting consequence of its mortifying conclusion.

Another wave of nausea pulls Evann back to the present. His eyes water as he retches again, his stomach forcefully expelling the remnants of his last meal in both directions.

Maybe you shouldn't've been such a pig last night. Pretty gluttonous to eat that much, don't you think?

He folds his arms across his stomach, praying for the cramps rippling through his abdomen to end, the queasiness too similar to the feeling he had in the moments before he ruined their day at Disney before it had even started. As Evann gasps for air, begging his angry insides for mercy, his mind wanders away on him.

———

Eager to show his parents what a big boy he was, he dressed himself, pulling on his new blue shirt, Mickey's oversized face on the front. Instead of Evann having to keep himself occupied like he usually did when he got up, his dad woke up early to play with him, and even let him have Lucky Charms for breakfast. They were on vacation, after all. There was a sour undertone to the sweet cereal, but it wasn't until they were in the rental car, a few minutes from arriving at the Magic Kingdom, that his stomach started to hurt. At first he tried to ignore it, far too excited to find out what was so magical about where they were going, but the closer they got, the worse he felt. He wanted to tell his parents, but they wouldn't stop talking, and he knew better than to interrupt. He waited as long as he could before finally shouting, "I really don't feel good!" moments before throwing up remnants of Lucky Charms and sour milk all over his brand-new shirt. Evann still remembers the disgusted look on his mother's face as she shrieked at his dad to pull the car over.

She pulled him from his booster seat with such force he wondered if his arm might pop out like a Ken doll's. While his dad leaned over the barrier trying not to be sick himself and his mom mopped up the mess in the backseat, Evann stood at the side of the road, scared and ashamed. He wondered why she was so worried about the car when there was puke all over Mickey's face, hoping she'd help him soon so that it wouldn't leave a stain. When it was his turn, she had him step out of his shorts. She stuffed them in a grocery bag and tossed them in the trunk. Next, she tried to pull off the shirt, but it got stuck on his ears. He squirmed as she yanked harder and harder.

"Don't you dare," she growled as he gagged at the smell. By the time she got the shirt off, his ears were burning, his eyes watering. For a moment, he was embarrassed to be standing in his underpants, but then he watched helplessly as she balled up his shirt and threw it in the ditch. He opened his mouth to protest, but she gave him a look, and he knew better. He fought back angry tears as she turned her Wet Wipes on him, scrubbing the rough towelettes vigorously across his face.

"Nice one, Evann. We were going to have ice cream today, but since we won't be getting the deposit back for the car, I guess we can't."

His cheeks stung as she continued to scrub.

"Jesus Christ, Ann! Get a grip. He didn't do it on purpose," his dad shouted over the traffic.

His parents spent the car ride back to their rental in silence while Evann sat in his underpants, his bare skin sticky against the damp booster seat, thinking about what he'd done. He held back tears as he realized the consequences: his new shirt was gone, his mom was mad at him, he wouldn't get to find out what was so magical about the Magic Kingdom, and, to top it all off, he'd lost the chance to get ice cream.

From then on, vomiting had been synonymous with shame and failure, and there had always been plenty of other things in his life to elicit those emotions; refusing to vomit was one of the few things he could control. Until today, that is.

As he crouches in the parking lot, he feels no less foolish than he had as a puke-covered toddler standing on the side of the I-5. Pulling up his pants—repulsed by the fact that he wasn't able to wipe first—he considers his options. With each passing minute, there is less residual dope circulating through his system, and pretty soon the agitation will become unbearable. Lying in wait: more and more cruel words and painful memories, more suppressed emotions threatening to overwhelm his fragile psyche.

———

He's done a lot of pathetic things—sleeping in a rat-infested alleyway, eating discarded food from a takeout bag, bathing in a public restroom—but he's never allowed himself the indignity of begging. But as he bends down to retrieve his bag, which sits mere centimetres from a puddle of his own shit, he realizes he's no better than any of the panhandlers he's looked down on—it's only that, until now, he hasn't been desperate enough. As he resumes his stagger toward Waterfront Station, stopping to dry-heave each time he catches a whiff of himself, he finally understands what true desperation feels like.

It doesn't matter what he has to do to get his hands on some junk —be it beg, borrow, or steal—he'll do it.

There is no way he's prepared to spend another hour sober.

14

Evann has never been so sick. He's known what it is to crave a fix, but this is like nothing he's ever experienced. No flu can hold a candle to the misery that pillages his body and mind with each passing moment. Milliseconds are stretched into hours; someone has him trapped in a time loop, forcing him to stay locked in the hell of his mind. All around him, they are watching him—laughing at him as he staggers aimlessly, aching to get something—anything—into his system.

I'm sorry you're such a failure, Evann.

You should be ashamed of yourself. I gave you everything, and still, look what you've become.

Why don't you just kill yourself, Evann? Nobody would mind. We wouldn't even miss you.

He swats away the voice—her voice—as he forces one cramping leg in front of the other, lurching forward as though being pulled along by his throbbing head. Through watery eyes, he sees tears—or snot or drool or maybe puke—drip onto the sidewalk. He just wants to curl up on the ground—to give in, to let go—but his possessed corpse keeps staggering on. Like a moth to a flame, it seems to know where to take him.

15

EVANN TRADES HIS VINTAGE 35MM NIKON FOR TWO TABS OF Percocet from an old guy busking at Canada Place, absolute thievery considering it should've returned double that, but he's hurting too much to bother bartering. He'd been prepared to beg for the money if it meant an end to his suffering. Having previously resisted the idea—reluctant to further widen the chasm between who he'd been and who he'd become—today that final thread of his tattered ego snaps and he's willing to surrender. As he turns to walk away, a little girl drops a five in the man's guitar case, and Evann has an epiphany.

Holy shit. Why have I never thought of that?

The busker isn't begging. He's creating. And that's different.

As the percs hit his system, the fuzzy outline of his new business plan comes into sharp focus. He cleans himself up in the washroom at Waterfront Station and makes his way back to Gastown. Evann selects three pieces from his sketchbook, carefully tearing along the perforated edges. Steadying his shaking hand, he writes *Art by Ev. $5 each* in beautiful calligraphy. He rips a blank page from the back, meticulously folding it into an origami box and setting it out in front of him. Then he waits.

Many slow down to admire his work but continue along once they notice the gaunt figure behind the display, his cleanest dirty clothes doing little to disguise the unshaven and unkempt man. Had they looked closer, they might've seen the gentle sterling grey eyes of a kind and hurting soul—those eyes holding a rare flicker of pride within.

The steam clock screams twice before he makes his first sale. The elderly couple, in their matching Vancouver T-shirts, smile politely, tossing the change in his paper box, but they don't linger, don't make small talk, don't look him in the eye. He's not surprised at the illustration they choose. It's one of his favourites: a majestic bald eagle catching a fish in her talons, set against the stunning beauty of Quatsino Sound. He drew it under the light of a propane lamp in a remote cabin on northern Vancouver Island, on what turned out to be the last fishing trip he and his dad took before he left for university. A heaviness settles in his chest as he watches the couple walk away—watches an item that he'd once cherished disappear into the crowd. Even his most cherished possessions are only worth the dope they'll return. He swallows hard against the realization of what that means about him.

"That's so cool, Mom! That dog looks just like Shadow!"

Pulled from his trance, Evann blinks away the past.

A child crouches in front of him. He watches as the boy brushes his blond curls from his face, studying one of the illustrations.

"Alex, don't touch the man's things," his mother says, reaching for his hand.

"It's o—" Evann clears his throat and starts again, focusing on the child. "It's okay." He can see the child's mother in his periphery, arms crossed, her discomfort evident in the tension of her jaw. He runs his hand down the back of his neck, the skin tingling with anticipation.

"Is Shadow your dog?" Evann asks.

The boy looks up, his deep brown eyes meeting Evann's. "Yeah, she was. But she got real sick, so she had to go away. But it's okay. She was old, and now she gets to play in doggy heaven."

His chest tightens at the innocence of the child's declaration, the earnestness of his gaze.

"Well," Evann says, "I know what it's like to miss your dog. It can be super hard, but it seems like you're being really brave."

Evann reaches out. The boy hands him the picture, understanding the request though the words are left unsaid. Pulling a pencil from his case, Evann works quickly and masterfully, the shaky hand of an addict temporarily replaced by the sure hand of an illustrator. For a few moments, his fears and insecurities fade away, his frenzied thoughts cease, and there is silence.

Returning the picture to the child, he hears the mother gasp. She crouches beside her son, her eyes filling with tears as she stares at the drawing. Evann has transformed the illustration: beside the dog, he's added a caricature of the boy, a head of wild curls, arm around his beloved pet.

"Can you believe it? It turns out the dog in my sketchbook was Shadow all along. I just didn't know it yet."

The woman reaches into her purse and pulls out two twenties.

In another life, maybe he'd have turned away the money, would've insisted on giving the sweet boy the sketch, would've considered it an insignificant price to pay to make them smile. But in this life, Evann is starting to fidget, the Percocet barely keeping the dope sickness at bay. So instead, he accepts the money, avoiding the mother's eyes, shame burning in his chest. He watches them walk away, leaning close and looking at his drawing together, and for a moment, Evann lets himself envy the bond between this unknown boy and his loving mother before carefully closing the lid on the box where he's learned to lock his emotions.

He has forty-five dollars in his hand, but in his mind, it's already spent.

16

WITH THE ARRIVAL OF AUTUMN COMES A DENSE CLOUD COVER, which hangs over the city. Hoping to escape the unrelenting rain, Evann spends his limited energy hauling his backpack from shelter to shelter before finally getting a spot, thankful not to have to spend another night lurking in the shadows of harbour-view mansions. Having never put much thought into the inner workings of a shelter, he doesn't know what "low barrier" means, naively assuming every shelter will offer the basics: safety, security, privacy—perhaps a place to take a hot shower, a locking door, somewhere he can lay his head down and get some sleep. He certainly isn't expecting it to have the amenities of a hotel, but he figures it'll be at least marginally better than a prison. Evann spends much of the night—crowded in a room with a dozen strangers, terrified of what might happen if he falls asleep—lying on his cot comparing the two: In prison, the doors lock —there are guards around to intervene if someone pulls out a shank. Here, there is nothing to protect him—no doors, no locks, no guards.

The guy in the bunk beside him mutters nonsensically to himself, leaning forward, tourniquet clenched between his teeth, his cell-phone propped against his bag, trying to get the vein between his first and second toes. Finally succeeding, he drops his uncapped rig on the floor between their beds and nods off, sporadic grunts and gasps escaping from his slack jaw, which hangs open, the light from his cellphone illuminating his toothless gums and weatherworn face. In the bunk above Evann, a restless man thrashes—side to side, back to side, side to back—over and over. His track-marked arm hangs over the edge of the mattress; as it catches the light, each twitch and spasm causes the shadow of the tentacled figure to gyrate along the wall.

Evann finally drifts into a fitful sleep. He's jarred awake in the early hours of the morning by a hysterical wail. Sitting straight upright, he struggles to distinguish his surroundings. The room is dark—the cellphone having either tipped over or died—and his eyes are slow to acclimate as he frantically tries to locate the source of the danger.

"Fuck sake! Wake him up!" someone shouts.

"Goddammit, he does this every fuckin' night."

His eyes finally adjust, and Evann sees the man a few rows over, thrashing in his bed. His scream is one of absolute terror—panicked and anguished—as though he's being tortured; as if his very survival is at stake.

A slight man shuffles toward the door, slurring fuck and shit and goddammit as he bumps his way through the darkness. He flips on the light, illuminating the room, which erupts in four-letter objections from his already agitated roommates. The man gently shakes his neighbour.

"Jesus Christ, Frankie, wake up, eh. You're okay, my brother. You're okay. No one here's gonna hurt ya."

Under the bright lights, Evann sees the elder—his back hunched, shoulders rounded, gently stroking the screaming man's forehead—hears his soft *shh, shh, shh* between the ongoing complaints of the other roommates. Startled awake, the man bolts upright, his distraught eyes scanning, his clenched fists raised and ready for a fight. The old man reaches out, taking hold of his hands, firmly but non-combatively moving the man's fists away from his face.

"Hey, my brother. Look at me, okay. Look right in my eyes. You're safe, Frankie. It was just a nightmare. You're safe."

In an instant, Frankie snaps out of it. His glossy eyes seem to come into focus. "Ah fuck, not again," he says, fighting back a sob. His head falls heavy against his chest.

"All right, that's enough. Turn off the fuckin' light," commands a booming voice.

The elderly man shuffles over to the wall, his long braid swaying over his curved spine. He flicks the light switch, plunging the room back into darkness.

Evann isn't able to sleep the rest of the night, the man's tortured screams rattling in his mind. He's never heard such a primal sound before, but he has a peculiar sense that he's experienced this very situation himself. As he wrestles with the feeling of déjà vu, he's haunted by the memory of the screaming.

Unable to face the notion of another night of hell, Evann makes yet another stupid and short-sighted decision and gives up his bed. Certain there must be greener pastures elsewhere, he doesn't consider that maybe he isn't the only guy tired of pruned feet, of sleeping outside, chilled to the bone. In sopping shoes that are starting to come apart at the seams, he walks the fruitless gauntlet, dragging his rain-soaked pack up and down Hastings. After several more nights of nocturnal wandering among the meticulously tended and tree-lined streets of Point Grey, he's finally able to find a space in a different shelter, only to discover that—although the people are different—the conditions are very much the same.

17

EVANN ARRIVES IN DEPARTURE BAY WITH TWENTY-SEVEN dollars and fifteen cents in his pocket. Fuelled by fear, he's spent the past week weaning for the trip home, his days dragging by in a state of ceaseless longing and his nights spent lying awake, staring at the underside of a stained mattress, the snoring of a dozen men augmenting the relentless racket of his mind.

Having sold off the remainder of his art portfolio, he's been managing to get by. But using, once a catalyst for creativity, has stripped away his artistic instincts. No longer does his pencil glide along the paper. No longer do the images arise, almost as if sculpted rather than drawn, the graphite a sort of chisel gradually removing material, exposing that which lay hidden within the page. What was once natural has become forced. His shaky hand has become unreliable, its muscles atrophied. In its place, a clumsy fraud, unable to carry out the intuitive movements that had once been effortless. In his graceless claw, the pencil strokes are too firm, too light, too defined, too subtle. Everything he produces feels flat and uninspired. He considers that perhaps his ineptitude is less physical and more psychological; maybe it's just too difficult to produce beauty while living a grotesque existence.

This trip home has already put a significant dent in his savings. He needs to look presentable if he has any hope of maintaining his cover, so he splurged to have his hair and beard trimmed ($14.85 he'd rather've stuffed up his nose). Add that to the cost of the two-hour bus ride to the ferry terminal (another $4), and the walk-on rate for the ferry ($16.90 plus $0.25 for some "Port Authority Fee"—whatever that means), plus the cost of enough pills to keep him coherent for three days of face-to-face time with his parents, and he's left with a twenty-dollar bill and a fistful of change. Growing up, he hadn't known what it was to worry about money. Coins on the sidewalk hadn't been worth the effort of picking up, nickels and dimes absent-mindedly tossed into fountains or tip jars. Whatever he spent was replenished without question. He'd never imagined that one day he'd be trying to make dollars out of pennies. After many failed attempts, unable to draw anything he's willing to sign his name to, he'll return to Vancouver with next to nothing—assuming he survives an entire weekend with his family.

With no money and no income source, he has no way to fund the intensifying demands of his narcotic mistress. Their relationship, once a warm and indulging love affair, has become a cold and depleting marriage, one that teeters on his continuing willingness to give more and more of himself while receiving less and less in return: his existence a series of transactions. Every withdrawal—whether money or an item or a remaining shred of self-respect—is followed by a deposit—snorted or smoked or swallowed—amounting to nothing more than a swap in time: time spent feeling like shit for time spent feeling nothing at all. These transactions are never one-to-one. The cost is always greater than the reward. Yet, he keeps going back, regardless of what it costs him, his hopes hinging on the impossible possibility that maybe the next will be as good as the first. The first is always the best: the first pill, the first rush, the first fix, the first minute; now relegated to the past, perpetually out of reach. Each day of his addiction is worse than the last: a series of cruel lessons in why it's called chasing the dragon, not catching it.

With very little dope running through his system, he was restless on the trip across the Strait of Georgia. Pulling out his sketchbook, he made another futile attempt at harnessing his anxious energy into something productive, rescued by a toddler who made a game of peeking at him over the seat. Evann played along, feigning surprise, pretending he didn't see her before she shouted "Boo!" He pretended to draw while she laughed hysterically, squealing in delight as she popped her head over the seat again and again. The game was a welcome distraction, but eventually she got bored of tricking him, so he returned his attention to the open page.

The limitless possibilities of the empty space felt overwhelming in a way it never had before. He let his mind wander, willing his hand to take over, eavesdropping on the happy family without meaning to. As he sketched, he allowed himself to imagine that he was the one scribbling a crayon masterpiece, that he was the one playing Simon Says, that he was the one singing "Twinkle, Twinkle, Little Star." But the longer he sat there indulging his childish fantasy, the more ashamed he felt. He tore out the page and crumpled it up, disgusted to see the outline of three faces on the page in front of him. Only the most pathetic creature—one with no self-esteem, no self-respect, no self-control—would envision himself in a life he had no business intruding upon. He spent the rest of the trip pacing back and forth on the ferry, avoiding that little girl and her parents. Eventually, he gave into his craving for a dopamine hit—the vending machine too great a temptation—and wasted three of his precious dollars on chocolate bars. By the time the crew announced their arrival at Departure Bay, the song was on replay in his mind, his own version of the lullaby, buried deep within his subconscious.

Little boy who whines a lot
Belly-aching, but for what?
Thinking that his life's so hard
Just ungrateful, no regard

That his mommy's sick and tired
Of her boy, the rotten liar

———

Undernourished and underdosed, Evann struggles to make it down the ramp, old wounds rubbed raw, his shoulders burning pathetically under the weight of his nearly empty pack. As he weaves through the crowded terminal, he fights to remain upright, fights the urge to snort everything he has on him to escape the painful memories haunting him.

Outside the arrivals area—impossible to miss next to her black and yellow Smart Car—waits his Auntie Barb. Despite the aching pain in his limbs, the subtle throb of an early headache making its intentions known behind each watering eye, he can't help but smile when he sees her. How fitting it is that his free-spirited aunt, a proud hippie who introduces herself as "Barb, but please, call me Barbee," has an eco-friendly car that undeniably resembles a bumblebee. Auntie Barb is nothing if not eccentric. Born seven weeks and three pounds too early, she grew up defying the odds—or perhaps defining them. As a child, her hair was such a pale tone of blonde it was almost translucent, right into her twenties, when—almost overnight— it morphed into the beautiful blend of grey and white that now hangs straight and silky, nearly reaching the waist of her tiny four-foot-nine frame. They've always shared a special bond. Perhaps she too knows what it means to be a little bit strange—to be the piece that doesn't quite fit. Perhaps that's why she has a soft spot for her only nephew, why he can always count on her to be a friendly face in his otherwise hostile family.

He's so distracted by the car, he doesn't immediately notice the balloon she's holding. She rushes over to him, the balloon dragging along behind her, bouncing frantically as if it is excited to see him too.

"Oh my God, Ev! It's so good to see you!" She wraps her arms tight around his waist, her head barely reaching his chest. "Happy

Birthday, buddy. I hope you don't mind it's a few days late. I wanted to tell you in person. You know how I feel about talking on the phone. So impersonal! And I thought that by the time you got your card in the mail, it would be late anyway, so I figured, why not just save the stamp and give it to you when I see you?"

Evann half listens as she chatters on, his mind drifting to the packet of pills carefully tucked away deep in his backpack, repeating the same calculations in his mind, reminding himself that if he greedily strays from his plan, he'll run out of dope before the weekend is over. He stuffs his bag into the miniature trunk and, with great difficulty, manages to get his long legs folded into the passenger seat, wedged firmly against the dash. As he carefully opens her hand-crafted card, it strikes him that his birthday passed unnoticed. Now that he's thinking about it, he doesn't remember seeing any missed calls. He's used to belated celebrations with his dad since he's always away for work, but this year, not even his mom or Nicole called. He pulls out his phone, double-checking there's no missed calls, no unread texts, no indication anyone left him a message. Clearly they all forgot—or perhaps they just didn't care enough to remember. A familiar ache radiates across his chest. He wants nothing more than to fix, to nod off to the beautiful place where his traumas, old and new, can't hurt him.

Lodged in the body of the bumblebee, Evann shakes away the hurt and returns his attention to the thoughtful card. His hands start to tremble with longing as he thumbs the three crisp fifty-dollar bills inside. It's more money than he's had at one time since he was robbed. He promises himself that in exchange for a weekend of hell, he'll treat himself to a belated birthday gift—a little something to help him forget what he's about to endure.

"Thanks, Auntie Barb. This is really generous of you," he says sincerely.

"Just don't tell your sister," she says, winking. "She only got forty. But she's already got more than she needs, and you know you've always been my favourite."

Evann's cheeks burn hot. Auntie Barb always manages to see the best in him, in spite of there being nothing good to see. It's her greatest gift. While others have always been able to see through his act, had somehow predicted he was destined for failure, she's believed in him. When his parents said he was too immature to move away, too undisciplined to bother with university, Auntie Barb stood up for him. When the family criticized art school as a fool's pursuit, she was the one to convince them that—given the tools and education —he could make a career as an artist. A knot of shame tightens in his guts.

"Anyway! Tell me! What's going on with you?"

"Uh, not much really." He wants desperately to steer clear of any topics that will force him to lie to his sweet aunt.

"I bet you've been drawing tons! I'd love to see some of your recent stuff."

"Sure, yeah," he says, shrugging politely.

"So how is school going?"

A tug-of-war plays out in his mind. Evann lets his hot cheek rest against the coolness of the window. He opens his mouth, the truth threatening to tumble out, but immediately thinks better of it. No good will come from disappointing her. He feels sick at the idea of lying to her, but he also can't stand the idea of stepping down from the pedestal she's placed beneath him, admitting that all of the potential she's seen in him has been nothing more than a carefully maintained facade erected to cover a deeply flawed foundation. It's too much for him to face. He carefully creeps toward the ledge between fact and fiction. "Uh, yeah, it was okay. Pretty tough," he says, disgusted with himself.

It's a lie, clumsily disguised in the semantics of past versus present, but she doesn't seem to notice. His throat tightens as the words leave his mouth—a coup against his brain, a trivial attempt to stop his sick mind from doing any more damage. He can't bear to broaden the brushstroke of his disappointment to stain his kind, caring aunt; to disappoint her would be to take the final step off that cliff.

"Is everything okay, Ev? You seem awfully quiet today," she says.

"Yeah, no, I'm fine. I just got up really early so I'm kinda tired." He cringes at the half-truth, turning away from her and hoping she won't notice the heat that has creeped up his neck, his ears burning bright red, as they always do when he lies.

It is true he's tired—in fact, he can hardly stop himself yawning—but in actuality, he needs another fix far more than he needs sleep. A more accurate not-lie would be to say something like: "I'm actually on a bit of a comedown, Auntie Barb, so I'm not feeling all that great. I only took a fraction of what I normally use to cope with the everyday burden of living, but this weekend I have to be on my best behaviour so I don't accidentally out myself as the homeless junkie I am now. So no, I'm not really fine. And yeah, I am awfully quiet."

But some things are better left unsaid.

"You're just like your dad—a man of few words. Why don't I shut up and let you rest," she says, patting his knee. "I'll wake you up when we get there."

He lets his eyes drift closed, knowing that no matter how much he needs to sleep, his deprived brain won't let him rest.

18

His arrival home is anticlimactic. His mom is with Nicole, no doubt basking in the attention her daughter will be receiving on this, the opening night of the ballet, and his dad's flight isn't in yet. Auntie Barb offered to buy him dinner, but he politely declined, and she didn't push. After she pulls away in the bumblebee, he begins his search for the stupid fake rock his mom keeps hidden in the front garden. As he fumbles in the dark, he wonders why his mom —obviously paranoid that someone will find the spare key, given it's in a new spot every time he tries to find it—doesn't just get rid of it. He can't help but laugh at the irony that she goes to such effort to keep people just like him from getting inside, yet here he is, traipsing through her flower beds. It's no longer amusing after five minutes of searching through the expansive gardens. Maybe instead of him having to stumble around, stepping over all the hostas, she could install a keypad like everyone else in the twenty-first century. Or maybe she could've thought to leave the front light on, knowing he'd be arriving after dark. Better yet, she could've cut everything back a month ago so the plants weren't left to slowly wilt, leaving a soggy mess of enormous decomposing leaves for him to search through. For someone who cares so much about appearances, she really is shit at keeping her gardens tidy.

He stomps the mud from his shoes and lets himself in, fumbling for the light switch in the dark entryway. He peels off his jacket, no longer accustomed to the tropical twenty-five degrees his mom insists on keeping the house. With great effort, the dog gets up from her bed, her tail wagging lazily as she lumbers out to greet him.

"Hey, my girl," he says, kneeling to scratch the old pup's ears. He sits down like a child, legs outstretched, his arms wrapped around her as she licks at him. "At least someone is happy to see me," he says, looking into her cloudy eyes. He sighs heavily against the aching in his chest, pushing aside the thought that she probably doesn't have many of these reunions left in her. She's showing her age in the greying fur of her face, the way she flops down on her hind legs, letting them splay to the side when she sits. She'd once been a proud protector of the house, but now she either didn't hear or didn't care to check who was rummaging around in the front yard. He kisses her soft head, tears stinging at the back of his eyes.

He walks carefully, his footsteps light as he wanders through the dark house and into the living room. Despite growing up here, he feels like an intruder, snooping around another family's home. Not much has changed, but he's been away long enough that the once-familiar space no longer feels like home. He studies the sign now hanging above the fireplace, his mom's cursive painted across repurposed pallets: *Family. Always. Forever. No Matter What.* Rolling his eyes, he thinks, *Yeah, sure.*

Below it, pictures line the mantel. He picks up a photo of the four of them at Long Beach, remembering how much fun they had building sand castles and chasing tiny crabs through the tide pools. It's one of his only happy memories of them all together, one of the rare times they didn't split off into their suitable pairings: mother with daughter, father with son.

Tucked to the back is the picture from the time they had professional photos taken. In it, they all wear bright smiles, standing arm in arm in their matching outfits. The story the photo doesn't tell is that Evann's white T-shirt is on backwards, a fresh grass stain hidden from view, his scraped hands tucked behind his back. His parents had been so busy arguing on the way across the park that his dad accidentally knocked him over, Evann's ruined shirt and bloody hand only adding to what had already been a chaotic morning. His mom used the rough fabric of her coat to scrub the dirt off his face, giving him a look that said *Don't you dare start crying*, and the Cartwrights managed to pull themselves together just long enough for the photographer to snap a few decent photos.

He looks at a photo of himself at karate class on the day he earned his yellow belt, wearing a proud smile that doesn't extend to his eyes. Photos of Nicole in various dance costumes over the years. A photo of her riding her bike. A sob catches in his throat. He took that photo: a perfect snapshot of the little girl she once was, an expression of pure joy on her face, her wispy hair sticking out from her hot-pink helmet. He got in a lot of trouble that day, having taken his mom's expensive new camera, but it was worth it; he was proud of his little sister, who had learned to ride a bike all by herself, and looking back on the moment now, he decides the spanking was worth it.

He makes his way to the kitchen, reads the note sitting on the island:

Ev,
Air mattress is downstairs.
Won't be home till late. Money in the takeout jar if you want.
See you after the ballet.
M

"Weird," he says to the dog, who's already fallen asleep, sprawled against his backpack. "What are they using my old room for?"

Leaving his bag and the dog behind, he goes to look. When he opens the door, his jaw goes slack. The formerly green walls have been replaced with a soft pink, so pale it's nearly white. He winces, not because he was attached to the old colour, but because he can tell the new one is Nicole's choice; he was never allowed to choose his own colours. In fact, the only time his mom did ask for his opinion, she painted his room something entirely different while he was away fishing with his dad.

"This just looks so much better, sweetie. The one you picked just reminded me a bit too much of baby shit," she explained innocently.

Evann didn't argue. He was used to her doing that kind of thing.

"Why can't he just have whatever colour he wants?" his dad asked. "It's his goddamn room."

She rolled her eyes. "Oh for the love of God, Bruce. We're not doing this. Come on, Ev. We all know you've never had an eye for colour. Which is why"—she continued before his dad could interject —"it's great you're so talented with a pencil!"

Staring into the room, no longer able to picture it as it was before, he can't quite pin down the emotion he's feeling. Hurt? Confusion? Betrayal? He—who was never allowed to hang so much as a poster on these walls—looks at his reflection in the enormous mirror spanning wall to wall, floor to ceiling. Affixed to the mirror is a ballet barre. The worn carpet has been replaced with laminate, and all the furniture has been removed. Knowing his mom, it's probably been donated to some "charity," her standing excuse for getting rid of things she no longer deems valuable. Shelves hang around the perimeter, displaying an impressive collection of trophies and ribbons. He isn't standing in his old bedroom, he's standing in what is as much a dance studio as it is a shrine to his sister. "Un-fucking-believable," he mutters to himself, slamming the door behind him.

Curiosity pulls him toward the open door of his parents' bedroom. He peeks his head through the doorway before crossing the threshold, drawn to the pile of cash sitting atop the dresser. He pockets a few bills and a handful of loonies and toonies, knowing they won't notice—people who have money never seem to keep track of it. Poking around the room, he casually notes the time, distantly aware that his dad will be home any moment. He also knows this will probably be the only time he has the house to himself. Helping himself to the medicine cabinet, he pulls out each bottle, laying them out on the counter one by one.

Venlafaxine. *Meh, not interested.*

Ativan. *Yup.*

Cialis. *Eww, fuck!* The bottle clatters into the sink.

Trazodone. *That would do in a pinch.*

Tylenol 3. *Same.*

Sumatriptan. *Uh, not sure what that is. Probably not.*

Jesus. She's got a fucking pharmacy in here.

Percocet. *Bingo.*

Pantoprazole. *Not interested.*

Zopiclone. *Hello, old friend.*

Hydromorphone. *Jackpot. Why does she even have these?*

He swallows a Percocet and lets an Ativan dissolve under his tongue while he surveys the buffet in front of him. He knows enough to be considerate in his selections. His mom has always been a pill popper—she obviously doesn't need all of these prescriptions, since half of them are well past expired—but if he gets greedy, there's a chance she might notice. He picks up the nearly empty Naproxen bottle and fills it with his choices, indulging in those that were tucked to the back, and taking only what he's sure she won't miss from the others.

"Hello?"

A shiver runs down his spine. *Fuck.* He hurries to put everything back as he found it, closing the cabinet. He meets his dad in the hall.

"Hey, Dad. It's good to see you."

"Uh, yeah. Hey," his father says, his tone flat. Bruce never has much to say. His size and presence make him seem more intimidating than he actually is, but there's something in his expression that makes Evann squirm. At this moment, he has no idea what his dad is thinking.

"What were you doing in our bedroom?" he asks in his usual matter-of-fact way.

Evann pulls the Naproxen bottle from his pocket. "I have a bit of a headache. There were only a couple left in the bottle so I figured it'd be okay if I took the whole thing." *When did lying become so natural?* "Sorry, I guess I should've waited to ask since I don't actually live here anymore." He isn't sure he means it as a jab, but it comes out that way. Bruce doesn't seem to notice.

"Nah, don't worry about it. Help yourself to whatever you need," he says, eyeing Evann suspiciously. "You hungry?"

19

FROM HIS BLOW-UP BED ON THE FLOOR OF THE UNFINISHED basement, Evann hears the flurry of excitement as his mom and Nicole come through the door at nearly eleven o'clock.

"Oh my God, Bruce! I wish you could've been there! She was absolutely flawless!"

A *thump*, a quick *snap*, and a *thunk*. The exposed joists creak, those beneath the recliner relieved of duty as the others pick up the weight.

"Hey, sweetie, congratulations! I can't wait to see you perform tomorrow."

He imagines their dad squeezing Nicole into a close hug, her head pressed against his broad chest. He tries to remember the last time he pulled him into one of those tight embraces.

Roused by the excitement, the dog slowly rises from the concrete floor beside him. He watches her, silently begging her to stay—to climb onto the air mattress, to rest her warm body against his—but even she seems to understand the familial pecking order. She lets out a low groan, the loose skin of her belly resting on the floor as she stretches, right hind then left, before lazily making her way up the stairs. No longer can the old girl take the steps two at a time. Evann listens as her arthritic legs carry her step by step—front, front, hind, hind—all paws landing gracelessly on each stair as she makes her way up.

The excitement carries on as the family walks through the entryway into the kitchen. Car keys clatter onto the counter. A purse —or maybe a gym bag, maybe a pair of ballet slippers—drops with a *thud*. Quite a task for the old dog, getting all the way up the stairs; probably the last time she'll bother with the effort of following Evann down the steep staircase to bed. Now, her long nails click along the floor above him, the rhythmic thrum of her tail against something solid—maybe a wall, maybe the leg of a chair.

He lurks in the basement as the family catches up; the mom and dad seeing each other for the first time in weeks; so much for the daughter to share with her daddy; the dog no doubt dozing close by. The forgotten son remains unmentioned, unseen, unacknowledged, an outsider, quietly listening from below. He waits pathetically— even crawls over to sit perched on the stairs—on standby, hoping to hear his name, hoping to be called upon, hoping to be considered.

He listens intently, but he doesn't hear mention of the son. Then again, the voices are a bit muffled, and he's too much a coward to show himself, so maybe—probably—he just missed it.

After some time, the house falls silent. It's late. Everyone must be off to bed.

———

Miscellaneous tablets and capsules—a mismatched cocktail—rattle as his finger searches. A blue oval pill scrapes up the inside of the bottle, set to the side, followed by a round white one. *These should do.*

Click. The lonely room plunges into darkness.

It's been so long since he's slept in a noiseless room, alone. Absent the snoring of strangers, the creaking of weight being shifted, the silence is deafening. The house groans, as if releasing a held breath.

The more he tries to ignore the percussive beating in his ears, the faster it becomes.

Click. A single bulb illuminates the room.

More rattling. He pulls out another round white pill—for good measure.

Click.

20

Feeling like shit, he's more than happy for Nicole to be the focus of the weekend. After waking from a night of broken sleep, he can't decide what, or how much, to take. He lays out his options, dumping his hand-selected Naproxen cocktail on the mattress along with the pills he bought for the trip. It's been a while since he had to consciously decide how much. He's been living fix to fix, buying what he can afford: sometimes that means he takes enough to pass out and ride around on the bus until the driver yells at him to get off; other times he hovers right in the sweet spot where nothing matters and nothing hurts and he can hold his head high and parade down East Hastings as if it's the Champs-Élysées. Most of the time, he barely manages to get enough to keep him from getting sick.

There's little room for error if he's going to achieve the perfect trifecta: a bit drowsy (but not so much that he'll slur his words or nod off), a bit indifferent (enough to keep his anxiety under wraps, but not so much that he can't hold up his end of a conversation), and a bit of a rush (but not so much that he blabbers on or makes an ass of himself).

The stuff from the streets is the riskier option, unlabelled tablets bought off a shifty lady he's seen around who, immediately after snatching half the profits from his illustrations, nearly ran him over with her scooter. He was left holding a bottle with a scratched-out label, the contents inside unfamiliar—certainly not a match to the last pills he bought, which had also been sold as Dilaudid. On one hand, he's intrigued by these mystery pills, hoping against hope that they might turn out to be a decent oxy knockoff. On the other hand, he's not willing to risk being fucked out of his head in front of his family; just being here—spending time face to face with them—is reckless enough.

He decides to set those aside for his emergency supply, reconsidering the rest of the pills. For a moment, he lets himself imagine what would happen were he to take them all. Gathering them in his hand, he allows them to slip between his fingers, to spill from palm to palm. His own worry beads, unbound, unrestricted—promising to set him free. He read about this once, the phenomenon of "the call of the void": nothing more than a benign manifestation of the psyche's twisted curiosity. It happens to everyone, but not everyone has the means or the motive. Not everyone spends their every day silencing intrusive thoughts. Ultimate self-destruction wouldn't be such a leap for someone like him, would it?

He watches them run from one hand to the other like sand in an hourglass, never letting the last pill drop. Would anyone really miss him? Would they even notice? Have they forgotten he's down here? The pills stick to his palms as he starts to sweat. It's intriguing—the void calling to him—but the thought of doing it makes him feel sick. Somewhere deep down he feels an unfamiliar sense of control, of power. Setting aside a Percocet and an Ativan, he pours the pills back into the bottle. He feels a sense of satisfaction; just knowing that he can, that it's up to him—that this is one thing they can't take from him —is enough for now.

———

Day two of not-quite-enough is not going well. Fortunately, his family —too naive, preoccupied, or perhaps indifferent—seem to assume he has a bad cold, so they keep their distance. No one questions his continuously running nose, or that he's wearing a heavy sweatshirt in the overheated house. The oven slams open and closed as his mom frantically prepares for Thanksgiving supper. Curled on the farthest end of the couch, Evann tries to ignore the crashing of pots and pans, the incessant slamming of cupboards, neither of which are helping his throbbing head, nor his steadily increasing agitation. He can't understand why she has to be so fucking noisy all the time, as if she's incapable of just setting something down rather than letting it drop with a loud thud. It's nothing new; she's known to crash through life, eliciting stares with her maniacal cackle, her *Here I am, look at me* demeanour, but he'll never get used to her boisterous way of being. Even more grating is her voice, which has only three settings: loud, even louder, and silent, though he knows better than to wish for the latter. He learned early in life that her silence was to be feared much more than her shouting.

Her record was thirteen days. Thirteen days of not speaking to him, not looking at him, not acknowledging his presence. It might've been a welcome reprieve—no yelling, no threats, no hurtful words or snide remarks—but as one week bled into the next, he was desperate to return to normal. He started to resent his sister—not more than a toddler—watching anxiously as she selfishly consumed what little love their mother had to give. The silence unmoored him, and he spent those thirteen days adrift, a small child all alone, forced to navigate without a compass.

What he did to deserve thirteen days of deprivation, he can't remember. What he does remember is how it felt. How the silence taught him just how much power she held over him, just how much he needed her, craved her attention, even if it came by way of criticism and putdowns. Every day was another day toward forever, and the fear of forever was crippling. His angst built every day, higher, higher, higher—until he was certain there was no room left in his cluttered mind; that his head would split open; that all of his stupid thoughts would spill out of his stupid head; that whatever he'd done would be out in the open and everyone would finally know all the reasons his mommy was right not to love him.

And just as the barometer inside his mind was reaching its breaking point, it was over. A switch was flipped, and she went back to normal.

He never did, though—never could shake his fear that hidden from sight, the pressure would continue to build, and that sooner or later, it would have to blow. From then on, every day was always a day closer to the possibility of an unending silence.

He unfolds himself from his couch cocoon, retreating to the basement, where he doubles down on his morning cocktail. Even the basement offers no reprieve from the bashing and banging. He lies face down, buried in blankets, counting his rapid heartbeats as he wills himself to forget about the precious powder carefully hidden away in his bag. The minutes pass in struggle, addiction and anxiety teaming up, trying to override fear and logic, trying to convince him that a little won't hurt anybody, that they probably wouldn't even notice. His skin grows damp, his breath hot as he exhales, laboured as he inhales, sucking the moist pillowcase into his dry mouth. Soaked in sweat, he pulls the blankets tighter over his head, too scared to emerge from his hiding hole, all too aware that the final barrier between him and a proper fix is the relative quiet and false sense of security afforded by his blanket fort.

The door to the basement swings open, slamming against the wall.

"Evann, get up! You can't just sleep the goddamn day away! Your grandparents are going to be here any minute."

He groans in response, but she's already gone, stomping across the house and up the stairs. He can just imagine her softly knocking on his sister's door, peeking her head in, and gently saying, "Nicole, sweetie, it's almost time for dinner."

Throwing the blankets aside, he rolls to the edge of the bed, the under-filled air mattress dropping him to the floor. The concrete slab feels refreshingly cold through his damp clothes, the familiarity of the unforgiving surface comforting in a strange sort of way. The sleeping arrangements might not be as cushy, but at least he's started to find his place on the streets. Out there, he's figured out how to blend in, whereas around here, the line between him and them is stark; he's nothing more than a placeholder to occupy a seat at the dinner table, a spectator to whistle and cheer for Nicole on her big day. Just another face in the crowd. He strains to push himself upright and pulls on a clean shirt.

"Evann! How many times do I have to tell you?"

"I'm coming," he says, knowing she won't hear him, knowing she's back in the kitchen from the muffled sound of her shout. He turns, looking once more at his backpack, the temptation threatening to pull him under. Hearing her stomp toward the open door, he heads up the stairs.

"Evann!" She's a silhouette in the doorway, her head bowed, reading something on her phone. She doesn't notice he's coming up the stairs until he's standing right in front of her. "Jesus Christ! Don't sneak up on me like that," she shrieks, holding her free hand over her heart. She flips the switch, illuminating his cave in the blinding light of a single bulb. "That's not actually what you're planning to wear, is it?" She looks him up and down, contorting her mouth into a disgusted snarl.

He follows her gaze over his plain black T-shirt and jeans, the nicest items remaining in his limited wardrobe. "Uh, yeah. What's wrong with what I'm wearing?"

"Watch your tone," she says, glaring up at him. "Have you looked in a goddamn mirror? You look like shit. We're going to a ballet, not some art show, and I'm not going with you looking like that. Can't you wear something nice? Or do you always have to dress like a fucking slob?"

"But, I don't have—" He's interrupted by a knock at the door.

"Enough. Just go let your grandparents in. I'll have to figure something out after dinner," she says, continuing to block the doorway. Her jaw tightens, an unsettling intensity in her eyes. "I mean, the clothes are one thing, but I don't know why you insist on keeping that goddamn beard. You look like a homeless loser."

He instinctively reaches up, running his hand along his facial hair. His cheeks burn hot, concealed beneath his beard, neatly trimmed for the first time in months. He flinches as she reaches past him. She raises her perfectly shaped eyebrows triumphantly, flicking the light switch behind him. She still has him. She knows it, and he knows it. After all this time—even after putting an ocean between them—he hasn't managed to escape the spell she has on him, the fear she's instilled in him. Taking a step toward him, she brings her hand to his face, her fingers finding a tuft of hair, pulling it taut, tilting his chin down until their eyes meet. She studies him, her eyebrows furrowed. "Actually," she says, her voice barely above a whisper, "I suppose it doesn't much matter. You've just got one of those faces that only a mother could love."

As unexpectedly as it starts, her unprovoked assault stops. Untangling her fingers, she pats him on the cheek. He watches as the veil drops, wiping the menace from her smile, the hatred from her eyes. Smoothing her dress, she fixes her mouth into a disingenuous smile as she moves away from him, answering the door herself while he follows, numbly observing the flurry of activity as his extended family jostles for space in the crowded entryway.

His dad, having heaved himself out of his recliner, towers over the crowd, reaching to take the jackets. Through the mass of bodies, Evann can feel his mother's icy glare, disguised behind her thin-lipped smile. Without words, he knows what she's thinking: he should know his place, should've been the one to step forward, to help his elderly grandparents out of their thick coats. Evann avoids her gaze, disoriented by the chaos. Auntie Barb makes her way through the door, dragging his forgotten balloon, its cheerful message lacklustre on the deflating carcass of crumpled foil, just enough helium remaining to keep it not quite floating, yet not quite flat. Nicole runs down the stairs, wearing her two-piece Dance Academy tracksuit, hardly recognizable with her garishly painted face pulled tight by her ballerina's bun, every hair glued firmly in place with sparkly gel.

"There's our princess," Gramps says, grabbing Nicole by the cheeks and leaning in for a wet kiss square on the lips. Nicole smiles politely, quickly wiping her mouth before she turns to Gram.

Amid the chaos, Evann catches the look exchanged between his parents. They see the balloon, and in the way that only a couple of twenty-odd years could pull off—subtle enough to remain unnoticed by the untrained eye—they silently communicate. But Evann has spent his life mastering those subtleties—those spaces between words where so much is said—and he sees their shared panic, imagines what they must be saying: *Shit...Did you call him? No, you usually call him! Goddammit, I can't be expected to do everything! It's fine. We'll just have to do cake tomorrow.*

"Oh darn it, Herb. We forgot the flowers in the car," Gram says. "You wouldn't mind running out to get them, would you, Evann? There's a little something in there for you too." She winks.

With the oversized bouquet of roses and a store-wrapped box of Purdy's chocolates in hand, he runs back to the house on his tiptoes, wishing he'd put on shoes before wandering out onto the damp drive-way. His mother's words repeat over and over in his mind like an accusation. He hates that she can see through him. But does she actually *know*, or has she just narrowed in on his deepest insecurities? Is what she used to say about being able to sniff out his lies true? Has she somehow used her motherly senses to intuit that her son has become just what she'd expected?

21

As the family moves from the kitchen island toward the dining room, he watches for the telltale signs: the flush of his mother's cheeks, Gramps doing his best to feign sober, his white nail beds betraying his grip as he lurches from chair to chair, making his way to the head of the table. Evann notes the empty wine bottles, four polished off in the span of an hour, his mother and grandfather—as customary—responsible for at least one apiece. Ann sways as she refills her glass, and Evann wishes he could retreat down to the basement, into the pills, out of his head. But he can't risk stepping away—can't allow his eyelids to grow any heavier, his senses to be further dampened.

Instead, while the others busy themselves, exchanging potatoes for beans, buns for roast beef, he does the only thing he can: he watches, and he waits. Taking his portion, he passes the items along, but all the while, Evann's attention is on his mother. He's spent his entire life observing her, studying her, trying to stay a step ahead of her. By the time he started kindergarten, he had her consistent cues mastered. When she rubbed her forehead, he knew to go draw in his room or take Nicole upstairs to play. A tight-lipped smile had a couple of meanings: when in public, it meant *Get over here, right now*, but at home it meant *Shut your fucking mouth before I slap it*. He knew when they had cereal for dinner, he needed to keep Nicole extra quiet the next morning, but those times weren't to be discussed when Dad was home. He knew to put on all his underpants if her eyes went wide and her jaw got tight. The extra layers didn't help a lot, but at least the wooden spoon might not sting so much if she was in a rush and didn't pull down his pants first. He knew that if she was talking on the phone, or to an adult, or watching TV, or reading, or she had a headache, or was tired, he wasn't allowed to ask her a question. That rule was revised to exclude emergencies, however, after he politely waited for her to finish her phone call before reporting that Nicole's hair was on fire; he had a sore butt for days after that incident, and even though his sister had been the one breaking the rules, it was somehow his fault for not noticing she was leaning over the flame, dipping her fingers in the melted candle wax.

Evann became very good at following rules, assuming he knew what the rules were. It became more convoluted any time the pattern lost its regularity; when she was into the wine, the rules had a way of becoming distorted and abstract. Sometimes she wanted him to crawl onto her lap to cuddle when she was watching TV. Sometimes she pushed him off and complained that he was always crawling all over her. That didn't apply to his sister, though; Nicole was always allowed to cuddle. Usually, he had to hold her hand when they crossed the street. Sometimes she acted like she didn't see him reach for her and instead he had to cling to her handbag, scared that all the bad things she said would happen to a kid crossing the road without an adult would happen to him—even though, technically, he was crossing with an adult, technically, he still wasn't following the proper rules. When his dad was away at work, Evann was responsible for making sure he and Nicole ate their cereal, brushed their teeth, packed their lunches, and were out the door in time to catch the bus. When he was home, their mom would get up before everyone, make pancakes, and pack their lunches. In his stupidity, Evann once started to comment on how it was nice to see Mommy in the morning, but across the table, he saw her eyes go wide, her jaw clenching behind a forced smile, and he knew to shut up. When his dad asked him what he meant, Evann broke one rule in order to comply with another as he fabricated a tall tale, watching her features soften as he carefully lied his way out of the hole he'd carelessly stumbled into.

And because it's become second nature, while everyone else is preoccupied with the peas and the gravy, casually chatting about life and work, sports and politics, Evann hasn't stopped watching, which is why he's the only one who sees the nearly undetectable look that Ann flashes Nicole as she reaches for a bun. Glance—eye contact—head tilt—insinuation—recognition—understanding—course change. To those not watching closely, there's nothing to see—Nicole simply doesn't want a bun, preferring an extra helping of peas instead.

"Ev. Your grandmother is talking to you."

He flinches at the heavy hand on his shoulder. His dad gives him a squeeze, gentle enough to seem casual, firm enough to convey a message. "Sorry," he says, refilling his glass. "I didn't catch that, Gram." He swallows hard, the bitter Malbec burning hot at the back of his throat. He's never acquired a taste for fine wine, but tonight he's sucking it back like grape juice. Interestingly, no one has said anything about his drinking, as though it's expected now that he's an adult. He's among kindred spirits. A bunch of addicts, each with their own vice: work, wine, power, control. He's certain that should they come to know the loving embrace of his China White, they too might add heroin to their lists. Of course, they'd be horrified at the idea, mortified at the suggestion that their sophisticated indulgences share any likeness with the obscene drug earmarked for lowlifes. He's happy to indulge in their pick if it provides a socially acceptable cover for the erasure he craves. Smiling politely, he turns to face his grandmother, lifting the glass to his lips.

"Oh, that's okay, dear. I was just saying how good it is to see you. Has it really been three years since you've been home?" With her hands tucked neatly in her lap, she looks helplessly weak next to the imposing presence of her husband, his enormous protruding gut draped in a cloth napkin, speckled with food that hasn't survived the long trip from his plate to his mouth.

"No, Mom. He's been away at school for just over two years," Bruce says.

He was also home at Christmas, but Evann doesn't bring that up. His grandfather sits up straighter in his chair. The hairs on the back of Evann's neck stand up, and before Gramps opens his mouth to speak, he knows what's coming. He knows that scowl—typical of a man who wears the look of displeasure beneath every expression. Even his clothing conveys his unhappiness, the button at his neck straining to contain the sagging skin of his miserable face. It's a wonder he can breathe. Evann inhales, steeling himself.

"You're not still wasting your money on that, are you, boy? Tell me you've come to your senses and found a real job by now," his grandfather says.

Evann picks up his wine again. The clatter of silverware on plates continues, but no one takes a bite. This scene is a familiar one, one that's been repeated countless times over the years. Looking between his grandparents, Evann wonders—not for the first time—how his grandmother, beautiful in every sense of the word, has spent her life with that mean old bulldog.

"Of course, we all know you're not man enough to get a job on the rigs like your old man, but I do hope you've got some plan for the future."

"Oh jeez, Dad," Auntie Barb says. "How many times are you going to bring this up? Let's not start with this again."

"You stay out of this, Barbee. I'm asking the boy a legitimate question. How exactly does he plan to support himself once he's done getting his 'degree'?"

Evann catches the glint in his mother's eye, the subtle curve of her lips before her smile is concealed behind her wineglass. She has that look: she knows where this is going, and she's relishing in it.

"I'm just saying," Barb says. "It's not the '60s anymore. Not every young man aspires to work on the rigs."

"What's wrong with working on the rigs? Look around. Seems like Bruce has done all right for himself. Wouldn't you agree?"

Evann scans the table. Nicole stares into her lap, pushing her abundant peas around her plate. Auntie Barb slides her chair back, excusing herself to the washroom. His father reaches for seconds, happy to continue the festivities after what, at least to him, has been nothing more than a brief interruption. Evann meets his mother's eye. She appears calm—bored even—spinning her diamond ring around and around. Without thinking, he moves his hand to his face, the pad of his middle finger running back and forth over the scar above his eyebrow, a permanent reminder of the consequences of being disrespectful, an ugly mark rendered by her beautiful stone.

"I just hope he doesn't end up leeching off the system, is all," Gramps says.

"I couldn't agree more, Herb. But that's something you'll have to discuss with your son." Ann holds her glass up in a cheers to her father-in-law, her mouth curved in a satisfied grin.

Nicole's fork hangs frozen above her plate. Beside Evann, his dad clenches and unclenches his fist.

"You and I both know he's over there wasting away his college fund, but your son thought we should support him, even though we both know it'll be our tax dollars that bail him out when he's serving lattes at Starbucks for ten bucks an hour," Ann says. It seems she has more to say, but she stops, shrugging instead.

She's baiting the hole, waiting for a bite. He'd caught a lot of hooks in the cheek before learning to simply keep his mouth shut. She's impatient, and without at least a ripple in the pond, she'll quickly divert her focus elsewhere. Her bass-mouthed co-conspirator reaches for a fresh bottle. Evann stares at her defiantly, the wine and the pills propping him up. Several beats of silence pass, and he takes satisfaction in watching the smirk evaporate from her face, which—if he's being honest—is really starting to show her age. Years of frowning have carved crevices between her brows. As a little boy, he always told his mommy how pretty she was; it was one of the only things that could elicit a reliably positive response. Now when he looks at her, he sees that no amount of Botox can mask the ugliness he knows to be hiding just beneath the surface.

His grandmother smiles nervously. "That's enough, dear. Evann is forging his own path, and if he thinks he can support himself by drawing pictures for a living, all the power to him. Anyhow, how is school going these days? Are you getting enough to eat? You're looking a little thin."

"It's—" Evann starts to say.

"My God, Dot. You say that about everybody." Ann laughs. "Christ, you even say Bruce is too thin, and just look at him." She tilts her head toward her husband, raising her eyebrows to make her point.

"I am," Bruce answers, his dry humour met with chuckles and eye-rolling around the table.

"Anyway," Ann says, "I think it's great Evann has lost some weight. You know how chubby he got during high school. It's nice to see him down a few pounds."

"I don't remember him ever being chubby," Barb says, returning to her seat with a fresh glass of wine in hand.

Why are you always so quiet, Evann? he thinks mockingly. *I guess it's probably because even when someone asks me a question, no one cares to listen to my answer.*

"What do you mean? Of course he was! Don't you remember? His nickname used to be Heavy Evvy!" Ann says, exploding into laughter.

"Oh my God, that's right," Nicole shouts. "We *did* use to call you Heavy Evvy! Oh my God. That's hilarious."

Ann dabs at her eyes and his sister picks up her phone, already bored of the conversation.

"Oh for heaven's sake. I really hope you didn't actually call him that. He was just tall for his age," Auntie Barb murmurs.

"No he wasn't! He was huge! But anyway, it's great that he's lost his baby fat. Although you can hardly tell when he insists on dressing like a slob all the time." She takes a long, slow sip. "That reminds me," Ann says, addressing Evann directly, "I really hope you're not planning to wear those filthy runners and jeans to the ballet tonight. Hopefully some of your dad's old clothes will fit you." She looks around for approval, getting a shrug of agreement from his grandfather. "In any case, it would be nice to see a bit more muscle on him. I imagine going to the gym isn't really your 'thing' though, is it?"

Everyone but Gramps fidgets uncomfortably, but Ann doesn't seem to notice. Without pause, she moves on to recounting Nicole's performance the previous night. The attack was uncalled-for, but not unusual, an expected byproduct of his mother plus his grandfather plus an abundance of wine. Even if any of the other guests happens to think she's out of line, no one dares stand up to Ann; more than one family dinner has ended with her pushing her chair back dramatically and stomping up the stairs.

Evann endures the rest of the meal in silence, thankful that in the dim of the theatre, no one will be looking at him. He doesn't want their attention. He doesn't want their pity. Doesn't care to make small talk, or to answer their rhetorical questions, or to wear the mask of a proud big brother. The only thing that will make him feel okay would be to feel nothing at all, and the only way he knows how to accomplish that is to do the one thing he knows he can't do—not here.

22

STRAINING AGAINST THE WEIGHT OF HIS EYELIDS, HE PEERS AT himself in the mirror—blinking, blinking, blinking—unable to see through the haze.

But of what?

Steam? Had he showered? He doesn't seem to be wet, though neither does he seem to be clothed—faintly aware of cold air brushing against areas that would otherwise be covered. Maybe. Maybe he just finished showering.

Fog? The mist of his hot breath accumulating on the mirror? No. His face isn't close enough. Not possible for his shallow breath to reach the mirror.

His eyes. Are they open? Have his eyelids collapsed under their own weight, unable to overcome the downward pull? Yes. No. They aren't open.

A simple answer, but the solution requires such vigorous effort.

Why is it that every movement requires such vigorous effort? Through slits, he fumbles his way into the shower.

Such effort it takes to convince his scrawny arm to take hold of the faucet. His mom was right: had he more muscle, he wouldn't be struggling so pathetically, his legs threatening to buckle beneath him.

Seated, such a relief, cool water pours over his flaccid body, collapsed in a contorted posture, his limp neck dropping, head to knees, arms listlessly splayed at each side.

Time passes—minutes, or is it longer?—the water running cold, until his captor suddenly removes the veil, exposing such pain!

Tiny icepicks push up through every pore. A pulsating pain throbs against the invisible vise encasing his skull. Every muscle aches against shivering tension. His eyelids, lighter—blinking, blinking, blinking—water streaming down his raised face.

———

Sleep has become an illusion in his life as an addict; when he takes enough junk, it's easy to fall into a shallow stupor, neither restful nor restorative, but if he doesn't take enough, he tosses and turns, memories surfacing like barely buried corpses, his mind struggling to differentiate fact from fiction, past from present, a saga of uneasy nights spent anguishing. On the streets, he worries about his safety. In the shelters, he worries about his stuff. In the basement, he worries about his standing, a fear so absolutely encompassing that it sends a shiver down his spine, holds his greedy nostrils at bay one day to the next because the risk is simply too great. It hadn't been his intention—his mind was far too detached from his body to have consciously contributed—but his hand made its selection: three sleeping pills and two painkillers. Plus the wine: too many glasses to count. Enough to account for the piercing pain behind his eyes, not enough to wash away the sting of what was said to him, about him. Face down in the pillow, Evann had been sucked away, willingly succumbing to a blackness that extinguished his thoughts, plunging him into the first real sleep he'd had in months. With the darkness had come absolute silence. No dreams, no thoughts, no awareness. Absolute nothingness —as if his body held vigil in the physical world, while his mind and soul escaped—perhaps to somewhere else, perhaps simply to nowhere.

———

Thrust back from his peaceful rendezvous, he finds himself stark naked, teeth chattering noisily. *But, how did I?* It doesn't matter. Grabbing the last of his Percocet, he coughs the pills down, his mouth coated in a thick paste. He checks again, confirming the time. He has no awareness of getting up. The piss all over the toilet seat suggests he had. Hours gone and unaccounted for. It's unlikely anyone came down to check on him when he didn't surface for breakfast, or again for lunch, but if they did, he doesn't remember. If they did, they'd seen him, and if they'd come close enough—taken off the blinders, allowed themselves to acknowledge that which is so painfully obvious —they'd know what he's become. And if they knew what he's become, they'd have come to realize that their worst fears about him had been naive, short-sighted—inconsequential even.

The truth is so much worse than anything they could've imagined.

23

EVANN OPENS HIS SKETCHBOOK ON THE DINING ROOM TABLE because other than going back downstairs and taking that entire bottle of pills—which he hasn't ruled out as an option—drawing is the only tool he has that might help settle his anxiety. It's been a long two days of biting his tongue and struggling to get by on far too little dope. Mercifully, his parents have gone out, and with just Nicole and the dog home, the house is quiet. He stifles a burp, the aftertaste of last night bubbling at the back of his throat. He swallows against a wave of queasiness, looking around the room, searching for something to draw inspiration from, something to distract him from the throbbing in his head, the burning in his chest.

The one thing that had always come naturally to him now feels like a chore, and as he finds himself once again staring at the blank page, he wonders if it truly had been as easy as he remembers. The idea that having a pencil in his hand used to unleash some mystical power—that an image would emerge from the page, meticulously detailed and brilliantly lifelike—now feels foreign and impossible.

The first time it happened, it was as if he'd entered a trance. His breathing slowed. His fidgeting hand found purpose, moving his pencil with blind certainty, as if it had somehow known what it was meant to be doing all along. He escaped inside himself, oblivious to the time, unaffected by the world around him, until—for some reason outside of his awareness—his hand set down the pencil just as reflexively as it had picked it up. He blinked and he was back in his body, utterly shocked by what he saw. Each movement, commissioned with certainty—by whom or what or why, he had no idea—had created something magnificent: an Allosaurus so closely resembling the one on his poster that his mom squeezed his cheeks painfully—accusingly—when he told her he drew it.

He didn't care that she didn't believe him; she always thought he was lying, so he figured he'd just have to prove it. From then on, his interest in dinosaurs became an obsession. Before long, he'd mastered Ankylosaurus, Raptors, Tyrannosaurus, Stegosaurus, and even Pterodactyl—which was tricky because the wings were really intricate. Every day after school, he drew crouched at the coffee table while *The Land Before Time* played on the TV, and each night before bed he read from his *Dinosaur Encyclopedia*, trying to memorize new facts to teach Nicole. It was too hard to impress his mom, and too easy to impress his sister, so he marked off the days on the calendar, counting the sleeps until his dad got home from work and he could show off his latest creations. He was finally good at something, finally getting attention for something he was doing well, rather than for something he was doing wrong. Even his mom sometimes said nice things about his drawings, letting him hang his best work on the fridge with Nicole's dance certificates.

Or she had. Before he ruined it.

He spent an entire weekend working to perfect a really complex rendering of a T-Rex head, carefully copying the beady eyes and menacing teeth, the serpentine tongue and intricate scales. Nicole stared, mouth agape, when he showed her the final product. "Whoa! You gotta show Mom this one," she said, jumping around his room. Her excitement was contagious, and he fed off it, but when he got excited, he got reckless. When he got excited, he misbehaved.

Together, they sprinted downstairs, his stocking feet slipping on the hardwood as he slid to a stop in the living room.

"Mom! Look what I drew!" he said.

"I'm on the phone." Her voice remained low, but she spoke through clenched teeth, pressing her palm over the mouthpiece. Still excited to show her, even then Evann didn't realize the gravity of his transgression—not until she hung up and turned on him.

"How many goddamn times do I have to tell you not to interrupt me when I'm on the phone?"

He stared at her feet remorsefully, hoping she'd be done being mad at him soon. He still really wanted to show her his drawing, held at his side.

"Look at me," she demanded, grabbing him under the chin and tipping his head back, forcing him to meet her gaze. "What is the matter with you? Your sister is only seven and somehow she knows better and you don't."

She tipped his head back even farther and he understood it was stupid of him to assume she wasn't expecting an answer. She always expected an answer. He heard Nicole quietly sneak up the stairs.

"Is that it then? Your baby sister is just smarter than you?"

Tears streamed down his cheeks as he shook his head no, unsure if that was the right answer. Maybe his sister *was* smarter than him. Maybe that was what was wrong with him. Maybe if he admitted that, she'd stop squeezing his face so hard, and if she stopped squeezing so hard, maybe the black spots would go away.

"I didn't think so."

His eyes betrayed him, ignored his pleading, letting more and more tears go.

"Smarten up, Evann. You're not a baby anymore, so stop acting like one," she said, giving him one final squeeze before releasing his face. His cheeks burned—the sting of shame and fingernail marks—as she wiped his tears on her jeans, disgust written on her face. "And quit crying, or I'll give you something to cry about." She grabbed the page from his hand, giving it a passing look. "Yeah. Great. Good job," she said, tossing it back at him.

The next time his dad was home, when he asked to see what Evann had been working on, he showed him the elephant he'd copied out of a book from the library. Evann shrugged off his questions. He knew better than to reveal what went on under his mother's regime. It was safer to let his dad assume that his dinosaur phase had simply ended.

Evann retreated further into himself. The little built-in desk tucked in the corner of his bedroom became his safe space, the place where he could go to escape. When he sat down and picked up a pencil, he fell through to a place of nothingness, a place where he could float—without pain, without judgment, without thinking—as if falling though a trapdoor somewhere deep within, freeing the boy from the hostility of his own mind. She couldn't get to him when he was in there, and she didn't care to, not as long as he was keeping himself occupied: out of sight, out of mind, out of her hair. In the long years during which his mere presence was enough to set his mother off, life was easier for everyone if he kept to himself.

And if he'd left it there, disappearing into the pages of his sketchbook, perhaps now he wouldn't be struggling to find inspiration where there is none, belonging where it's never existed. Perhaps he wouldn't be shivering in his sweat-soaked clothing, trying to distract himself, trying to think of something—anything—other than the bottle of pills rattling for his attention. Had he known the dangers lurking, maybe he would've been more cautious, more careful. In the beginning, the feeling was so similar that he didn't consider the risk, didn't consider that there might be more than one trapdoor—more than one way to escape into nothingness—didn't see how different they really were.

Instead, he believed his own self-absorbed lies for far too long: told himself that drugs helped him be more social, a better student, a more prolific creator. He doubled down, even as pills became powders, once in a while became all he could think about—long past the point of knowing but not admitting—until one day, he found himself sleeping behind a dumpster, the stench of strangers' piss and rotting food a welcome reprieve from the sour stink of his own unbathed skin and unwashed clothes. It took that long for him to realize that he was falling rather than floating. But by then it was too late. The trapdoor had slammed shut.

24

THE DOG LETS OUT A HEAVY SIGH AS SHE RISES FROM HER BED and trundles over to lie on the cold tile. Her head resting in her paws, she looks at Evann, her greying eyebrows twitching as she watches him from across the room. She's been the subject of many of his pieces, including the abstract acrylic hanging in the entryway, which he had to submit for his university application. Unlike some of the other "artists" he's encountered, especially those on the streets, his work never features vibrant colours or dripping blood or missing eyeballs or needles sticking out of the subject's neck. He's always had a knack for drawing faces, animals, and nature scenes. His portfolio has included lifelike renderings of Willie Nelson and an elaborate illustration of a peacock that shimmered off the page, despite being portrayed in pencil. The beauty of his work has always been in the details, in the seemingly effortless way he captures the intricate feathers on an owl, the wrinkled skin of an elephant, the glacial peaks overlooking the crystal clarity of Joffrey Lake. From where he sits, he can see the painting. To his realist eye, the piece is grotesque. He despises it. He is—was, at least—happiest with a pencil in his hand. It isn't the medium that irks him, but its garishness: the bright colours give it an ostentatious feel, the piece begging for attention rather than commanding it. His mother knows how much he hates that painting, which is likely why it's the single piece of Evann's artwork she's ever had framed. It stares at him mockingly.

He sits up straight, cracks each knuckle, and sets out his tools in the same order he always does. As he lightly sketches the outline of her face and paws, the image begins to take shape. He doesn't get too fussed about getting it exactly right. Instead, he works carefully to get the placement and proportions of her features accurate. Next, he begins adding the details, the short strokes of his pencil meeting to form arrows, which will produce the texture of the Labrador's fur, starting around her greying eyes and working his way toward her dark ears, his strokes sweeping from the bridge of her nose down toward her jowls. Uncharacteristically impatient, he grows frustrated, his watering eyes making it impossible to focus in on the fine details. Nicole studies him as she pours a glass of water and moves to stand behind him. She stays quiet, watching over his shoulder, as he moves from pencil to pencil. His head is throbbing, heart rate accelerating to keep time with his agitation. He sits back. There's something off in the proportions, something not quite right. It takes him several moments to pick out the spot near the eye where the page has puckered, the clean lines distorted by a tear left unbrushed, allowed to fall carelessly from his exhausted eyes.

Her voice startles him. "How many times you think you've drawn her?" she asks, sitting across from him.

He shrugs, reaching for his pencil and returning his attention to the page, though he's lost all interest. If she wasn't watching, he'd crumple it up and throw it away. He closes his eyes and visualizes the flap of heroin hidden away downstairs, trying to imagine the rush he'll get once he's finally free to deposit it up his nose.

"Remember how long it took us to convince Mom and Dad to let us get a dog?"

He can't help but smile. Of course he remembers. It's hard to believe more than a decade has passed. That was back in the days when they were teammates, two kids doing their best to pull one over on their parents. It took a month-long campaign to convince them. Nicole deployed crocodile tears and pouty lips and her cutest smiles, while Evann spent his recess at the library typing up their list of promises, spelled out in Comic Sans. They each signed the contract— Evann helping his sister, who couldn't remember how to write her name—before presenting it to their parents after weeks of extra good behaviour.

> 1. *We promise to pick up there poo*
> 2. *We promise to take her for walks*
> 3. *We promise to through the ball for her every day*
> *Sined,*
> Nicole + Evann

Their mom and dad found their commitment impressive, and hilarious, and the contract—broken almost immediately after getting the dog—still remains pinned to the corkboard in the mudroom. They wanted to name the new puppy Harry, but their parents argued Harry wasn't a great name for a girl dog, so Mrs. Potter had been the compromise.

Nicole leans over to scratch Mrs. Potter behind the ears. "Not gonna lie, I kinda miss how you always used to draw pictures for me," she says.

He forces himself to look at her, pressing his lips into a half-hearted smile. He's adored her since the day she was born. That has never changed—but she has. She was once his best friend, the one person he was able to rely on, but as she grew older, he saw more and more of their mother in her. He sees the way she looks at him now. The poorly veiled disgust is far too familiar.

The sweet little girl who used to sneak into his room and cuddle in beside him, tell him that Mommy hadn't meant it, that she'd just lost her temper, that she really did love him—that girl is gone. Sitting across from him now is a young woman who is growing more callous, more self-absorbed, more manipulative, and it makes him feel sick. The apple doesn't fall far from the tree, and he learned not to overlook his sister's capacity for cruelty the hard way. Once Nicole realized how much her dance meant to their mother, realized that just allowing Ann to dress her up and treat her like a real-life doll guaranteed her carte blanche, she used it to get whatever she wanted, even when it came at his expense. So as much as he'd love to push aside his hurt, to chat with his sister, to confide in the person he'd once been able to talk to about anything, he knows better than to trust her. Anything he tells her will get back to their mom eventually. He's not about to make that mistake again.

"I, uh—" she hesitates, her gaze on the dog, "I know Mom and Dad forgot your birthday, and that Mom's totally trying to play it off like she was just so busy with the ballet, or that they just wanted to surprise you, or whatever, but I... I just think it's kinda a shitty thing to do—to pretend we didn't all forget when we obviously did—so, like, I'm sorry I forgot."

Evann shrugs. "Don't worry about it."

He looks over the sketch, decides to try to salvage it. She rolls her eyes and pulls out her phone, obviously not satisfied with his indifference. The room is quiet, the sound of her breathing filling the space between them. Another thing she's picked up from their mother: her unconscious habit of treating each breath like a savoured drag off a cigarette. Inhale: hold, hold, hold, hold. Exhale: the pent-up breath rushing to escape through her nose in an irritating *pffft*.

Pffft. Pffft. Pffft.

Again and again and again.

It's almost too much to stand, the *pffft* and the scratching of his pencil scraping along the pad—what should be soundless, effortless, fluid—coming together disharmoniously, grating on his last nerve, his hidden reserve tugging him toward the basement like a magnet. The chair teeters on two legs as he pushes himself to his feet.

"Are you okay, Ev?"

He pauses, scanning her face, trying to read her expression.

"Uh yeah. I'm fine. Why?"

"I don't know. You just seem, like..." She searches for the right words. "I don't know. Off, maybe? Like not quite yourself."

He lowers himself into the chair, suspicious, but curious where this will lead. He starts shading around the dog's ear. She has a unique way of talking herself into a corner when given the space. Usually, once her foot is firmly in her mouth, she'll either double down, change the subject, or walk away. But something in her tone seems earnest.

"I just mean, like, it must be really hard for you. Hard, you know, to live over there and to keep pursuing your passion, even though Mom, like, *constantly* talks about what a waste of time and money an arts 'degree' is—yeah, like, she actually does the finger thing when she says *degree*. And I was just thinking about how that can't be easy."

Evann doesn't respond, the sound of his pencil scratching along the paper filling the space. *Well, considering you know me, like, so well, like, I guess you should, like, know.*

"Anyways, if you're not okay, or there's something wrong, or you want to talk or whatever, you can tell me," she says. "And, like, don't worry. It's not like I'd tell Mom and Dad or anything."

He weighs his options and decides to give her the out. "Thanks. If I ever need to talk, *or whatever*, I'll let you know. But I think I'm good for now."

"Okay, good," she says. "But also, I actually think you're really talented. Maybe Mom's wrong, and you'll make something of yourself." She shrugs casually, obliviously unaware that her words land like a punch to the gut.

Ho-ly fuck. She really can't help herself. I don't think she even knows she does it.

"Like, maybe you could be one of those people who gets rich on

YouTube or something. Like, make time-lapse videos as you draw or record tutorials, or whatever."

It's not a half-bad idea, he has to admit.

"Yeah, maybe. Or maybe my sister the professional dancer will support me when Mom's fears come true and I'm forced to work at Starbucks for minimum wage."

Nicole snorts. "Uh, yeah. Not likely." He rolls his eyes. Of course she can't let even an offhand hypothetical comment slide. "I'm not going to be a professional dancer. No fucking way."

He looks up, surprised. "What do you mean? Mom said some school is probably going to offer you a scholarship."

"Yeah, probably," she says, picking at her nails. "But I hate danc-ing. I only do it to keep Mom happy. Like, I'm not going to lie, I do like the attention sometimes, but I didn't ask for all this." She waves her arm around, as if everything in her vicinity relates to her—as if the world truly does revolve around her as she's been conditioned to believe. Evann is stunned, unsure how to respond. "It's just too much sometimes, you know. Like, I used to really love dance, but now there's all this pressure. Mom convinced Dad to pay a bunch of money to convert your bedroom into a studio for me, and now there's no getting away from it. I mean, I worked my ass off to get ready for this weekend. I was so excited to finally get the lead, but the whole time I was up there, I was just wishing it would be over. It's like my entire life has to be dance, but sometimes I just want to be a normal teenager." Her eyes are glassy when she looks up from her lap. "I know it's stupid, but do you have any idea how long it's been since I've had pizza? I honestly can't even remember. It's ridiculous. She tracks everything I eat. I dance every single day, and I'm not even allowed to eat a piece of fucking pizza."

———

As he lies on his flat air mattress, an insufficient stand-in dissolving under his tongue, he replays their conversation again and again, wondering how he'd been selfish enough to believe that her role as the golden child was so much better. Neither of their lives has been easy. Each of them has a role to play, but until now he hasn't seen that each of them has suffered: while one spends his life being deprived, the other is being suffocated.

25

Topped up, he returns to his drawing with a renewed sense of equilibrium and a fresh eye, but, more than anything, with nothing better to do. Having spent the preceding months hustling, scrounging his way to the next fix dollar by dollar, the hours now pass sluggishly, time a plentiful currency, open for him to spend however he chooses. It's a cruel irony that he's unable to spend it the only way he wishes to. His eyelids hang heavy, his eyes sleepily tracking the rhythmic movements of a hand holding a pencil. Back and forth it moves, like a metronome, his head falling forward until it hangs limp, hovering just above the page. Thoughts flutter by, just out of reach. He stares at the hand, no longer certain it belongs to him. He considers asking it to do something, just to see what will happen, but he can't keep his eyes open long enough to make it worth the mental effort.

His head jerks, startled awake by the front door slamming, keys clattering on the entry table. It takes a moment for him to understand where he is, what he's doing, why his neck is so stiff. He must've nodded off, the pencil still hanging loose in the hand, which he now recognizes as his own. Stomping into the kitchen, his mom lets her purse drop to the floor with a *thud* before pouring herself a glass of wine from the box on the counter. She sighs, retreating to the living room. Evann rubs his aching neck and returns to filling in the details of the dog's nose.

"Been a while since you drew the ol' girl, eh?" Evann startles as a heavy hand drops on his slender shoulder. He tenses uncomfortably under its pressure. His dad lowers himself into a chair, leaning in close. "You know, bud, your mom was pretty upset you didn't bother to come up for breakfast," he says in a low voice, turning to check that she's watching TV, not eavesdropping on their conversation.

Evann shrugs. "I wasn't feeling that good so I slept in."

"She made waffles, just for you. You know her and Nicole don't eat that stuff anymore. But you decided sleeping-in was more important."

Evann closes his eyes, fighting the urge to pull away from the touch. "I didn't mean to. I was really tired. I slept through my alarm. But I didn't realize it was so important to her." His dad looks at him with a doubtful expression. "Not like she's too stoked on me being home anyways," he says under his breath.

Bruce raises an eyebrow, and Evann knows better—has had this unproductive conversation a dozen times before—knows that no matter what he says, his dad will always take her side. But he's hovering in that unrestrained space—where his inhibitions are lacking, his resentment overflows—and he really can't help himself.

"What's that look for?" Evann asks, squaring his shoulders to face his father. "I don't think it's a state secret that Nicole is the favourite. Mom doesn't exactly try to hide it." He swallows against a lump in his throat as he wills himself not to cower, not to crumple under the weight of his father's glare like he's done so many times before.

"Don't start with that shit, Evann," his father says, rubbing his hand over his jaw.

"Am I wrong?"

"We're not doing this again, all right? I know you think she's hard on you, and maybe she is, but it's only because she cares about you. She wants to see you succeed."

"Yeah, Dad, that's what you always say."

The sentiment is nice, but talk is cheap. He turns away, unwilling to let his dad look at him, afraid he might see the gloss of his eyes, the pinpoint pupils, the tug-of-war at play within him: his mind telling him he has nothing to lose, no reason to put up with her insults, while his heart begs him to do more, to be more—to earn their love, their admiration, their acceptance. He tunes out as he considers what his dad said. *She cares about you. She wants to see you succeed.* Evann has never been any good at math, and he's certainly never been able to figure out the complex algebra necessary to make her actions add up to anything resembling care. She made that perfectly clear years ago, at this very table. He picks up his pencil, but his hand hangs ineptly over the page as his mind drifts.

———

"Why didn't you just tell me you were struggling so much? Or do you just enjoy embarrassing me in front of your teachers?" She wouldn't look at him as they walked out of the counsellor's office. She'd been reticent during the meeting, politely nodding along while Ms. Taylor went on and on about how badly his grades had slipped in the second half of the semester.

He *had* told her. It was nothing new that he was struggling, it just happened that he'd gotten a bit more lax, worrying more about hiding the booze on his breath and appearing sober than paying attention in class. But even at his best, his grades were never high enough to meet his mother's expectations, so he didn't see the point in trying anymore. He'd never been a strong student, and no matter how many times he'd asked for help—especially with math, which he just couldn't understand, no matter how many times he went over the examples—her response was always the same: he simply needed to try harder, to practice more, to ask the teacher. Yet, she acted surprised every single time his report card was littered with C's. There was no use in arguing with her. She was never wrong. One way or another, the fault always fell to Evann.

That evening, she made him sit at the kitchen table so she could "keep an eye" on him. He stared at his textbook, hoping the numbers would magically reveal their secrets, struggling to concentrate with cupboard doors slamming and pots smacking down on the countertop. Just as she put the water on to boil, the phone rang. "Jesus Christ, Evann. What did you do now?" Ann mumbled as she looked at the caller ID.

"Hello, this is Ann speaking," she said in her artificially cheery tone. She put the phone on speaker and continued preparing dinner.

"Hi, Mrs. Cartwright. This is Dale Kline calling. I believe you spoke with my colleague, Ms. Taylor, in regards to your son, Evann?"

A heavy pit of dread settled in his stomach. Why was he calling? Mr. Kline's classes were the only ones he did well in.

Ann let out a heavy sigh. "Yes, Mr. Kline. Ms. Taylor and I went through Evann's issues at length this afternoon, and we've set out a plan to get him back on track. In fact, tomorrow I'll be calling around to get him a private tutor because, believe me, his father and I are just as unimpressed with his performance as you are."

"Yes. That's great to hear," Mr. Kline interjected. "It's just that I felt compelled to add my perspective."

Ann's head snapped up, her eyes meeting Evann's.

"Yeah, we really appreciate that, Mr. Kline, but as I said, we'll ensure he gets the support he needs to prevent this from becoming an ongoing issue. In fact, he's sitting right in front of me working on his homework as we speak." Her tone was mellow, but Evann could see she was quietly seething. She picked at her nail polish, tiny flecks sprinkling the countertop, her gaze fixed on him. She didn't have to say a word for him to know what she was thinking.

"I understand that, Mrs. Cartwright—"

"Ann. Please call me Ann. Mrs. Cartwright is my mother-in-law," she interrupted.

"Absolutely. Sure, of course. Uh, yes. As, uh—as I was saying, setting aside some of his grades, which I gather you are well aware of, there's no denying Evann is immensely talented. He's not only excelled in every arts class—photography, art studio, media arts—but he's also very active in the arts club. In fact, one of his photos is displayed in the library." Mr. Kline paused. She didn't react, silently responding with a blah-blah motion as she sipped from her glass. "As you probably know," he continued, "he's designed the yearbook cover for the past three years. He's really quite exceptional."

Ann set down her glass and returned to preparing dinner, no longer fully invested in the conversation. Snapping a fistful of spaghetti, she leaned over to speak into the phone.

"So what exactly is it, Mr. Kline, that you have to add? How is being quote-unquote exceptional at drawing going to help Evann succeed in the real world?" Her tone dripped with sarcasm, and Mr. Kline stumbled over his words for several seconds before continuing.

"Wow. Okay. Well, Mrs.—, Ann, I, uh, I was calling because I have been teaching for a long time, and I've never seen a student with as much natural talent and potential as your son. And with all due respect, not every kid is cut out to be a doctor or plumber or an accountant." He took a quick breath, leaving no opportunity for her to interject. "And I think that if we could collectively foster his potential, that there's a really good chance he could be accepted to a reputable university and could go on to be very successful. I clearly hear your concerns about his grades, and I share those concerns—he won't be able to go on to any post-secondary education if he doesn't pass the core curriculum—but I do think that we should start supporting Evann so that—should he decide to—he'll be prepared to apply to universities next year."

Ann stirred the sauce and strained the pasta, passively listening as Mr. Kline outlined his ideas to support Evann: exchanging biology and chemistry for earth sciences, dropping math for essentials of math, and having him meet with the career counsellor to look at potential university options. She was quiet for several minutes after hanging up.

"Well, Mr. Kline sure had a lot of nice things to say about you," she finally said. "But you need to be realistic, Evann. Take whatever classes you want. It makes no difference to me, but your dad and I aren't going to support you forever, so whatever you decide to do, you'd better make damn sure it'll pay your bills."

He ate dinner that evening in the company of his textbooks while his mom and sister sat in front of the TV. He replayed Mr. Kline's words over and over in his mind. He'd never thought about a career in the arts—hadn't considered it to be a possibility.

The thought consumed him for weeks before he started to tug at that thread, cutting back on the drinking, focusing his time and attention on creating his portfolio. His mother retaliated in her own ways, subtly undermining his efforts. As she publicly encouraged him to do whatever would make him happy, privately she was explicit in her view that he was wasting his time, and that—if she had anything to say about it—he wouldn't be wasting *their* money on his childish fantasies.

———

"Are you listening to what I'm saying?" Bruce asks, pulling Evann out of the past. "Sometimes you need to be the bigger person. Understand that she's your mother, and she loves you more than anything."

"Yeah, well, it doesn't always feel like that."

"And—" Bruce says loudly, then nervously checks that Ann hasn't heard before continuing in a lower tone. "And understand that without her, you wouldn't even exist. So you'd be wise to show her a bit of grace, young man."

"If she loves me so much, why is she always such a b—" the word catches in his throat. He crossed that line once before, and despite having six inches on his dad, he doesn't dare allow it to pass his lips again. "Why can't she just leave me alone? She's always got something to say."

"Oh come on. You're not talking about what she said at dinner, are you? Jesus Christ, Ev. You need to toughen up," he says. He leans back in his chair, interlacing his hands behind his head. The message is clear: the matter is closed, and there's no place for further discussion. "She was just pulling your leg. No need to take everything so seriously. Learn to have a goddamn sense of humour."

26

HE TRIES. HONESTLY, HE DOES. BUT THE SYSTEM MAKES IT damn near impossible for people *like him* to execute their rights. The line between a right and a privilege is no longer fixed, no longer permanent, no longer fundamental, now that he's allowed himself to fall below the poverty line—decided to co-exist with the criminals and the junkies. He now belongs to the lacking class. The less thans. The have-nots. Those without money, work, status, willpower, luck, self-respect—or perhaps many of these things—in the eyes of those who have never themselves wanted for anything. Poverty is a filthy swamp, and Evann is deep within the bog, putrid and full of sludge, reeds camouflaging the shore, leaving no discernible escape. Once a person falls in, the water laps against them, soaking their clothing— creeping up pant legs, saturating up to the waist, tugging at the length of a shirt—the downward pressure ever increasing, pulling them deeper and deeper. Overcome with the exertion of remaining upright, it's easy not to notice the mud shackles around their ankles, the rising level of the water licking at their chests, their collarbones, their earlobes—threatening to suck them into the underworld.

From the comfort of their perches high above, the others—the people who, but for class and privilege, are really not unlike *them* at all—might watch in disbelief, oblivious to the struggle occurring beneath the murky water. How can they not see—*those people*—how can they not see that if they simply work harder, of course they can climb from the pond? How can they be so lazy, so unintelligent, so unmotivated? Aren't they even willing to *try*? How can they not see the ladder out—plain as day—just there behind the tall grass? Of course, *those people* are drowning in poverty; after all, if *those people* weren't so complacent, perhaps they wouldn't have waded out in the first place.

———

As he stands in the downpour, lined up on Election Day, his parents' words are heavy on his mind. They made their feelings on the matter perfectly clear as they drove him to the ferry terminal, and even though he felt a bubbling anger deep within his gut as they rambled on and on—about the snowflakes and the Libtards and the drama teacher who was intent on corrupting the country, killing the oil industry, offering handouts to anybody and everybody who didn't have the strength, the integrity, the will to provide for themselves—in the days following their chilly departure, Evann has been conflicted. To do nothing would be to disobey them. To do what he feels is right would be to disrespect them. To do what they expect would be to once again cave to the covert power they still hold over him, long after he no longer lives with them, off of them, or in service to them.

He waits anxiously among the other good citizens, having deliberately taken the bus far from the downtown core, away from the other people *like him*. He feels like an imposter in his freshly washed clothes, his hair combed, clad in his once-quite-expensive Arcteryx jacket, the rest of his belongings stowed safely—he hopes—back at the shelter. As rain cascades over his hood, soaking through the soles of his worn shoes, a taunting whisper mocks him.

Why bother? You'll never be one of them. Just accept who you are. Come back to me. I'll make everything better.

He shakes the voice away. He's here. He's going to exercise his right. He's going to cast his vote. It's as much an act of rebellion against his parents' authoritarian lecture as it is a delusional attempt to prove the validity of his existence. If he votes, he's contributing; if he's contributing, he's a good citizen; if he's a good citizen, perhaps he's still superior to the lowlifes who inject the government's money into their veins.

He wants to believe that he's the kind of man who will defend his principles, do what he feels in his gut to be right, but the voice in his head reminds him that he's merely a boy masquerading as a man—that time and again, he's proven himself as one without principles, one who doesn't know right from wrong. He thumbs the flap of heroin tucked in his pocket—the reward he'll allow himself once he's done the right thing—but the debate wages in his mind, and he's having trouble seeing both sides objectively through the white powder clouding his vision.

As the line creeps through the double doors, he pushes back his soaked hood, the warm air trapping a damp mist against his skin. The sudden heat is suffocating, the floor unsteady beneath him as he unzips his jacket, forces himself to take slow deep breaths. He scratches at a scab as the queue slowly moves forward—his latest vice a satisfying stand-in now that he's pillaged his fingers, each nail ripped from the tender flesh beneath. He hadn't realized he was doing it until he saw the evidence reflected back at him: open sores glossy with serous fluid, barely sealed scabs flaming angry red and speckled with dried blood, lining the nape of his neck. Now that he's started, he can't stop. He quickly wipes his bloodied hand on his jeans, hoping the rotund woman at the registration table doesn't notice.

"Voting card," she says, holding her hand out expectantly.

"Uh, I'm sorry?"

"Your voting card," she says, slower this time.

"I, uh, I don't think I have one." His ears burn with embarrassment. He can feel their heat against his cold hand, which has disobediently returned to picking the scab.

"Did you register to vote, sir?"

"Not—no, I don't think so. I didn't know I had to. I've, uh, I've never actually voted before." His blunt fingertips struggle to get under the scab. He anxiously rubs the area with his pointer finger.

"O-kay then," she says, glaring up at him. "I'll need to see a piece of government-issued photo ID."

He hands over his ID card, fighting to keep both hands by his sides and away from the raw skin of his neck.

"Sir, this is expired. I need a *current* piece of government-issued photo ID."

His rough skin rubs abrasively, escaping into the discomfort. It's probably the fingertips aggravating the thin skin of his neck, but as his mind spins faster and faster, he wonders if it might be the rough scab aggravating the fingertips. He pulls his hand away, forcing himself to focus on the very large, very impatient woman staring at him. He watches her say something, unable to make out the cryptic message, too focused on the slash of cherry-red lipstick staining her front teeth. After a long blink, he tries to refocus, turning his attention to the wild nest of hair plopped atop her head.

"I'm sorry?" he asks.

She sighs impatiently. "This piece of ID," she says, waving it in front of him, "is expired. As in, no longer valid." She discards the card on the table between them. "So, do you have a *valid* piece of ID? One that is not expired?"

Evann racks his brain, distracted by the wild fluttering in his chest. He digs through his wallet in search of his student card, hoping it's not expired too.

"Will this work?"

She stares at him from beneath raised eyebrows, waiting for him to place the card in her outstretched hand.

"Yes. I can accept student ID, but I'll also need something with your current address on it."

The room around him is getting fuzzy. He's becoming unmoored, the floor beneath him tilting unpredictably. Shallow breaths catch in his chest as he scrambles to come up with an innocent excuse to explain that no, he cannot provide proof of address. His mind comes up empty.

"I, I'm—you know what—I'm sorry I wasted your time. I'll, uh, I didn't bring anything with me, so I guess I'll have to come back."

She hands back his card, eyeing him up and down before looking to the next person in line. As he turns to walk away, he's sure he hears her say, "Mm-hmm, I'm sure you will."

Evann sits down on the sidewalk—the sidewalk, in the *good neighbourhood* where the *good citizens* regard him with confusion, perhaps not used to seeing people *like him*, seated in *this* part of town, seemingly without regard for the wet pavement or how it soaks through his cleanest jeans, his underwear, and into the lean flesh of his shrivelling frame. He struggles to slow his breath: *Inhale 2-3-4, exhale 2-3-4, inhale 2-3-4, exhale 2-3-4,* he repeats over and over.

PART II

It is impossible to understand addiction without asking what relief the addict finds, or hopes to find, in the drug or the addictive behaviour.

DR. GABOR MATÉ, *IN THE REALM OF HUNGRY GHOSTS: CLOSE ENCOUNTERS WITH ADDICTION*

27

"Fuck me, kid. You ain't easy to track down."

Evann shields his eyes from the glaring beam pointed in his face, the gruff voice behind the flashlight unmistakable. What isn't clear is how he found him, or why he's come looking.

"Nice place you got here. Looks like you're keepin' warm," he says, sticking his head in through the unzipped doorway. "Fuckin' reeks in here, though."

He doesn't doubt it. Evann hardly draws a breath of fresh air these days, time divided into fixes rather than hours. Now that he has the tent, he's given up on playing the shelter game, preferring the certainty of living alone, even if it means he has to shit behind bushes and under overpasses. Had he been keeping track, he might've known it's been nineteen days since his last shower, eleven since he last ventured out of his fetid cave. He might've heard that Spider has been asking around about him. Maybe then he would've realized he isn't as anonymous as he likes to believe, that people have come to remember the lanky kid with the expensive gear and the vacant eyes.

The tent was an innocent enough pinch from his parents' basement, along with an enormous duffle bag stuffed with a sleeping bag, his old wool coat and hiking boots, several pairs of thick socks, base layers, and his waterproof jacket and pants. Evann figured he could use the gear to survive the cold winter; his parents just assumed he was planning a camping trip. What they didn't know was that hidden in the toe of his boot was a carefully wrapped diamond pendant. He hesitated, but only for a moment, before deciding his mom would probably never notice it was gone. Even if she did, she was always losing things. She wouldn't even miss it. He pawned the pendant for a week's worth of junk and has gradually been trading or selling most everything else.

Christmas came and went in a church basement, in the company of strangers—misfits like him who weren't welcome elsewhere, no different than any other day. He sent a quick email telling his parents he wouldn't be home for the holidays. He didn't bother to explain why. They didn't bother to ask. Maybe a part of him was testing them —giving them a chance, giving himself a chance. Hoping for an out. In the darkest days of winter, he had been ready to admit to them the full extent to which he'd fucked up his life, to disclose his depression, his anxiety, his all-consuming addiction. But they didn't ask, and so there had been no explanations, no raised voices, no tears, no apologies. No "Why aren't you coming home?" or "Is everything all right?" or "Is there anything we can do?" Just a few hundred dollars transferred into his empty account, sent in place of connection. Their money was withdrawn and redeposited, spent up his nose by the time the ball dropped on 2016.

It was in those weeks—as winter greedily snuffed out the light of day, blanketing the hours in disproportionate darkness and depleting the air of its warmth—that Evann really started to lose touch. Maybe it was the short days and long nights, the lack of vitamin D, or the utter hopelessness that finally got to him. Maybe it was the way the coastal clouds settled over the North Shore Mountains like a lid, smothering the city. Maybe it was simply the nature of addiction. Each moment felt exhausting, punctuated with the misty puff of his breath—a visible reminder that although he was still alive, he had ceased living.

The worst part had been the flashbacks. Vivid visions haunted him ceaselessly; nightmares indistinguishable from memories, daydreams indistinguishable from hallucinations. They all felt so raw, so real. His only reprieve was in the ever-closing window of oblivion immediately after a fix. No matter how much he hustled, how much he snorted, how much he smoked, how much he willed his mind to go blank, he could not escape.

His heart would thump faster and faster—angst overflowing into panic—the flutter within his chest moving into his stomach, as if a hysterical bird was battling to break free. There were no nails left to chew, his teeth idly roaming over each fingertip, finding no loose edges to catch, settling instead on angry skin, picked and pulled and ravaged. When he could no longer stand it, he'd give in, spending what he had for a few precious moments of nothingness. And then, from behind drooping eyelids, his chin settled unnaturally against his chest, he'd watch, as if through the eyes of an invisible onlooker: an all-knowing presence.

The child was writing something, his brow furrowed in a look of absolute concentration. Behind him, the lights of a Christmas tree twinkled, reflecting off the meticulously placed bulbs, the gifts positioned just so beneath the tree. The boy tapped his pencil against his temple, his feet swinging several inches from the floor. He sat this way for a long time, silent with his thoughts, before hopping from the stool and delicately taking hold of his paper, mindful not to crease it. He padded out of the kitchen and into the den, a large black dog lazily following. The boy crouched down at the coffee table and fixed his gaze on the gaming console. Carefully, he copied out the letters he saw, sounding each one out: P-L-A-Y-S-T-A-T-I-O-N.

The boy concentrated, his tiny hand gripping tight around the thin

pencil. The task took him a long time to complete, each letter meticulously printed and erased over and over until he had them just right.

Satisfied, he skated down the hallway in stocking feet, the dog close
behind him. In the living room, a woman was stretched out on the sofa,
her blanket-wrapped legs resting on the reclining footrest. The room
was dim, the lights of the Christmas tree and the television dancing
across the woman's face.

"Mommy?"

The woman didn't respond, and he seemed to understand that
although she had heard him, it wasn't an acceptable time to speak. He
took a step back, surveying his work. He felt proud of his resourceful-
ness. Copying the letters off his PlayStation had been quite clever. He
hoped his mom would think so too.

As the boy waited patiently, he studied his letter again, his smile
fading as he realized how many smudge marks his heavy-handed script
had left. He bowed his head, trying not to panic, focusing on the words
they'd practiced reading at school:

Dear Santa,
I have been good this year. For Christmas, I am wishing for...

From the television came his cue: "...and on the next Judge Judy."
"Mom?" he tried.
This time she answered, her gaze remaining fixed on the TV.
"Can you help me spell out controller?"
"Why do you need to spell out controller?"
He hopped up on the couch beside her, being extra careful not to
crinkle the page. Not taking her eyes off the television, she turned her
palm up. As she grabbed the list, butterflies danced about in his chest.
She was not being extra careful!

"You already have a PlayStation. Why would you ask for another
one?"

"I don't want another PlayStation, I want another PlayStation
controller," he said, eager to explain himself.

She raised an eyebrow.

"I want to ask Santa for another controller so I can play Crash *with Nicole."*

She shook her head and sighed. With a flick of her wrist, the paper floated into the boy's lap, her thumbprint leaving an indent.

"That's a nice thought, but your sister is too little. She's not going to play videogames with you. Ask Santa for something else."

The boy's chin wobbled in the way it did when he was trying his very hardest not to cry. He fought back tears, determined not to let a single drop fall onto his letter, which was already at least a little bit ruined by all the erasing, plus the way the paper was now crinkled on the edge.

The woman turned to the boy and sighed. She ran her hand through her vibrant red hair, her angular jaw clenching impatiently. "There's no need to cry about it," she said. "Just ask Santa for something else."

She didn't understand. Now he would have to erase what he'd written, and nothing could ever really be erased; the outline always stayed behind, even with the most careful erasing. Plus, it was almost Christmas—only four chocolates left in his calendar—and now he'd have to think of something else to ask for.

It was no use. His time was up. The commercials advertising mesothelioma lawyers and prescription drugs were over. The next episode was starting.

It had been a benign enough situation—ordinary even. Hardly noteworthy in the life of a child who had endured far worse. But for one reason or another, that memory—or hallucination, or dream, or apparition—had pushed him over the edge. It had nagged at him until he could no longer ignore what he'd always known to be true: Where there should've been love, there was rejection. Where there should've been acceptance, there was shame. Where there should've been comfort, there was a backhand, a dismissal, a snide remark. Through the eyes of an adult, he'd seen what no child could understand. Once he'd peeked behind that door—began to consider what it must mean about him if even his own mother couldn't love him—there was no going back. Shortly after, he moved into the tent. Away from the holiday spirit bullshit; away from the charity, the pity, and the hand-outs; the fake smiles and insincerity. He knew that he was losing touch, was no longer able to distinguish past hurts from present. And a shelter was no place to lose his mind—no place to battle one demon with another. He made the decision in the middle of the night, bumping his way out of the bunk room. A skiff of crisp white snow covered the muck of the Downtown Eastside as Evann walked and walked and walked, desperate to get away—as if distance would lead him further from the pain.

"Whatsa matter, kid?" Spider says, flipping the unzipped sleeping bag off Evann's legs. "Don't tell me you forgot your old pal?" Evann shivers, not at the cold breeze that funnels in through the open door-way, but at the conniving sneer on Spider's ugly face. "Don't tell me you forgot about the deal we made?"

His thoughts rattle in his head like a tin low on mints. It's been months since they've seen each other. Evann doesn't know what the man wants, too close to his last dose to fully comprehend that a dealer only makes a house call if there's a debt to collect. He rubs his eyes, trying to bring the situation into focus.

"Maybe this'll jog your memory, eh?" Spider steps back, two enormous heads taking his place.

The hairs on the back of Evann's neck stand up. Swallowing against the chalky paste in his mouth, he tries to place them. Why does he know those faces? Hot bile burns in his throat. As his eyes adjust to the dim light, he catches a glimpse of the chain, dinky and insubstantial around the thick neck. The pendant is unique and unmistakable: a golden lure, hand-hewn—only two ever made. The other one hangs around his father's neck. Phantom hands fumble beneath his waistline, his heart pounding in his chest as he relives the terror he felt pressed against that dumpster.

"Looks like you recognize these fellas," Spider says through the canvas walls. "I do hope they didn't rough you up too bad, but your little girlfriend mentioned you scare easy. Figured you'd try to worm your way outta our agreement, so I decided to collect a little collateral. But even that didn't seem to keep you honest. See, maybe you're too stupid to realize it, but while you been reliving your days as a Boy Scout, I've been coverin' for you. Lotta motherfuckers a lot more dangerous than me looking for you, kid."

Evann stares wide-eyed at the dark faces. He tries to make sense of what he's hearing. Girlfriend? Spider must have him mistaken for someone else. The only thing he remembers about their conversation is how good the dope was, and he'd offered to pay for that. Spider said that was a gift—hadn't he? What the fuck did he agree to? What deal? People are looking for him? Looking to harm him? That doesn't make any sense. Does it? He pays upfront, tries to stay out of the way, keeps to his own. At least he thinks he does; there are a lot of hours unremembered and unaccounted for when his body is out hustling without his brain. Maybe he's done some bad deals—pissed off the wrong people.

A thick hand around each ankle pulls him from his thoughts. Pain shoots up through his tailbone as they deposit him in a heap at Spider's feet. He tries to pedal back, coming up against a wall, the three men looming over him. He ducks his head, wishing they'd just get to it—get the shit-kicking over with—so he'll have an excuse to spill the tears that are threatening to betray his fear. He gives a passing thought to how long it's been since he was coherent enough to relieve himself, suddenly sure it's been long enough that he's about to piss himself.

"Now, lucky for you, I'm a pretty forgiving guy, all right. So I'm willing to give you a chance to redeem yourself. Maybe even get some of that cash back," Spider says with a wink.

28

THE THICK AIR IS OPPRESSIVE, UNCOMFORTABLY WARM AND musty. Too cold outside to crack a window, the bus rattles toward Granville Island, smelling of clammy skin and stale breath. Water carried in on jackets, caps, and umbrellas rains onto the slippery floor. Evann, having boarded before the dozens of others seeking refuge, sits cramped next to the damp window at the back of the bus, the overhanging fat of a stranger's enormous abdomen crossing the boundary of the seat, pressing against him. Evann doesn't notice, or maybe he just doesn't care, the pressure of the man's belly a sort of comfort, a weighted adipose blanket to help calm his anxious mind. A quick sniff would do the job, but he's too scared of what he might say or do if he allows himself the luxury.

With about ten grams of smack on him, Evann is headed to meet a "distributor" on Granville Island. He received his first assignment earlier this morning, meeting Spider and his guys on the front porch of the haunted house near Strathcona Park. He's certain Spider chose the location on purpose—to send a message, to get in his head— knowing it would make him twitch to return to the place they'd first met. He hadn't known exactly what to expect, but he recoiled when Spider opened the lid on the Slurpee cup, exposing the baggie—the largest volume of powder he'd ever seen.

"No way, man," he said, his voice cracking as he started to back away. He stopped as Spider's guys took a step toward him, raised his hands defensively. He knew there was no getting out of it. If Spider had managed to track him to his hiding hole, he was serious about having this so-called debt repaid. "Fuck. Come on, man. You said I'd only be taking small amounts."

"Ya, I know what I fuckin' said, kid. But you fuckin' said you'd help me out with some deliveries, and you been skirtin' around it long enough." Spider stepped forward brashly, thrusting the cup toward Evann. "I helped you out, and you fuckin' owe me. Time to pay up, my friend."

His vision narrowed, focusing on the cup. In front of him was an innocent-looking item, but if he was stopped with its contents, it would easily get him locked up. Also in front of him was an aggressive and unpredictable man. It had been a couple days, but his ribs were still tender from their last encounter. After Spider's guys had dragged Evann out of his tent, hanging him by his armpits like a marionette, Spider had reminded him of the power he held over him, recounting with pride just a few of the things he'd done to earn his reputation as a "hardened criminal," a "repeat offender," a "danger to the public."

Spider had told him about the time he broke into some old guy's house, tied him up, and took off with his dead wife's jewellery. He'd made sure Evann understood that his only regret was getting caught, said he should've known better than to take the diamond ring to a pawn shop. He also had no remorse about the time he pulled a shank on a pervert in Kent, jammed it into the freak's neck, all the way to the melted plastic handle. He'd barely missed the carotid, boasting that he would've been happy to serve extra time for that one if it meant one less degenerate on this planet. He'd spared no detail, describing how his hands were covered in blood by the time the guards pulled him away, how—given another opportunity—he'd aim for the femoral artery instead.

Spider hadn't expressly stated what he was willing to do if Evann refused to deliver for him, but he hadn't needed to. As Evann was dropped in a heap outside his tent, given a swift kick to the ribs to punctuate the point, he understood that either he'd prove his allegiance to the powerful and notoriously unstable drug dealer, or he'd be as good as dead.

With a shaking hand, he took the cup, settling the details of the drop location. As Spider and his men started to leave, Evann called out after them, "Hey! Uh—where, uh—where do I put it?"

Spider looked back, disgust sweeping over his ugly face. He waved his hand dismissively as he continued to walk away. "Fuck if I care. Stuff it up your fuckin' ass if you want. I don't give a shit. Just make sure it gets there." Without turning back, he shouted over his shoulder, "And my guy'll be weighin' it, so don't for a fuckin' second think about skimming me, you little prick."

Evann wasn't entirely sure if Spider had been kidding about stuffing it up his ass. Maybe he'd actually expected Evann to put it down his pants like he was Billy Hayes in *Midnight Express*. Locked in a bathroom stall at the SkyTrain station, he considered his options before deciding on a couple of things: First, the baggie was way too flimsy, so there was no way it would remain in one piece if he tried to stuff it anywhere, not to mention that it might break in transport and kill him—or, more embarrassingly, pour out of him like he was a goddamn powdered sugar dispenser. Second, as someone who had never tried putting anything up there, inserting a dry baggie the size of a golf ball wasn't how he intended to lose his anal virginity. But he also knew he couldn't carry it around in a worn paper cup with a transparent lid, which is how he ended up protectively holding a venti Starbucks cup with *Evan* written on it—as it always is because having two *n*'s is a stupid way of spelling Evan, a curse his parents had thoughtlessly placed upon him in their first, and perhaps most annoying, slight against him. He hopes that none of the other miserable and soaking-wet passengers notice his shifty eyes, or that he isn't drinking his "coffee."

Painfully under-dosed, he pants anxiously, the musty smell of coffee on the fat man's breath making him feel queasy. The scabbed skin at the back of his neck prickles, begging to be picked, but his arms are pinned. He presses his flushed forehead against the cool window, reviewing the plan.

Take the #50, heading westbound. Get off at West 2nd Avenue at Anderson Street. It should be twelve stops. Walk to the market. When you get there, text the number: "Hey man, when do you wanna meet for coffee?" If the response is "Does noon work?" go to the men's room at the west end of the building. If he responds "How about next weekend?" go to the men's room at the east end of the building. You'll know it's him because he'll be combing his hair in the mirror. Say "Pardon me" as you pass behind him. Pick a stall, take a piss, and leave the package behind. When he's made the exchange, he'll "forget" his coffee cup on the sink where you'll be washing your hands. Do not make eye contact. Do not look at or touch the cup until he's gone. Wait for him to leave and count to one hundred before walking out.

Wait... that doesn't make sense. How is he supposed to exchange the package if he's already gone when I get out of the stall? Shit. No. That's not right either. I just stand there and wash my hands and he'll bring the cup out. Is that it? Okay, take a deep breath. Focus. What did Spider tell you?

He's lost track of how many stops have passed, unable to keep count as he reads the script through in his mind over and over. His calf starts to ache as he mindlessly bounces his leg, though he's too preoccupied to notice his knee being rubbed raw by the metal frame of the bus. Careful to hold the coffee cup perfectly upright, Evann plans how he'll extract himself from beneath the fat man's belly. His pulse hastens as he contemplates the situation. What if the man does not, or will not, or cannot, move when he needs to get up? What if he misses his stop, unable to free himself from under the flab? What if he

171

has to climb over the man's lap? Should he face forward, so his crotch ends up in the man's face, or face backward? Which would be the less uncomfortable option? Less uncomfortable for him, or for the fat man? Is the fat man's comfort or discomfort really his concern, since there'd obviously been no consideration when he allowed his enormous gut to flop over the boundary of his own seat? Why did he think it would be better to be semi-sober for this trip? Now his anxiety is running rampant, and he can't see straight, and he can't think clearly, and if he could just take a couple of pills maybe his brain would work properly. Shit. Did he miss his stop? Now he's really lost count. Hot bile burns in his throat as the display flashes the next stop: W 2nd Ave @ Fir St.

Evann is suddenly overcome with claustrophobia, the pressure of the man's weight no longer comforting, but suffocating. He can't breathe. His rapid shallow breaths aren't enough. His body can't survive with such little oxygen, and that's assuming the stale air in the stuffed bus even contains enough oxygen for everyone. Don't people exhale carbon monoxide? Or is it carbon dioxide? Either way, he needs oxygen, and he's pinned by this fat man, breathing in other people's expelled carbon-something-or-other, and he's getting dizzy, and his vision is getting blurry, and he absolutely has to get up this moment because he's pretty sure the next stop is his stop anyway.

"Please, can I get up? I need to get up. This is my stop," Evann says, the words frantically spilling out.

The man looks at Evann. His bushy eyebrows knit together at the sight of the tall but quite skinny man with the alarmingly wide eyes.

"Uh, yeah, of course. No problem." He lifts his considerable mass away from Evann with ease. "Oh, I'm so sorry, pardon me," the man says as he nudges people standing in the crowded aisle.

Evann clutches the coffee cup. *Don't hold it so tight,* he scolds himself. *You're going to crush the fucking thing.* Eyes downcast, he jostles his way past the other passengers, fighting to reach the doors before the bus pulls into the next stop. The doors open and he jumps down, pulling in heavy breaths of fresh air. Staggering to the shelter of the bus stop, he sits down, bringing his hands to rest on his knees, continuing to gasp for breath. It's several moments before he realizes his mistake. There, in his hand, balancing atop his knee, sits the Starbucks cup, but the lid is missing, its illicit contents plainly visible for anyone to see.

29

FOR A MOMENT, EVERYTHING STANDS STILL. THE LABOURED breath catches in his chest. His rapidly beating heart seems to slow, a stalling engine—*thunk, thunk, thunk*—against his sternum. Everything around him fades away as his eyes fixate on his exposed secret.

In a blink, he's back, frantically scanning the sidewalk, searching —silently pleading—for the lid. When could he have dropped it? Is it still on the bus? How will he explain himself if someone asks about the contents of his cup? His mind races, incoherent thoughts catapulting one after another. Incapable of logic, his panicked brain continues to bombard him with nonsensical prompts. *You must've left it on the bus. If you run, maybe you'll be able to catch it.*

Evann takes a deep breath, preparing to chase after the bus. As he presses down against the bench, he feels the soft give of plastic crumpling beneath his hand. Grasping the disfigured lid, he forces it onto the cup, struggling to get his damp, uncoordinated hands to cooperate. Another deep breath, and for the first time since sitting down, he looks up and looks around. There's a teenage boy absorbed in his phone leaning in one corner of the bus shelter. An elderly man with a white cane sitting at the other end of the bench hums to himself. Pedestrians hurry by, heads low, rain hoods lifted in protection against the torrential downpour. He's not surrounded by police cars. No one is on their phones, alerting the authorities about the paranoid man carrying a takeout cup of heroin. *I'll have a venti Flat White, full shot of blissful numbness, one dry mouth, maybe a sprinkle of constipation, extra powdered sugar, and... I should probably also have a shot of Narcan—on the side*, he thinks, laughing maniacally. The old man turns in his direction and shrugs before moving his unseeing gaze away. No one even notices Evann. No one cares. Beneath his brand-name jacket is a tall, clean-shaven white man, and from a distance he can still pass as one of them.

30

By the time he enters the market, he's soaked through. Even his waterproof jacket is no match for the West Coast storm. He stuffed the goods—cup and all—inside the breast of his jacket, praying that would keep it dry enough to stop the powder from disintegrating into the consistency of royal icing. He refuses to consider the possible consequences of not making this exchange. What should've been a five-minute walk turned out to be at least twice that; in his panic, he'd leapt from the bus one stop too late, but in his agitation, he trudged the wrong direction for two miserable blocks before he was able to regain his bearings.

Water puddles around his sopping shoes as he removes the cup from his jacket, relieved to see the exterior appears relatively unscathed. Setting the cup atop a garbage can, he blows into his hands, thawing his unresponsive fingers just enough to send the message. The reply is immediate: *"Does noon work?"*

Back in his university days, he and his classmates frequented the public market. Within walking distance of the campus, he spent many afternoons wandering through the crowded building, searching for inspiration for his next project and snapping photos of the vivid colours and the eclectic mix of old and new architecture. The atmosphere had become somewhat familiar to him, but today he feels utterly disoriented. His stomach churns at the thought of wading through the packed venue. What if he accidentally drops the cup? Or the lid pops off again? There are so many people in here, there's probably a lineup for the bathroom. What if another guy enters the stall before his contact has a chance to make the exchange? Does Granville Island have a police force? No, it must be under the VPD's jurisdiction. Evann runs his hand through his saturated hair as he scans the crowd, anxiously making note of the security cameras: there have to be dozens, covering every millimetre of the building.

Smarten up, he scolds himself. *If you don't want people to notice you, stop acting so fucking suspicious. Just do a lap, take a piss, look around at a few kiosks, and get the fuck out of here.*

To his relief, after orienting himself and finding the men's room at the west end of the market, there is no long lineup, no uniformed officers waiting to arrest him, and only one man standing in front of the mirror. The man begins combing his hair when Evann walks in.

Does he know it's me? Spider didn't send this guy a picture of me, did he? Jesus Christ. What the fuck am I doing here? This was such a fucking stupid thing to get involved in.

He takes a deep breath, fixing his gaze on the muddy floor, and walks behind the man.

"Pardon me," he says, careful not to bump into him as he makes his way to the last stall. Locking the door behind him, Evann steadies himself, leaning against the cold wall tile as urine drains from his bladder. Unlocking the latch, he rushes to leave. The door swings open and he stands frozen in place, realizing he's still holding the cup. "Oh, shit," he murmurs, slowly turning to set the cup on the toilet paper holder.

He keeps his gaze down as he reaches into the sink, warm water cascading over his icy hands. He meticulously scours every surface of each finger, washing the dirt and grime out of the jagged ridges of his ripped fingernails. Resisting the urge to look into the mirror, he waits for the man to make his move. The seconds stretch excruciatingly, though perhaps that's just the illusion, time distorting in relation to the aberrant pounding of his heart. He still has three fingers left to scrub when the man returns from the stall, the dull *thud* of the cup against the stainless steel countertop startling Evann. He doesn't dare look at the man, who quickly washes up and leaves, wiping his wet hands on his legs.

1-1000, 2-1000, 3-1000, 4-1000, 5-1000, he counts, trying to slow his breathing to match the count. *Inhale, 2, 3, 4. Exhale, 2, 3, 4.* He has to restart several times, his deprived brain drifting to think about when he'll finally get his next fix. When he's sure he's made it to at least one hundred, he reaches for the cup. He's done it; it's over.

He picks it up, the cup virtually weightless in his hand. He starts to pant, unable to breathe beneath the weight of his fear. He's in way over his head. Here he is in a public washroom, where he's delivered enough drugs to get himself charged with what? Drug trafficking? A felony? He can't even imagine what will happen if he's caught, how long they'll put him away. What Spider will do to him—to his family —if he doesn't show up. Or worse, if he shows up empty-handed. He was supposed to get money in exchange, and the guy—who he hadn't even glanced at in passing—walked out with the drugs and left him with an empty cup. And he'd been told, no matter what, not to look in the cup, but now he doesn't know if he should look inside it, because even if he confirms it's empty, what can he do about it? The guy is long gone.

Evann stares at himself in the mirror, searching for any semblance of his old self within his gaunt, unusually bare face. And even if the guy is still somewhere in the market, there are hundreds of people here, and it's not like Evann knows what he looks like; not like he can just walk up to a drug dealer and politely ask for the money.

Sweat trickles down his spine, sending a shiver throughout his body. He lets out a whimper when the door bursts open, his knees buckling as he grabs the counter for support. Through the door runs a frantic boy, followed closely by his dad, the child making a run for the nearest stall. The father smiles apologetically at Evann. "He really had to go," he says.

Staring into the reflection of his vacant eyes, he once again attempts to pull himself together. *Inhale, 2, 3, 4. Exhale, 2, 3, 4. Inhale, 2, 3, 4. Exhale, 2, 3, 4.* The cup rattles in his unsteady hand, and he feels something shift within it. He hurries past the father and out into the crowded market.

Should I go back into the bathroom to open the cup? How much is a golf ball of heroin worth? Has the arrangement changed? Maybe Spider accepts e-transfer?

Wandering without direction, conscientiously matching his pace to that of the other patrons casually perusing the kiosks, Evann tries to figure out what to do. Just as he decides to make his way to the other men's room, he hears his name, spoken like a question.

He turns around and comes face to face with Dani and her partner Amy. *Fuck. Fuck. Fuck. FUCK!* His legs wobble beneath him; it has been an excruciatingly long morning with no food, an inadequate dose—not even enough to take the edge off—and far too many close calls. He's utterly exhausted and running out of reserve. He fights back tears, forcing his mouth into a manufactured smile.

"Oh, hi, guys," he says, leaning in to give Dani an awkward one-armed hug, careful to keep the cup upright and out of reach. He lifts his other hand in a half-hearted wave to Amy before resting it against the back of his neck, his fingers clawing mindlessly at the scabbed skin. He hopes they can't smell the fear and sweat trapped beneath his raincoat.

"I almost didn't recognize you," Dani says, looking up at him. She smiles politely, but Evann senses her judgment. It's the first time they've seen each other since he moved out of her place months ago. "You look so different—like, uh—well, I don't really know what it is." she says, her voice wavering.

Evann forces a clipped laugh, shrugging. He doesn't trust himself with words; he's feeling too agitated, too depleted, too irrational, jonesing harder than he has in weeks.

"So, uh, what have you been up to? I was surprised not to see you back at school this semester."

Is she making a statement, or is it a question? Or is it a rhetorical question that doesn't actually warrant an answer? He's never done well in uncomfortable social situations, never quite sure what's expected of him. The pills had helped a bit—before he found out drugs have a point of diminishing return. He stares dumbly at Amy's shoes, ridiculous combat-style boots with chunky heels and laces up to her shin. He blinks again and again, not trusting his eyes. The boots are covered in a colourful mandala, which doesn't make any sense, because who would ever buy a pair of boots like that, or, for that matter, sell a pair of boots like that? She must've painted them herself, although they don't really have the textured appearance paint would produce. How long has he been staring at her stupid boots? He needs to get out of here; needs to get some junk in his system before the cramps start.

"Ev?"

"Yeah, sorry. I'm just, uh, really busy, and I kinda have somewhere I have to be, so I gotta go," he says, turning to leave. He feels a hand grab hold of his arm. Panicked, he pulls himself free, gripping his cup firmly. "Don't," he pleads. "Look, I'm sorry. I really have to go."

"Shit, sorry. I didn't mean—I just—" Dani stammers, unable to untangle the words into a coherent thought. "Listen, I hope you're doing okay, Ev. We never see you around anymore. We're worried." She squints up at him, trying to meet his eyes. He avoids her gaze, looking to the door. "Anyway, I can see you need to go, so just—you know, take care of yourself, okay?"

Another statement, or question—or question within a statement—to which he doesn't know how to respond.

"Yeah, thanks," he finally says, excusing himself.

As he rushes to get away, fighting the instinct to take off running, he can feel the eyes on his back. But he doesn't care. He doesn't care what's in the cup, or what judgmental Dani and her judgmental girl-friend think of him. He's of a single-track mind: *Get to Spider, get your fix.*

31

"You're—you're kidding, right?" Evann says, his jaw releasing in disbelief. He runs his hand along the stubble of his cheeks.

"Oh come on, kid. Don't be a fuckin' drama queen." Spider laughs as he returns the tiny packet to its place in the bottom of the cup. "What difference does it make to you?"

He doesn't see Spider's guys hanging around, but he can feel their menacing presence in the shadows, waiting for him to fuck up. Evann squeezes his eyes shut, pulling in a long deep breath in an effort to settle his agitation.

The difference is immense. Evann had agreed—well, not agreed, he certainly hadn't asked to be extorted—to move heroin in exchange for money, not in exchange for more drugs. Not in exchange for fentanyl. That hadn't been the deal. The difference is that because he hadn't known ahead of time, now, perhaps self-righteously, he can convince himself that he never would've agreed to this transaction. In reality, he's powerless against this man. Worse yet, he's indebted to him. Out here, debt isn't simply forgiven, it's paid—with money, with goods, with services, or, if all else fails, with a life. Burying those thoughts, he tells himself that if he'd known what he'd be carrying back, he would've refused. The deep breathing isn't working. An irritated heat creeps up his neck and into his ears.

"Are you fucking kidding me right now?" Evann's jaw clenches as he struggles to keep his voice down. "This shit is killing people all over the goddamn place."

He's seen the red-and-yellow posters plastered everywhere in the Downtown Eastside, alerting users of the risk:

WARNING
ON AUGUST 9TH THERE WERE 16+ OVERDOSES FROM HEROIN POSSIBLY CUT WITH FENTANYL

More than six months later, the numbers have only continued to climb.

"Jesus Christ, kid. Get a fuckin' grip, all right?" Spider sneers, exposing his cracked and rotted teeth as he steps closer. Glaring up at Evann, his putrid breath fills the space between them. "Look, I know you're new to this game, but I've got fuckin' news for ya, big guy. *All* this shit's been killin' people. All of it. For fuckin' years!"

Evann staggers back, wiping Spider's foul spittle from his cheek. Spider steps closer still, yelling now, his right hand flailing wildly as he clenches the cup in his left.

"And you have no fuckin' idea what it takes to survive out here, okay? No clue. You think I wanna sell this fuckin' shit? Any of it? No. But I don't got no other way to make a livin', and I don't got nobody left. All of 'em are fuckin' dead, and that's what you can't seem to get into your stupid fuckin' head." He takes a breath, his nostrils flaring. "See, us addicts, we don't get to pick and choose. We do whatever the fuck it takes to live another day out here, kid, and I just sell whatever the fuck the buyers are askin' for."

Evann stands in stunned silence. He's been on the receiving end of Spider's anger before, but this time, beneath the fury, he senses pain. As a damaged man himself, looking away—looking anywhere but *at*—has become habitual. Averting his gaze allows him to guard his deepest deficiencies, protect himself from the inevitable scrutiny, although, in his broken heart, he knows it's all he deserves. Of course, he knows what Spider looks like, but he doesn't *know him,* and there's a vulnerability in his words that lands with a sharp point in the centre of Evann's chest. He forces himself to look directly at him, to study his face: the lurid tattoo, the pockmarked skin, the jagged scar pulling at his lip, leaving him with an unrelenting snarl. He looks closer, meeting his gaze. In Spider's eyes, he sees a lot of hurt. He knows nothing of Spider's upbringing, his story, the where's or what's or why's or how's that have led him to this life, but the details are inconsequential. Spider and Evann have each suffered, and hurt people hurt people. More than that—maybe because they don't know anything different, probably because they don't believe they're worth any better—hurt people hurt themselves.

Several moments pass before Evann fully processes everything he's just heard.

"Wait," he says. "Did—did you just say you only sell what people are asking for? Are you saying people are *asking* for fentanyl? Like, they're taking it on purpose?" The idea is unbelievable. There's no way anyone down here doesn't realize how dangerous that shit is.

A quick walk down East Hastings is all the proof they'd need; there's guaranteed to be at least one paramedic crew working on a downed junkie right there on the sidewalk.

Spider looks dumbfounded, the crevice between his eyes deepening. "Jesus Christ, kid. You really are fuckin' green, aren't ya," he says, shaking his head in disbelief. "How you survived out here alone for even a week is just un-fuckin-believable, it really is."

Evann stares blankly, unclear if he misunderstood initially, or if the answer is so blatantly obvious, he should be able to keep up.

"What d'ya think us old-timers use? I'd be willing to bet you didn't just start snortin' heroin out of the blue." He pauses, waiting for Evann to confirm his hunch. Evann looks down at his feet, his cheeks burning under the dark heat of Spider's stare, the expectation of a smack across the mouth. "There," he says, pointing. "Like I say. Kids like you don't wind up on skid row in an instant. First, they try somethin' harmless: weed, booze, maybe a pill now and again. The lucky ones do it for fun, and it don't ever cause 'em no trouble. The unlucky ones—the ones like us—we got somethin' wrong up in the brain. Some of us got somethin' we're runnin' from, or some shit we're tryna forget—you know, from being a kid or whatever—and some of us just got somethin' about the way we're wired, so once we try it, we're hooked. We can't never stop."

Evann is having trouble following, his own thoughts preoccupied by his intense craving. He nods along anyway, thankful Spider and his guys haven't kicked the shit out of him for losing his temper.

Spider continues, "Right, so, once the weed and booze stop workin', you move onto somethin' stronger. Maybe you try painkillers, or downers to take the edge off a bit, or you and your buddies have a quick bump before you head out for the night. But then that stops workin', and you need more, or somethin' stronger."

Evann nods again, struggling to understand where this is going.

"Don't you see what I'm sayin' here, kid?" Spider asks, suddenly animated. "What's a junkie do once the smack's not enough, eh? Once snortin' it's not enough, then smokin' it's not enough?"

Evann looks away, picking furiously at the skin along his hairline. *What the fuck is the right way to respond to these kinds of questions?*, he asks himself for at least the third time today.

"Inject it! Don't you get it, kid? A guy like me'll spend his entire fuckin' life chasin' that first high, and before he knows it, he don't got nothin' left—no money, no home, no family. So instead of usin' to get high—I mean, of course ya still wanna get high, but it ain't never as good as it was that first time—he starts usin' just to avoid gettin' sick, just to cope with all the shit that's gone wrong, and it takes more and more and more until it takes over a guy's life, you know. This shit's fuckin' evil, man. It'll take everything you got. But us old-timers," he says. "We can't keep on with the smack forever. It don't work like it used to. And this new shit, fentanyl, or whatever, it's like a godsend for us old guys, you know. Like fifty times stronger they say, and it's way cheaper. Ya, it's real good stuff. Don't need nearly as much of it to get a good rush."

Evann wishes he didn't understand, but of course he does. It happened so fast. One minute he was experimenting—innocent, in control. Then something had started chasing him—or perhaps he was the one doing the chasing—and he started picking up speed until he was running, faster and faster, the trail disappearing beneath him. A foot snagged on a hidden root, balance thrown off kilter, arms flailing before finding a branch to grab on to—a momentary relief—only to have the branch break. And he hasn't stopped falling. He hasn't wanted to admit to the power of the unquenchable beast he's welcomed into his life. But with snot dripping onto his upper lip, burnt fingers on shaking hands swiping it away, of course he knows. Because even as Spider rambles on—about all the friends he's lost over the years, all the ways "them fuckin' cronies" should be doing more, could be doing more to secure safe drugs for people like them, how "the establishment" likes to blame the dealers, make it seem like they're somehow responsible for their customers using too much, getting themselves killed, like they don't appreciate this is a business, don't even consider how bad it is for that business to have customers dying—the only thing Evann is thinking about is when he'll get his next fix.

———

And later, he doesn't care. Not when he huddles in the farthest stall in some dingy bathroom, not when he's crouching over an unflushed toilet, not when he opens his tiny packet, not when he sucks his prize clean off the toilet paper holder with a brisk sniff. Perhaps he should feel fear after coming face to face with that which has killed so many, should think a bit harder about what might be hidden within those indistinguishable granules. But instead, it's a jovial reunion—old friends reconnecting after time spent apart. A brief moment of jubilation, and then calm, the captive bird in his chest relinquishing the fight.

So comfortable, so at peace, it's tempting to stay—maybe even have a brief nap—here in his metal enclosure, leaning against the filthy wall, the poster taped to the stall door fading further and further away, warning people like him of the risk they're taking.

32

GRADUALLY, THE COLD RECEDES, THE FROZEN GROUND GIVING way to the season's first blooms. It's his Gram's favourite time of the year, and once upon a time that made it his favourite too. Pink and red and orange and yellow tulips balance on delicate stems. Now that it's spring, he sometimes finds himself wandering through Stanley Park. When he manages to hit the sweet spot—that perfect dose that allows his body to function independently as his mind takes respite, consciousness dissolving as the venom melts to vapour—he'll make his way to the Rose Garden, as if pulled by a magnetic force.

The first time it happened, it was startling, disorienting, just as it had been to wake from a sleepwalk as a child. He looked down to find himself wearing clothes that were his, but he had no recollection of dressing, no recollection of walking away from the streets of skid row, through historic Gastown, beyond the bustling business district, past the cruise ships and the float planes and the tankers of Coal Harbour and into the park. It was a substantial enough walk while sober, let alone in the wobbly fawn stagger his long legs adopt under the influence. He can't explain why his unguided vessel continues to make this illogical pilgrimage, but he finds small comfort in returning to his body to find it's carried him to the magnificent gardens.

Staring at the tulips, Evann marvels at the polarity: beautiful flowers sprouting from invisible bulbs, pressing through the earth and arduously reaching toward the sun, all while he shrivels and shrinks, his choices and circumstance maliciously plucking away his petals, one by one.

Spider never did return his money, and Evann didn't have the nerve to ask the terrifying enforcer with the bulbous forehead and the wandering hands for his necklace back. But to his credit, eventually, Spider did stop coming around. An optimist might tell themselves the debt's been repaid, that there's a decent man buried deep beneath the dealer's rough exterior, but Evann suspects it's because he can no longer play the part. Even a neatly trimmed beard and his old brand-name clothes can't mask what he's become.

Somewhere along the way, he more or less stopped eating. First, he tightened his belt one notch, then another. Then he had to poke his own holes, cinching it tighter and tighter around his protruding hip bones, his loose jeans hanging like drapes. It only became a problem because he didn't notice—too busy glancing behind him—as his pants slipped from his withered frame, which is how his thousands-of-dollars, two-years-of-braces, once-perfect smile became the grotesque mess of chipped and greying teeth now rotting beneath scabbed lips. The connection between face and sidewalk was certainly the catalyst, but his incessant craving for Slurpees hasn't helped.

He had that first bad fall—the one that left him with a mouthful of pennies—while trying to skitter away, not wanting to find out the hard way whether the rumours he's been hearing are true. He was preoccupied that night, consumed by the animalistic instinct to protect himself, paranoid that the group clad in Canucks jerseys was pursuing him—preparing to make him the next victim. He's heard there are people just waiting to take from the destitute, to grind them into the sidewalks on which they rest their hollowed husks, to piss on them as they sleep it off, to spit at them as they hold out their hats, to remind them that they're unwelcome, unwanted, unworthy—but not unseen. The rumour mill has been churning; just last week, he heard about some guy minding his own business—Wely cheque cashed, ready to score a point—swarmed by a group of guys out on a stag. They damn near kicked the poor guy's face in. At least, he's pretty sure that's what he heard. The nightmares are back, and it's getting harder to tell fact from fiction. Regardless, the fear he feels is real.

To make matters worse, he's back to living in a shelter after nearly perishing in a hell of his own making. An untended butane burner carelessly left aflame ignited the mass of blankets he was passed out under. He made it out of that one, but barely, and only thanks to a stranger who didn't stop to consider that a life lived in a dilapidated tent probably wasn't a life worth saving. The guy was out on a run and noticed black smoke billowing from the ravine below. Evann woke to frantic shouts—"Hello! Is there anybody in there? Get the fuck outta there! The tent is about to go up!"—and managed to scramble through the hatch with his grab bag just as flames engulfed everything he had left. Scurrying up the hillside, he didn't notice the enflamed material sizzling into his skin, too busy dodging half-spent butane bottles that were shooting into the early morning sky like rockets. With that, he had no choice but to nurse his wounds—minor, all things considered—and with nowhere else to go, he was thrust back to the shelter, back to swimming upstream in a system intended to drown those relying on it.

The seared flesh on his forearm has blistered and sloughed off, leaving him with palomino splotched skin, dirty brown against vibrant pink. It's slow to heal, the tender flesh throbbing beneath the shrunken skin, but the nurse at the clinic gives him a sidelong look if he asks for painkillers after his dressing change and sends him away with an extra-strength Tylenol, telling him that's all he should need since it's barely even a second-degree. In his coherent moments, when he allows himself to feel it, the pain provides a twisted reassurance that—at least in the physical realm—he must still be alive.

Smoking an extra point takes care of the pain in his arm, but there's no reprieve from the itching. Invisible to the naked eye, he can't figure out what it is he's caught—maybe mites, probably bedbugs from one of his nasty bunkmates at one of the nasty shelters —but his skin crawls day and night. Sometimes he swears there must be ants tunnelling beneath his skin, preparing to house their colony deep within his tissue. He picks feverishly—frantically—trying to stop the invasion, but his stubbed fingernails are no match for the quick-moving insects. Covered in scabs and scars, gyrating in a rhythmless jitter, it's no wonder Spider has let Evann off the hook. He must've realized the well has run dry, that he's extracted all there is left from a once pliable pawn—that what Evann is doing to himself is far worse than anything he could be forced into.

Each day in Evann's ever-worsening life plays out like a sadistic adaptation of a *Choose Your Own Adventure* book. He'd loved them as a kid—had dreamed of being the main character in the wild tales— but he's lost that enthusiasm, having found himself trapped in a story where each branch leads to another dead end.

SCENARIO ONE:

It's 8:00 a.m. After an anxious night tossing and turning—your minuteless cellphone and a few dollars cash stuffed inside your boxers—you head out onto the streets. You can't stay at the shelter, which is now closed for the day and won't reopen until 4:00 p.m. This particular shelter doesn't accept intakes until 9:30 a.m.

Time to choose your adventure!

OPTION A:
You decide it's best to hang around nearby until they're accepting intakes.

OPTION B:

You decide to head over to Howe Street, because you've heard there's a place over there that—if you're lucky enough to get one—holds beds for returning guests, which would save you from having to play this game every day.

LET'S SEE HOW THIS PLAYS OUT:

OPTION A:
You hang around, hoping to get on the list for a bed tonight. With a couple of hours to kill, you figure you'll head to the soup kitchen and line up for breakfast. You didn't really account for how heavy your bag was getting—or perhaps how little muscle mass you have left—and you're feeling extra drained after yet another sleepless night. It takes longer than expected, and by the time you get to the community centre, there's a lineup half a block long. Now you're faced with another choice:

1. Wait in line, prioritizing a hot meal over a (semi-)guaranteed bed.

2. Head back to the shelter and hope you're in time to get your name on the list.

OPTION B:
You sling your cumbersome pack over your shoulder and set off on the nearly two-kilometre walk to Howe Street. It's only slightly uphill, but you've been prioritizing drugs over buying food, and your diet of Big Gulps and stolen KitKats isn't cutting it. When you get there, you find out they don't start intakes until 11:00 a.m. Now you're exhausted and hungry and you still don't have a spot to sleep tonight, so you're faced with another choice:

1. Hang around nearby until they're accepting intakes.

2. Head back to the other place, because at least it's closer to the soup kitchen, and you're pretty sure (fingers crossed) they'll still have a spot for you.

SCENARIO TWO:

You're an opioid addict. You wake up in the morning (is it really waking if you can't be sure you were ever sleeping?) and you're immediately consumed by the need to use. Life would be a lot easier if someone would just write you a script for painkillers. You didn't get a bed last night so food, shelter, and security are objective concerns. But, you're physiologically and psychologically dependent on opioids—your brain no longer able to produce that feel-good hormone, dopamine, on its own—so food, shelter, and security will have to take a backseat for now. You prefer pharmaceutical narcotics—percs or dillies or oxys—when you can get them. Sometimes you swallow the pills so the high lasts longer, but if you're feeling real desperate—to quiet the asshole in your head, to dull the screaming pain in your arm—you crush them up and snort them. With the pills, you can function (somewhat) normally, rather than nodding off in public, but heroin is just so much cheaper and so much easier to get. Plus, it's not like you have anything important to do, so what's the harm in spending another day on the nod?

Time to choose your adventure!

OPTION A:
You connect with some guy you've never met in some dark corner of the city and hand over all the money you have on you to buy one, maybe two, pills. Depending on what you manage to get your hands on, maybe they'll cover you for the day, but you could just as likely be looking for your next fix by lunchtime.
OPTION B:

You connect with some guy you've never met in some dark corner of the city and opt for heroin instead, knowing it'll only get you to lunchtime. But at least you've got plenty of cash left, so you can buy another flap later, plus get some food in your belly.

LET'S SEE HOW THIS PLAYS OUT:

OPTION A:
Dilaudid crushed and snorted, you're ready to face the day—or rather, the next few hours. You're feeling elated! Every anxious thought that was plaguing you earlier has disappeared. You have no worries, no pain. You feel as though you've taken the perfect antidote, a magical cure for the relentless sense of worthlessness you carry. For now at least, you're not uncertain or pessimistic. For now, everything that is wrong in your world feels pretty all right. But don't get ahead of yourself! Once the high wears off, you'll remember you've spent all your cash. You'll be jonesing for a fix, so it'll be back to the hustle for you!

OPTION B:
You're well aware of the dangers of buying powder, but at this price, heroin is hard to beat! Luckily, it's up your nose, and you don't have the bandwidth to think about all the shit it could've been cut with—baby powder, corn starch, laundry detergent, powdered milk, maybe even a little cocaine or fentanyl. You're feeling elated! Every anxious thought that has been plaguing you has...
You're not aware of any worries, or any pain, but you're also not aware of much of anything else. You've nodded off, and while your brain is no longer online, your body has developed a mind of its own. You're distantly aware that your arms and legs are getting really heavy. Everything feels so heavy.

Unable to bear the weight of your head and torso any longer, your upper body starts to pitch forward. You jerk awake, fixing your sights on a bench—just five steps away. Just four steps. Three steps. Shit, you're on the nod again. Wake up. Almost there. Two steps. You lie down on the bench and let yourself be sucked into the trance. It's not very comfortable— the taxpaying citizens seem to think that making benches and entryways and bus stations uncomfortable will somehow change the fact that you need somewhere to nod off—but you're not occupying your body anyway, so you don't mind. You repeat this cycle for the next several hours. When you wake up, you've still got dope left, *and* you still have some cash on you. As a bonus, you have no appetite, so you can use your extra cash to buy more junk later!

Day after day passes without notice, slipping between the cracks in much the same way Evann does. Sometimes he wakes to find himself admiring the tulips, other times he wakes next to a puddle of his own puke, his neck aching and a brick texture indented into the side of his face. Once he woke up with no shoes, something that might've shocked him in his previous life. But in this life, there are no winners.

Some take, and some are taken from.

Some survive, but too many don't.

33

EVANN SLIPS THE SLENDER PACKAGE OUT OF SIGHT, LETTING HIS good arm hang casually, the weight of the beef jerky pushing gently at the cuff of his sleeve. By the time he pays for a bottle of Coke and a bag of salt and vinegar chips, he's managed to stash three jerky strips, a couple of KitKats, and, most practically, a bottle of knockoff Tylenol. Not a bad haul for two bucks.

He went to school with a kid whose dad was a kleptomaniac. The guy spent his entire adult life in and out of jail, and it didn't seem to matter whether or not he had the means, he simply couldn't resist the thrill of pocketing items and walking away with them. As the story went, this guy got off from stealing, in a perverted, sexual way. His picture was posted at stores all over the mid-Island—defaced with phallic sketches and vulgar slurs—and that still didn't stop him from walking into the grocery store, loading up a cart full of steaks, and walking out. The meat was long gone by the time the store sent the security footage to the news, but the gossip was just getting going. Teenagers can be ruthless, and that poor kid's dad was all the talk; they hadn't even tried to be discreet, and a fantastically unlikely story spread through the school like wildfire, about all the disgusting ways in which that guy had violated the raw meat. Evann, who was often on the receiving end of his classmates' cruelty, hadn't participated in spreading the rumour, but he also hadn't done anything to stop it.

Sometimes he sees that kid in the haunted faces of the street people living out on Hastings—gaze downcast, the corners of their mouths perpetually pulled downward as if, at any moment, they might burst into tears—and he feels a pang of guilt in his gut.

He's not like that, though. He doesn't steal for the thrill of it. In fact, even though he's getting pretty good at it, he feels a deep shame every time. It's funny how quickly the lines of morality soften and shift when survival depends on it. Now he takes what he needs, when he needs it, but it was only a matter of months ago that he first stood in the aisle of 7-Eleven considering stuffing something— anything—in his pocket to temper the gnawing emptiness in his stomach, only to scurry from the store, a phantom ache in his cheeks. He stood outside, rubbing his face, hot with embarrassment, just like it was as a child, the only time he'd ever stolen anything.

———

His mom stopped at the corner store to buy a pack of smokes— something Evann understood to be a secret that she only did when his dad was away, and not to be discussed, ever. He was just a kid, eating five-cent candies straight from the bulk bin. She found him stuffing a gummy worm in his mouth. The hairs stood on the back of his neck as he felt her presence behind him.

"Evann David Cartwright," she said through clenched teeth. He knew he was in really big trouble just by her tone, her voice a low growl. "What the fuck do you think you're doing?" she said, putting extra emphasis—as always—on the f-word. He often wondered if that particular word required special effort. It must be hard for her to say with her jaw tight like that. Sometimes he whispered it to himself when no one would hear, practicing it both ways; he wanted to make sure he'd know how to use it properly when he was old enough. He turned toward her, not daring to finish chewing before swallowing the enormous gelatinous blob. She reached down and grabbed his chin. His head snapped back, and for a moment, her face was obscured by black spots. He willed himself not to cough on the saliva dripping down his throat, his eyes watering at the effort. Not for the first time, he wondered if she kept getting those ridiculously long fake nails reapplied so she'd have a handy weapon to hurt him with, without causing a scene. Her nails dug into his tender cheeks as he blinked away tears, forcing himself to meet her gaze.

"Answer me." She tightened her squeeze as she pushed his head farther back.

His mind was spinning, trying to understand what he'd done to upset her. *Is she mad that I'm eating candy before dinner?* he wondered. *Should I get some for Nicole? Is she mad that I'm not sharing?*

He opened his mouth to speak, but that only made room for his flesh to be squished painfully into the gap between his teeth. His cheeks felt like they were being stretched, and once again tears threatened to escape from his blurry eyes. *Are my cheeks like Silly Putty? Can they rip apart? Will they bleed? Would Mommy do that?* He started to panic, silently begging her to let go.

Unable to form words, he did his best, sputtering, "So-wah, maw meh." He made a plan to practice talking while pinching his own cheeks in private so he didn't sound like he had a jawbreaker in his mouth the next time he found himself in this situation. She released her grip, her narrowed eyes holding his gaze in that intense way that made him want to squirm away and hide.

"Excuse me?"

"I'm sorry, Mommy," he said, daring to shift his gaze down to his feet, extra relieved his cheeks didn't end up bleeding all over since he was wearing his new shoes. They were his first pair with laces, and he'd finally mastered tying them himself. His dad had even showed him how to do a double knot so they wouldn't come untied when he was playing at recess. His mind wandered, replaying the steps over in his head: loop the bunny ears and then cross them over each other, poke one through the hole and pull extra tight.

"You will look at me when I'm talking to you," she said, forcing his head back until he was looking up at her.

The candy was sitting like a rock in his stomach. "I'm sorry, Mommy," he tried again, hoping she'd see he meant it because suddenly he really needed to use the washroom.

"That is stealing, Evann. What do you not understand about that?"

He wasn't sure if he should answer. Sometimes when she asked him questions, she got more mad if he answered. But she kept glaring down at him—the passing seconds marked by the thumping of his heart in his ears—so he decided to be honest.

"I didn't know that," he said sheepishly. Just a week earlier when they were shopping at Costco, she'd handed him and Nicole each a cookie to eat in the store. He was having a hard time differentiating the two situations. He'd been hungry in the store then and it was okay for him to eat something, but today, when he got hungry, that obviously wasn't okay.

She released him, looking down at him with disgust. "Don't be an idiot, Evann. And don't you *dare* lie to me. You're old enough to know better."

He made a note to add *dare* to the list of words to test out in private. He began to squirm, the pressure in his bladder starting to build.

"Stand up straight," she said, pulling him upright by the arm. "You're going to tell the lady what you've done and you better hope she doesn't call the police because if they knew what a bad boy you are, they'd take you straight to jail with all the other bad people."

Dragging him by the arm, she marched him over to stand in front of the till. Even on his tippy toes, he was far too short to see the woman on the other side. "Excuse me," his mom said, her voice having morphed to the especially sweet tone she used when she was irritated, but pretending she wasn't. "My son has something he needs to say to you."

She gave him a subtle push forward. He arched his head back, attempting to see over the counter. His mom pulled on his shirt, sending him stumbling backward until the top of the counter came into view. His ears burned red, his cheeks stung from their near miss with being ripped into pieces, and the pressure in his bladder was edging toward pain.

He kept his gaze lowered as he said, "I'm sorry, ma'am," his voice hardly a whisper.

His mom bent down, pinching the tender skin at the back of his neck, and hissed into his ear. "Like you mean it."

He met the lady's eye, her face revealing her confusion. "I'm sorry, ma'am," he repeated.

"What for, sweetie?"

"I got hungry, and I ate some of the candies. My mom says that's stealing, but I didn't mean it." He felt his mom tense beside him, could tell he'd said something to upset her.

"That's not true, Evann," she said in that sweet voice. "You know stealing is wrong."

He took the extra tight pinch on his neck to mean *Don't make me look bad, you little shit,* so he tried again. "I really am sorry. Please don't send me to jail. I promise I won't do it again."

Tears pricked at his eyes as he struggled to keep his gaze fixed on the cashier. She smiled down at him, but that only made the situation more confusing since she was acting like it wasn't that big a deal, but his mom was acting like it was a really big deal. He didn't know if the cashier was just pretending to smile so he wouldn't run away because the police were already on their way, or if it was a real smile because this really wasn't such a big deal.

"Don't worry, sweetie. I won't call the police. This time," she said with a wink. "Thank you for the apology. Let's not let this happen again, okay?"

A tear streamed down Evann's reddened cheek. He didn't realize he'd grabbed hold of his crotch, urgently needing to use the toilet. Several minutes later, he stood in the store's tiny staff washroom, tears freely flowing down his face, hot and wet, like the urine that had soaked through his underwear and into his jeans, uncomfortably sticky against his skin.

Later that evening, he overheard his mom on the phone as she sat on the back porch, drawing long drags off a contraband cigarette.

"I don't know what to do with him. Do you have any idea how fucking humiliating it was to have to apologize to that woman? I could tell she was judging me, like it was my fault the little bastard stuffed candy in his mouth the moment I turned away—and then, to top it all off, he pisses his pants and tries to lie about that too? He's a pathological liar. There's something fucking wrong with him, I'm telling you. As if anyone would believe he actually spilled water on his crotch. I mean, my car reeks of piss. Jesus fucking Christ."

———

Butterflies swarmed in his stomach as shame took root deep within his being; like an invasive vine, those roots have only grown deeper and more robust with time. At least now the ugly feelings are only temporary; once he trades his stolen goods for the few bucks he's short, the shame and self-hatred will drift away with the smoke off his pipe.

34

THE SKELETAL FIGURE HAUNTS HIM, TRACING HIS STEPS, lurking in the background, ready to expose itself unexpectedly. Eerie with its dull hair—left too long—gaunt cheeks covered in an unkempt beard, clothes hanging from its slouched frame, the figure disgusts him. It's best not to acknowledge it. Best not to look too intently or get too close. Despite its withered frame, its height is imposing, intimidating.

For weeks he's averted his eyes, stared at the sidewalk, crossed the street, all in an effort to evade the figure, but everywhere he goes, there it is, waiting for him to look up. To dare look into its hollow eyes. Waiting for him to recognize his likeness in its reflection.

He prefers to spend his days in the shadows. In the dank alleyways and along the boarded-up streets, he can fade into the shame and filth. Among the graffiti and dumpsters, the rats and trash, the lost and disembodied, he can continue his meagre existence anonymously. But it isn't only in shops and cars and mirrors that the soulless figure haunts him. He sees it in the vacant stares of his comrades, in the names and dates and details memorialized in spray paint and

Sharpie, splayed on the walls and sidewalks, covering the concrete and plywood of the Downtown Eastside.

How many of them had died in the days and weeks and months before anyone took notice? Before *they* decided that the dead and dying—the less thans littering *their* streets—were worth tabulating? Thirty percent certainly hadn't been enough. Thirty percent more dead, one year to the next, and yet nothing had been done. It was a problem of *them*, of *those people* living *that life*, out *there*. After January, when the unnamed lost congregated to become a startling statistic, seventy-six haunted souls sucked away and drowned in the depths of their addiction—maybe that would finally be enough to perk some ears, to get some Minister-of-This or Doctor-of-That's attention. No. That didn't do it either. Which is why, as the first month of 2016 rolled into the next and into the next and into the next, the death count continued to climb.

The statistics swept through the street in a series of did-ya-hear's and can-you-believe-it's and when-the-fuck-are-they-gonna-do-something's. The residents were rapt with fear, soothing themselves with pills and vapours, powders and potions—the pain of losing yet another friend, yet another acquaintance, yet another familiar face too much to bear without.

Month after month, the poor, the oppressed, the addicted, the mentally ill, the homeless, and the marginalized continued to die at staggering levels. Long before the government took notice, long before the public took notice, the cries from the trenches went ignored.

It wasn't until *they* started dying, until *their* sons and daughters and brothers and sisters and nieces and nephews and friends and coworkers started to perish, that the numbers stopped being statistics to track and started being humans to mourn.

By April, apparently enough *worthy* souls had died—or at least enough to warrant the declaration of a public health emergency. Rumours swirled around what that might bring: Clean drugs? Decriminalization? Policy change? But in the end, it was nothing

more than conjecture. The response was abysmal: warnings, awareness, Narcan kits. Perhaps enough to spare the life of the casual user
or the weekend partier, but inexcusably blind to the underpinnings of
addiction, the realities of homelessness, and the decades of oppres-
sion blanketing the streets of Vancouver.

Yet still, Evann clings to his kit like a lifeline, because it's all that's
being offered.

Always within reach—though practically speaking it's nothing
more than an untethered rope. Alone, it's just a prop: swabs, syringes,
needles, the antidote, conveniently packaged and clearly labelled. All
the fixings to save him—to reverse the poison he and the others *like
him* could ingest or inject or inhale at any moment. But alone, it's just
a kit. Alone, there's no one to open it; no one to snap the vial; no one
to withdraw the lifesaving medication into the lifesaving syringe; no
one to screw on the needle; no one to inject it into his lifeless body—
thigh, arm, ass; no one to pump on his chest, to blow air into his lungs,
to call for help. So really, it won't be the lethal dose of narcotics that
will kill him. It will be the loneliness.

He hates himself for it. Hates how pathetic he's become, how he
clutches to that fucking kit as if it will make any difference. Hates
that no matter how many times he's heard the wail of sirens, scanned
the names and condolences scrawled across memorial murals, he's
still stupid enough to hope he'll be one of the lucky ones—as if there
is such a thing as luck for people like him.

He's no longer able to escape. Smoking a point or snorting a line
provides only the briefest relief before he's thrust back into the repulsive mind of his wretched self. How sick he must be to hope—to pray
to a god he knows can't possibly exist—that someone else will be the
one to buy the bunk, that he'll be spared. For what? To continue
living his disgusting existence among the filth and squalor of skid
row? To passively observe as one meaningless day bleeds into the
next? To kill himself slowly over hours, days, months—maybe even
years—rather than in a matter of moments? Isn't that what he's trying

to accomplish anyway? To extinguish his thoughts, feelings, and memories—the very pieces that make up his being?

He wants to believe it's only the *real* junkies dying, the pincushions tying belts and shoelaces and tourniquets around their limbs, recklessly injecting muddy slime directly into their bloodstream. It's an unravelling thread of hope, and it's the only one he clings to because it's the only thing that distinguishes him from them. In reality, he only chases because he doesn't have the stomach for injecting; if he did, he'd be no different.

On three occasions—in three moments of absolute desperation—he's tried injecting: once with an empathetic stranger's help and twice at the supervised injection site, where a kind InSite nurse helped him prepare the rig, find a vein, and stick the needle into his skinny arm. Each time he wrapped the tourniquet tight, the squeeze of his skin sent him back to a simpler time, when the big kids would chase him and he—the slowest— would have his arm twisted in a painful snake bite. The cool alcohol swab tingled against the bulging vein in his wrist. He took a deep breath, swallowing the surge of bile pushing against his esophagus, and plunged the needle through the skin, holding his breath as he felt the subtle pop of it poking through the vessel wall. Three separate times, however, when he pulled back on the plunger, saw the flash of his blood enter the syringe —his literal blood intermixing with what has become his lifeblood—he passed out cold. After the third time wasting good smack, he decided the effort wasn't worth whatever the prize might be—though he'd likely think otherwise if he ever made it far enough to find out.

The feeling of a rush is now a hazy memory, one he isn't certain ever actually existed: were the euphoric highs of earlier days experienced or imagined? He no longer gets even the slightest pleasure, settling for a few hours of relief from the pain of his very existence. But it's the longing—the aching desire—for the feeling of the firsts that holds his attention; mirages feeding the delusion that, with stubborn pursuit, surely the feeling he's after can be recaptured. It's become a ritual, and it now dictates every aspect of his life. But the periods of relief—of balance—are growing shorter and shorter with each passing day. Fear grips him even as he snorts a line or smokes a point. The fear of dying—of who he's become, of the darkness that suffocates his spirit—has become all-consuming.

He is trapped in a nightmare, startled and repulsed, yet remiss to the scene in front of him, the world around him. It's happened so insidiously, this gradual acceptance: what was once a doorway now substitutes as a room, an unlit stoop now a private haven, a chunk of cardboard has become a mattress. Modesty is overlooked, security is no longer, the walls around him graffiti-adorned in a crude and tacky wallpaper. The putrid smell of piss and garbage and human filth had —not too long ago—caused his stomach to turn, his nostrils to sting. But it has all—somehow, bit by bit—become normal.

Evann looks around, taking in the wasteland, the place where he lives and eats, pisses and shits and pukes, where he spends his fleeting highs and his jonesing lows, where he has made neighbours and then watched them die, and fear consumes him. He feels an urgent sense of desperation to escape this wretchedness, but in a vicious paradox, the only way he knows how to cope with the unrelenting terror is to use.

35

FOR THE SECOND STRAIGHT DAY, EVANN IS SURE HE WILL DIE. Ironically, he didn't realize he was about to die as the bunk entered his bloodstream—uninvited fentanyl riding in through a heroin trojan horse, in an invasion that nearly cost him his life. Even if he had, would it have changed anything? Maybe. Maybe not. Time and again he's learned that fear alone is a dull blade in the battle against addiction. Fear itself is perhaps the only constant. Somewhere along the line, the magnet was flipped, and what should be a repellent had become an attraction. How many times had he performed the ritual and gotten away with it?

Wake up.

Immediate craving. Brain and body are angry. It's been too long since the last hit.

Hopefully drugs on hand. If so, use. If not, figure out how to get some. Nothing is off limits. Sell his stuff, sell other people's stuff, scrounge for change, reach into garbage cans, beg, borrow, steal.

Use.

Still breathing. Not dead. Must've been okay stuff.

Balance restored. Chemical keys fit into receptor locks.

March of the haunted junkie. Nod off, collect bottles, wander the streets.

Relief fading. Think about using. No sense resisting. Never strong enough to fight it.

Use.

Will this be it?

———

The clock reads 10:50 a.m. Sleeplessness has left him disoriented. Minutes resist becoming hours. Day and night have become indistinguishable. The calendar on the wall has been changed to Tuesday, which is how he knows it's been two days since he went under. Two days since he came back up, gasping for air. Two days since she hadn't.

They weren't supposed to tell him, but he saw it as he staggered to his feet: the black tarps, the strobing lights, the tiny hand, charred fingers limp and drained of life. He should probably be grateful to her; had he gone down first, he wouldn't be here, sicker than he's ever been. Had the paramedics not been there, trying to force life back into her departing corpse, her frail frame collapsing under their efforts, had they not been there pushing futile breaths into her contorted chest, it's likely he too would've been zipped into a bag.

He watched it happen through the wavy distortion of his teary eyes, transfixed. A freakishly skeletal woman about his age—her skin so pale it was nearly translucent—and a much older man frantically scrambled to pack up their rigs. Spoons filled with bubbling tar, syringes with caps clenched between teeth, recycled needles ready to pull up the poison—all prioritized over the pile of bedding they'd been wrapped in. Evann watched absently as the two hurried to leave the doorway, staggering farther into the dank alley. It took him a while to realize that within the discarded blankets lay a perfectly still girl. Her crumpled frame was so slight, she looked almost childlike. He watched as the first responders pulled her out into the open, one starting chest compressions as the other drew up a dose of Narcan. After sticking the needle into what little muscle was left in her tiny toothpick leg, the paramedics continued rhythmically pumping her chest. With each push, the needle in her thin arm—splayed out above her head—moved up and down. "Twenty-eight, twenty-nine, thirty." He listened to the honk of artificial breaths squeezed in through her slack jaw before they resumed, the invisible metronome reset back to one. Something in the rhythmicity of it was strangely settling, and Evann's eyelids grew heavy. The last thing he remembers was wishing he had the energy to move, to get away from the girl with the needle in her arm, her ribs breaking under the weight of those trying to bring her back to life.

They brought him back, and that's when he saw her. The guilt of seeing her lifeless body is the only reason he accepted the laminated card, allowed the kind paramedic to look him in the eye, to tell him about a place accepting walk-ins. He didn't deserve that stranger's kindness—is still surprised, in fact, that anyone in a uniform has any compassion left after reviving junkies hour after hour, shift after shift, month after month—but because he felt compelled to accept the help that didn't reach that girl, he staggered into detox that night.

The nice people—the ones who welcomed him, explained the rules, smiled at him, heads tilted sympathetically with pity in their eyes, as if he were an abandoned dog—say it's still too early. Some score—they told him about it, but now he can't remember—isn't high enough. They kept him up late that first night obtaining a comprehensive history, not that he would've been able to sleep anyways. They explained how important it was for the team to know exactly what drugs he had in his system; he fought back tears as they watched him struggle to pee in a cup. They searched through his belongings, taking his long-dead cellphone and his sketchbook.

He's spent every moment since being injected with Narcan in agony. Not a moment of sleep, not a moment of reprieve from the guilt and shame. Not a moment without that scene playing like a film on repeat.

By hour forty, he's oscillating from hot to cold, his burning skin damp as he shivers violently, the ache deep in his bones, radiating to every muscle in his body. Each time he makes a run for the toilet, he's surprised there's anything more to give, his cramping stomach mercilessly emptying top and bottom. "The worst is nearly behind you," the nice people say as the first tablet of Suboxone dissolves under his tongue. If only clearing the drugs from his system was all it would take. No matter how sick he gets, he's unable to purge the memory of seeing her corpse.

Four hours later, he stares at the ceiling in his small room, the most comfortable accommodation he's had in months, unable to concentrate on anything but the constant throb in his head. He's been fed a regular diet of Advil and Imodium since his arrival, a seemingly futile attempt to counteract the dope sickness. During intake he downplayed his symptoms, not wanting these caring people to see him as a loser junkie, not wanting them to feel sorry for him when he was the fortunate one. Suffering is a privilege. Only the living get to suffer.

They check on him every hour. "One," he lies when they ask him to rank his anxiety on a scale of one to four. "Not too bad right now," when asked how intense his cravings are.

By the time he admits to himself and the team just how agonizing his symptoms are, he's in moderate withdrawal. Coming up on fifty hours since his last fix, and fifty-plus hours since he last slept, the pain is unbearable. His anxiety is crippling. He hasn't been able to keep down food or water. His skin crawls, his vision blurs, his head pounds. Even the tiny sliver of sunlight peeking around the blackout curtains is too much for his enormous pupils to filter, too much for his deprived brain. He's desperate for a fix—his body and brain begging him to go—but right now, he can hardly manage to lift his head off the pillow.

The door creaks open. Evann cowers beneath the blankets, a scared animal hiding in his cave.

"I need to see if you're ready for another dose, Evann," the nurse says.

On the first hourly check, he agreed to take another Suboxone, admitting that he wasn't feeling any improvement. On subsequent rounds, she agreed not to turn on the lamp, assuming that he was being honest when he said, "I'm fine, thanks. I just have a bad headache. I don't need any more right now."

Now, four hours after taking the first tablet, she says she needs to do a proper assessment. She clicks on the small lamp, illuminating the dark room. Evann slowly sits up, pulling the blanket from over his head. Snot drips down his face. He compulsively wipes away the tears streaming down his cheeks, interrupted only by his constant wide-mouthed yawning. He crosses his arms over his abdomen, eyes darting around the room.

"Evann? Are you feeling okay? You don't look great."

Well, no shit, lady, he thinks but of course doesn't say. "Uh, no. It's pretty bad now," he admits.

"Okay," she says. "Let's go through the SOWS score again. So, I can see your eyes and nose are running, can you hold your arms straight out?"

Evann lifts his arms, his achy muscles twitchy and tremulous against the strain of their own weight. She grasps his wrist, pressing her fingers gently on his pulse.

"All right." She writes something down. "You don't seem to be sweating too much?"

Unsure whether that's a question or an observation, he says nothing.

"Are you still having loose stools? Still vomiting?"

Squatting behind a dumpster suddenly seems less humiliating than discussing his bowels every hour. "Uh, yeah. Not much improvement there."

"Have you managed to keep any of the electrolyte drink down?"

The last time he tried, he barely made it to the toilet. "No, but I haven't tried in an hour or so."

"All right, Evann. I'm going to get the medical director to come see you. We expected you'd be feeling better after the second dose."

Dr. Portmann comes in a few minutes later, a look of concern in his gentle eyes. In their initial intake, the doctor shared how substance abuse recovery became his life's work after his own brother lost his battle with addiction in the early 1970s.

"So, tell me what's going on, Evann. Michaela here is worried about you."

How the fuck should I know, you're the doctor. Just the thought of saying something so disrespectful to someone of superior status evokes the phantom sensation of nails digging into his cheeks. He doesn't want to admit it—to himself nor to this kind man—but the cravings have become all-consuming. How was he stupid enough to think he can get clean? This is no different than anything else he's ever tried, another line on the long list of failed endeavours. The only thing he's ever managed to succeed at is getting himself hooked on drugs.

"I'm quite worried you're in the territory of what we call 'precipitated withdrawal.' It usually passes, but it can be agonizing, and if I'm being honest, in my experience most people leave detox and go back to using rather than push through it."

Evann can't bring himself to meet the doctor's gaze, humiliated that even here, having been given all the tools, all the right people, all the support, all the medication, he's proven himself a disappointment, yet again.

"So, what are you suggesting, sir?"

"Please, call me Simon. I know I look old, but *sir* feels a bit too formal for young men like ourselves." Dr. Portmann gives Michaela a cheeky smile.

He can see that the doctor—Simon, rather—is just trying to connect with him, and he appreciates the effort, appreciates how kind and compassionate they all are. Evann forces his mouth into a tight-lipped grin, all he can muster. He rests his head on his knees, the darkness of the blankets providing a moment of relief before the throbbing behind his eyes resumes.

"What I'm saying, is you're very sick, Evann. And I'm very worried about you. I think we all underestimated your tolerance."

Evann doesn't lift his head as he nods along. He tries, he really, honestly, tries to pay attention, but he can't comprehend, can't hear him over the compulsive thoughts that have taken over the space in his head, expanded to every cell in his body.

You'll feel better once you get some dope.

You're going to die if you stay here.

These people don't understand. They've never gone through this.

Your parents already think you're a failure.

That girl isn't coming back no matter what you do. Why put your-self through this?

"Do you understand what I'm saying?"

"Um, not really," Evann admits. "I'm sorry, I'm feeling really out of it. It's kinda hard to concentrate right now."

"We don't know that Suboxone is the right approach for you, Evann. I understand it was our goal—everyone's goal, really—to get you started on a partial agonist rather than the methadone program, but your withdrawal symptoms are too severe to safely continue with the Suboxone."

The kind-eyed doctor and the compassionate nurse sit with him as his facade collapses, as the agony of pain and loss and rejection flood out of him in gasping sobs. When the effort of crying becomes too exhausting, they gently explain the next steps, but the only thing he hears is that he's failed.

36

He lets it ring once, hangs up, returns the phone to the charger, and shuffles back to the TV room. He tells himself he'll try again later. Maybe he'll be stronger in an hour.

Of course, he doesn't know the exact time it happened—not the exact time of death, nor the exact time of resurrection—so he's decided to count from his first dose of methadone, which means he has ninety-two hours of sobriety.

He's well aware of how pathetic that is—like those ridiculous parents who insist on saying their kid is "twenty-five months" when any normal person would say "just turned two"—but he doesn't dare think in terms of days yet. It's hard enough to think in terms of hours. They're still titrating his dose, so he's too high to top himself up with junk—that would be a sure way to kill himself again—but too low to do anything more than wander around the shelter. Right now, every minute since the pipe rolled out of his flaccid hand feels longer than the last.

The waitlist for a treatment bed is lengthy, and he can't afford to give up his place at the shelter if he has any chance of remaining sober. Without applying for social assistance, he'll remain trapped in no man's land, but he feels sick to his stomach every time the support workers bring it up. He can see his father's face, can imagine the shock, the shame, the disappointment he—a hard-working, tax-paying, Conservative-voting citizen—would feel if he knew his own son has become one of the leeches he so despises.

Evann saw it first-hand over Thanksgiving, the way his mother rolled her eyes when the news camera panned over the turkey dinner being served to the less fortunate, the way his father snorted in disgust, said how much easier life would be for everyone if those invalids would just get a goddamn job instead of suckling at the government's teat. Rather than taking the hand-out, Evann shuffles around in donated PJ pants, cinched tight around his thin waist, keeps his bed made and the communal kitchen tidy, and attends NA meetings.

Today, he's exhausted after a long night lying awake, thinking about what the counsellor said in yesterday's group:

Shame. Disgust. Self-hatred. Do any of these ring a bell? On their own, they're just words, but I'd be willing to bet they're pillars in your life as an addict. Can any of you sitting here honestly say you haven't felt ashamed of yourself? Disgusted by the things you've done? Is there anyone here who didn't pick up the pipe or the powder or the rig as a way to punish themselves? That's certainly why I did it. I didn't know who I was, and I didn't like the glimpses I saw between fixes, but instead of taking accountability, I chose to punish myself—because that's what I believed I deserved. And I tell you what, that became a self-fulfilling prophecy. Believe you're a bad person, you'll make bad choices. Believe no one cares about you, you'll put up walls, block out those who do. Believe you don't deserve better, you'll make damn sure you never get it.

So, to be successful in recovery, we need to let go of the past—not forget about it, not deny it—but let it go so we can focus on being better every day. And that starts with forgiveness. Maybe that means forgiving those who've hurt you, those who've taken from you, those who weren't there for you when you needed them most. Maybe not. But there is one person you absolutely must be willing to forgive, and that's yourself. Because if you don't forgive yourself—for the person you've been, the things you've done, the people you've hurt, whatever it is that brings up that lump in your throat—you're just going to carry on punishing yourself.

Evann isn't sure he buys into it—any of it. That guy finished off by saying it all links back to the Twelve Steps, to some mystical guiding principles, to some path to sobriety that involves turning power over to some god, to surrendering and accepting and making amends. It sounds to him like a lot of buzzwords.

What about accountability? What about the unforgivable? What about the people like him who've done nothing to deserve a second chance but were "given" one, as though it weren't a matter of chance, but some divine intervention? As though there's some all-powerful being handing out get-out-of-jail-free cards like this is some twisted game of *Monopoly* where Commercial Drive isn't a property for purchase, but a trapdoor straight to hell. Wasn't that girl worthy of a second chance? They had both landed on the same square. They rolled the same dice. Why was he allowed to keep playing, but her piece was flicked off the game board? Did this "God" they keep referencing not think she deserved a second chance—a chance to roll again? Did their "God" not think she deserved a shot at the "forgiveness" they keep preaching about?

He wants to have hope, wants to believe that, with time, something will shift, and he'll be ready to see a clear path forward. Maybe he's rushing it. Maybe ninety-three hours will feel different than ninety-two. Maybe he just needs to be patient, maybe even wait until he's made it to an even hundred before he can expect the message to resonate; perhaps then he'll even feel secure enough to stop counting in hours altogether. Maybe then he'll allow himself to acknowledge that four days have passed. What if four days simply isn't enough time either? Maybe it's more realistic to expect this elusive shift after six days sober. Maybe by then he'll be able to acknowledge that his survival hadn't come at her expense, that it hadn't been a one-or-the-other type scenario. Maybe then he'll be able to do what he needs to do—to reach out, to start making amends, to take back his life.

But at that point, why not see about measuring in weeks?

He can't think like this. If he lets himself, he'll live the rest of his life chasing tomorrows. So, although he's angry, and he's scared, and he's confused, although he isn't ready to drink the Kool-Aid just yet, he reminds himself that he's already wasted enough of his life; he has no intention of going back to the bar for the "Free Beer Tomorrow" day after day after day, which is why every hour, he drags himself away from the reruns of daytime television, over to the phone where he lets it ring once, hangs up, returns the phone to the charger, and shuffles back to the TV room.

Maybe it's not time yet, but it has to be soon. His sobriety hinges on it.

37

"I DIDN'T KNOW WHO ELSE TO CALL."

He didn't actually expect her to answer. Certainly didn't expect she would agree to meet him. Not after everything that's been said.

It goes generously unasked, and therefore left unsaid, that he's missed three doses, the pharmacy now refusing to dispense his methadone until he's reassessed by a doctor. But he's too ashamed to explain that. Too ashamed to admit that he's clinging to the wagon by the skin of his teeth.

"Thank you. Honestly, I didn't know who else to call," he repeats, nervously scanning to make sure there are no other familiar faces around. She hasn't asked what it's for, and he hasn't offered. It's gracious of her not to; though, at this point, it won't change anything.

They make small talk, awkward and superficial, old hurts masked behind indifferent expressions, the sting of past transgressions lingering just below the surface.

"I know this hasn't been easy on you, so—"

"Don't," she interrupts. "We're not doing this right now."

He feels himself starting to spin, face to face with his past. Her sterling grey eyes—something they once shared—seem to shine in a way his no longer do. The juxtaposition between what is and what could've been—what had actually happened and what was said—is more than he can stomach.

"You look like shit, by the way. When's the last time you slept?"

"I've been stressed. But this will really help," he says, holding up the makeup bag. "I just need to get back on my feet."

She holds her shoulders in a shrug, a look of doubt crossing her face. "I guess we'll see."

"Okay, well, uh... thanks for this. I really appreciate it." His skin burns hot. This is a mistake. He knows she's angry, but he didn't expect her to look at him with such hatred. He isn't strong enough for this—not yet. "Anyways, I'd better get going. I have somewhere to be."

She doesn't argue. Perhaps she senses it would be a waste of time. In his mind, he's already gone, and they both know it.

He reaches forward to hug her, but she takes a panicked step back. He wants nothing more than to pull her close, to wrap his arms around her as he has so many times before. "Shit. Sorry," he says, fumbling for his phone instead.

She waits for him to hit Send before taking a reluctant step toward him. She stiffens as he pulls her close, whispers into her hair.

And then he's gone, leaving her and his past behind him.

———

Dope in hand, he limps up the footpath to the lookout point. Sleeping rough has turned his youthful body into that of an arthritic elder. This spot has always been his favourite place to come, a peaceful retreat, somewhere to clear his head; it'll be worth the pain of climbing the steep embankment.

Soon, he won't be in pain.

Soon, he won't feel anything.

The sunlight sparkles on the water. He opens his sketchbook, flips to the last page. The illustration is perhaps the most incredible thing he's ever drawn. It's certainly the most meaningful.

His mind wanders obsessively to the powder in his pocket, but this is too important. He's nearly finished, but he has to make sure it's perfect, that every detail is just right. Withdrawal racks his body, cravings rip at his mind, but he forces himself to continue until, finally, it's complete. He signs and dates it, then tucks it safely back in his bag.

He pulls out the baggie, tilts it back and forth—watches the powder slide side to side like sand in an hourglass. It used to freak him out, the idea of the last grain of sand falling, the idea of watching as time runs out, but now, it doesn't bother him. It's an inevitability; time, just like sand, is finite, and choosing to look away doesn't change that. He understands that now.

Resting back, he watches the early summer sun fade to dusk before bringing the powder to his nose. One sharp inhale, a series of violent sniffs, and Evann begins to drift into the twilight.

His mind wanders to something he read as a child, something he hasn't thought about in years. It explained how excruciatingly painful it is for whales to be lifted from the water in those slings. It made him sad all those years ago, not just because he loved watching the belugas at the aquarium, but because he could relate to them: he also smiled without being happy.

Maybe he's like those whales. Maybe that's what's wrong with him. Maybe he too was delivered somewhere he would never belong, but instead of being released from the torturous pressure of the sling, he'd been left to hang—left to spend his life being crushed under his own weight.

He lays back into the grass, feeling himself drift into blissful oblivion. As the poison flows through his veins, his breathing slows.

Caught somewhere between here and nowhere, the dream comes as it had when he was a child.

He's on a ferry boat, crossing the Strait of Georgia. The captain announces a pod of orcas off the port side, causing a flurry of excitement. As everyone rushes to the windows, the ferry flips over, submerging him into a mystical aquarium, where he is alone, perfectly at peace, a pod of orcas swimming just beyond the windows. He holds his breath as the enormous animals watch him curiously—as if he's the one in an aquarium.

The dreamy image begins to blur, and he feels himself gradually slipping away. It's often said that drowning is a peaceful way to die. Perhaps it's true. A feeling of futility and finality washes over him. He knows his fight is over, that he's finally able to slip away. The unrelenting suffering, the guilt and shame, the pain and betrayal, all float away as water fills his imagined aquarium. He feels no fear, and as he takes his final breath—as he drifts away—he finally knows what it is to be weightless.

38

"Hello there. I'm looking to speak with Ann or Bruce Cartwright."

She cocks her head, pinning the phone as she continues to apply the finish coat. It's nearly nine o'clock. She can't imagine who could be calling this late, but after the same number popped up on the caller ID for the third time that day, she begrudgingly picked up. "Speaking," she says, blowing gently on her wet nails.

"Mrs. Cartwright—"

"Please, call me Ann."

"Sure. Ann. I'm sorry to call so late. I'm calling about your son, Evann. Evann is your son, is that correct?"

Jesus Christ, what is it now? "Yes, Evann is my son. What in God's name has he gotten himself into this time?"

PART III

Addiction is always a poor substitute for love.

DR. GABOR MATÉ, *IN THE REALM OF HUNGRY GHOSTS: CLOSE ENCOUNTERS WITH ADDICTION*

39

BRUCE

ANN HAS ALREADY GONE HOME BY THE TIME BRUCE ARRIVES AT the hospital. He hopped in a company truck and started driving to the airport as soon as he spoke to her, not even thinking to ask which city he was flying to, which hospital their son was in, or what had happened—not until he found himself standing at the security check-point, unable to present a boarding pass. All she said was "It's bad." Well past midnight, he jogs up to the locked doors, which open to reveal the orderly chaos of the ICU. The beeping alarms and ringing telephones are disorienting against the competent calm of the staff, quietly going about their routines. He takes three steps into the room before he turns and walks out to speak to the nurse.

"I'm sorry, I think I was given the wrong room number," he explains. "I'm looking for my son, Evann. Evann Cartwright."

He spent the entire flight thinking about the day he met his son. He'd barely made it to the hospital in time to be there when Evann entered the world, making him a Daddy. All the incredible things he'd been told about becoming a father were true. From the moment he looked at their perfect baby, felt Evann's tiny hand grasp on to his finger, he knew there was nothing he wouldn't do to love and protect that little boy.

Bruce looks down at the man before him, this figure lying in a hospital bed bearing no resemblance to Evann. Even beneath the matted beard and the breathing tube, held in place by stickers high on his cheeks, he can see the sores, the cracked lips, the hollowed eye sockets. There must be some mistake—a mix-up. This guy is about twenty pounds lighter than Evann was the last time he was home, and that was only in October. Surely, he couldn't have changed that much—become *this*—in eight months. Bruce watches the man's heart beating behind his ribs, the line in his neck throbbing gently with each beat. He reaches down to touch the ID band around the man's swollen wrist:

CARTWRIGHT, Evan

DOB: 04/10/1995

That proves it: Evan with one *n*. Just as he'd suspected—as he'd tried to politely tell the nurse—this isn't his son.

He glances at the man's face again, pushing aside what he knows to be true but can't bring himself to see. There must be a mistake. Another Evan Cartwright with the same birthdate. His son—his Evann—can't possibly be this man. His Evann is probably at home in bed, or working late on an assignment. His Evann is a good kid, clean-cut. But isn't it also true that Bruce has missed a lot throughout the years? Can he really claim to know his children when he's only been around for a quarter of their lives?

He'd only thought it fair to let Ann hold the parenting reins; she'd always had a much better handle on what the kids were up to, what they needed, what was best for them. Bruce moves closer, trying to see past the tubes and wires and machines, willing himself not to see his son beneath the clutter. An unthinkable idea is forming in his mind; if this is Evann—this battered man lying before him—did Ann know their son was in trouble? Has she kept it from him?

He shakes the thought away. She and Evann might not always see eye to eye, but that doesn't mean she doesn't care about him. How many times has he heard her say "I don't have to like you, but I do love you" to their son over the years? Sure, sometimes she's cold and withdrawn, but underneath that is a warm and affectionate mother.

If either of them is guilty of withholding the full truth, it's him.

Bruce pulls out his cellphone, taps on Evann's name under Recents. His chest burns at the memory of their last call, but he pushes that away. That doesn't matter right now. If he can just hear his son's voice, know he's all right—that this is all an unfortunate misunderstanding, that some other Cartwrights are the real victims—they can sort out their differences later. He holds his breath as it starts to ring. Led Zeppelin comes on, muffled and distant. It isn't until the tune starts again that Bruce realizes why he recognizes it. It's "Stairway to Heaven," Evann's favourite song.

———

The nurse provides a perfectly logical explanation for how they'd come to identify Evann, but it doesn't explain how his son was found pulseless and blue, with no ID, nearly no belongings, and a lethal combination of heroin, fentanyl, and something called benzodiazepines in his system. It's so unbelievable, Bruce has the nurse write it down for him, sure that he's misunderstanding her in his sleep-deprived state.

In the back of the taxi, he rereads her note, folding the paper and tucking it back in his pocket. He intends to go home and catch a few hours of sleep before he and Ann have to return to the hospital in the morning, but when he unlocks the front door, sees Evann's painting of Mrs. Potter staring back at him, he grabs his truck keys and pulls the door closed behind him. He's ten kilometres from home by the time he realizes where he's going.

With the light of his cellphone, he follows the path carved through the dense forest, dwarfed by the towering western hemlock and Douglas fir trees. Making his way through to the concealed clearing, he climbs carefully down the steep staircase and onto the beach below. At low tide, the rocky beach is exposed, driftwood strewn across the shore. First light is peeking over the horizon as Bruce walks toward the water, the rounded rocks giving way to soft, wet sand that squishes beneath his boots: the perfect stuff for building a sand castle.

He thinks back to the day they spent as a family at Long Beach. The kids were quite young—they must've been because once Nicole started to dance, their weekends were earmarked for rehearsals and competitions. Ann packed the cooler, and they drove north, winding their way up island, past glacial runoffs and old-growth forests. He can still hear the waves lapping against the shore, Evann's giggles as a tiny crab crawled in his hand, Nicole's squeals as he tossed her in the air until his shoulders ached—and then until he collapsed onto the sand, laughing and pleading, "No more, sweetie, Daddy's arms can't handle anymore." Ann sat on a blanket reading while he and the kids waded through the tide pools, searched for starfish, collected spent sand dollars in their buckets, and made an elaborate castle, complete with a moat to fortify its walls against the encroaching waves. They drove back in silence, Ann and the kids asleep—the kids snoring from the backseat, Ann with her face pressed against the window—but he hadn't minded. It was one of the best days of his adult life. He pitched the idea of making it an annual thing, and while she seemed enthusiastic about it, in the years that followed there was always a reason not to go: it was too much work to pack up the kids, there was this or that dance thing, it wasn't worth Ann being carsick the entire drive.

As the tide begins to approach the shoreline, he finds a dry log to sit on, resting back against the bluff. He's surprised to see his watch reads 5:30 a.m., suddenly aware that he is still wearing his work clothes fifty-odd hours later. He watches the grey sky give light to the glowing sunrise, feathery clouds moving across the bright orb peeking over the mountains. If Evann was here, he'd know what that cloud formation is called, whether those are stratus or cumulus, and he'd know what they mean; he pays attention to those sorts of things, takes interest in those things around him that others might consider mundane. If Evann was here, he'd be hunched over his sketchbook, or crouched behind his lens, capturing the beauty of the moment, the intricacies of his surroundings. Or would he? Perhaps the old Evann, the version Bruce knows and remembers. But what about the real Evann—the version he saw in that hospital bed?

Bruce has worn the mask of a man being strong, but now he's exhausted—he can't hold it back any longer. He can no longer ignore the relentless squeeze around his heart, the hollow feeling in his stomach, the pressure of tears pooling behind his eyes. With no one around to witness, Bruce allows himself to weep.

———

His nose is raw, his eyes red-rimmed and puffy, when he pulls his wife into a tight embrace. He feels her tense in his arms, but he doesn't care. She can put on a tough exterior, but he knows she's hurting too.

"How are you holding up?" he says into her hair.

Ann shrugs. "About as well as can be expected when you find out your son is a junkie, that he's overdosed, and that he's going to die—all in one day."

Bruce pulls away, puts his hands on her shoulders. "We don't know that, Ann. I talked to the nurse, and she didn't say that. So until we hear otherwise, we need to stay positive."

"Sure, Bruce," she says, looking at her watch. "Why don't you go shower. I'll make some coffee."

He tries not to let Ann's words bother him as the hot water washes over his aching back. It's no secret that she and Evann have never been particularly close. He'd seen it the moment the doctor laid the infant across her chest. While he'd been overjoyed to have a boy, imagining playing catch in the backyard and teaching him how to cast a line, Bruce saw the not-so-subtle signs of Ann's disappointment. He knew she'd started to fill the nursery closet with cute pink outfits, convinced—for whatever reason—that she was carrying a girl. He figured that after she had a chance to get some rest, she'd snap out of it, but she didn't. Two days after giving birth, she couldn't even talk about what to name their son without crying, which is why the task of formally naming Baby Cartwright was left to Bruce. It was important to him that his boy have a timeless name, something strong and traditional, but also something a little different. Everyone they knew had named their boys Michael or Christopher or Joshua, and he wanted his boy to have a name that wouldn't be too common, but also not something weird. He ran it by Ann, who said she liked it. It wasn't until he started to fill out the paperwork for the birth certificate that the alternative spelling occurred to him. Hoping to help his wife connect with the new baby, he figured, *Well, what the hell.*

What had been intended as a thoughtful gesture had not been well received. She called him at work the day Evann's birth certificate arrived in the mail, crying about how some moron at the government had misspelled the baby's name. He'll never forget that phone call, holding the receiver away from his ear as she shrieked into the other end. "Jesus Christ, Bruce! What do we do? I can't believe some fucking idiot would think we'd spell Evan with two *n*'s." Obviously, he had to tell her it wasn't a mistake—the last thing he wanted was to subject some poor government official to the wrath of his hormonal, sleep-deprived wife—but he took a lot of flak for that decision, and his naming rights were forever revoked. When their daughter came along a few years later, he wasn't even consulted.

———

"Where's Nicole?" Bruce asks, pouring himself another strong cup of coffee.

"At a friend's house."

He holds the mug close to his face, the heat from the enamel radiating to warm his hands, the fragrant steam rising to settle on his chin. "Okay. I guess we'll just swing by and pick her up on our way to the hospital."

Ann pauses, her mug suspended halfway to her mouth. "You're kidding, right?"

"What do you mean?"

"You don't actually think we're going to bring Nicole to see him like that, do you? I mean, my god, Bruce, I can hardly look at him. I am not going to traumatize my daughter by forcing her to see him like that."

"You can't be serious, Ann. He's her brother. He needs his family."

"Wow. Listen to you, Mr. Hypocrite," Ann says, setting her mug down. There's an alarming intensity burning in her eyes. "Not last week you were droning on about how much money the government is wasting on these people. How you can't believe all the nonsense about addiction being a disease when it's so obviously a choice. Calling them the 'plague of our time.' So what's changed, Bruce? Now that your precious son has gotten himself wrapped up in it, your opinion is suddenly different?"

He rubs at his temples, attempting to gather his thoughts, searching for the right thing to say. She isn't wrong: he did say all those things. But debating politics and ideology doesn't seem important right now. "Okay," he finally says. "We'll give her the choice."

"Fine. But don't you think for one second that I'm going to force my daughter to do anything she's not comfortable with."

"Fine. She's old enough to drive, she's old enough to make decisions for herself," Bruce says. "While we're at it, don't you pull that 'my daughter' bullshit. She's my daughter too, and she's stronger than you give her credit for."

40

ANN

No mother wants to admit—not even to herself—that she feels anything but unconditional love for her own child, but as Ann stares at her son through watery eyes, tubes protruding from between scabbed lips, sweat pooling in the concave of his chest, all she feels is disgust.

She tries to pull her attention away from the repulsive corpse in front of her, its chest rising and falling as though it's alive. But it isn't. It looks like it is—the monitors and machines harmonizing in a symphony of fabricated continuance—but the doctors and nurses have pulled no punches: they're waiting on a couple more tests, but it's likely their son is already dead—legally speaking.

Leaning back into the uncomfortable chair, she reaches for the paper cup, wishing it was full of wine rather than orange juice. She scrolls through her feed, filled with posts of happy families, normal families—the kind without dead children or secrets to keep—feeling the familiar sorrow tightening in her throat. She can't help but take stock of her life, to look back at everything that has led to this point and wonder what she's done to deserve so much heartache. She closes her eyes and allows herself to fantasize about how simple—how wonderfully perfect—their lives might've been if Nicole had come along first. Deep within her being, Ann knows if that had been the case, they wouldn't have had another. Had their beautiful princess arrived first, as Ann expected, she would've insisted on not having a second, and their lives would've been so different.

The glass door slides open, just enough for the nurse to slip in quietly. Ann watches her exchange one IV bag for another before slipping out, closing the door silently behind her. Her husband is snoring softly, his head resting on the side rail. The sour smell of sweat hangs in the air. Pasty excrement crawls out from under the sheet through a tube, sliding into a sack. She supposes it's better than the alternative—which she assumes would be Evann shitting the bed —but the closed system doesn't help much; not even the tray of peppermint-scented shaving cream placed on the floor below the bag can mask the intolerable stink. The smells are enough to make her eyes water. Worse still are the rotten teeth, chipped and grey—teeth that were once perfectly aligned thanks to the thousands of dollars they'd spent on orthodontics. She doesn't know how Bruce can stand to be that close.

She was so young—barely more than a teenager—when she and Bruce started their life together. When he walked into that diner, she certainly hadn't expected him—or any of the men who tipped generously in the hopes of taking her home—to become anything more than a meaningless fling to pass the time. She'd always been a wanderlust spirit: while her girlfriends were talking about falling in love, getting married, and having a family, she was daydreaming about backpacking through Europe. The day after she graduated high school, she walked out of her parents' house with not so much as a goodbye. Her life crammed into a backpack, she hitchhiked across the country, setting off on what she hoped would be the first of many adventures. She made it to the West Coast before running out of money, landing in the small town entirely by happenstance. When her future husband walked in and ordered a coffee, she was working a double at the diner, strands of long brown hair slipping loose from her hair tie, her feet and ankles screaming in protest of ten hours in heels.

She watches her husband sleep. His hand twitches, clasped around his son's, and she makes a mental note to remind him to wash his hands when he wakes up. He might not mind wiping the beads of sweat from Evann's scabbed brow or holding his hands—which are foul, the crevices so embedded with dirt and grime that even the twice daily bedbaths haven't cleansed them completely—but the last thing they need is to catch whatever Evann might've picked up doing whatever he's been doing to land himself here.

———

There was something about Bruce—right from the beginning—that drew her in. He was tall, handsome enough—in an ordinary sort of way—but there was something in his demeanour that she'd found intriguing. He seemed confident, sure of himself, but not in the usual cocky way. He was kind and generous, but not in the way of other men who seemed to expect something in return. She was used to men paying attention to her; in fact, with her size two waist and a perky set of boobs, she was managing to make a pretty decent living as a waitress. But when she spoke to him, he held her gaze and leaned forward. He listened intently, as if there was nothing more important in his world than to hear her list the specials. Ann, who loved to be the centre of attention, wasn't used to *that* kind of attention. He didn't just look at her body, he looked at *her*.

It all happened so fast. In hindsight, she barely knew the man she agreed to marry, but when he presented her with a two-carat oval solitaire and the promise that she'd never have to work another day in her life, of course she said yes; it was the safe choice. He was stable, secure, and predictable—qualities she'd never known in a man. He was selflessly kind-hearted, endlessly patient and forgiving, and, above all, he treated her like a princess.

In the lead-up to their big day, they settled into a comfortable routine. She quit her job at the diner, and—much to the disapproval of her future in-laws—they moved into their new home together. She was allotted a generous allowance and was free to do as she wished while he was working away three weeks of each month. She'd never been happier, allowing herself to dream about European adventures.

They weren't particularly careful to prevent it, but when one month became two, she cried on the edge of the tub. As the urine evaporated, so too did her dreams—in their place, two distinct blue lines. At just twenty-one years old, Ann wasn't ready to have a family, but weeks away from their wedding day, there was no way she could share her reservations with Bruce—not when he was overjoyed with the news. She quietly chastised herself. Assuming they could keep the pregnancy hidden until after the wedding, there was no reason to feel anything short of thrilled.

By all standards, the day had the makings of a fairytale wedding. Bruce's family paid for the entire affair, right down to the lavish custom-made gown with its long train and intricate beadwork. Her hair and makeup turned into an arduous process, interrupted each time she had to run to the bathroom to dry-heave over the sink, tears streaming down her cheeks as she expelled nothing more than bile. She spent most of the morning crying, worried the dress wouldn't zip —that the tiny bump would betray their secret. Fortunately, she passed it off as nerves and managed to squeeze into her gown, a care-fully placed bouquet hiding any indication of the bastard life growing within her.

In the end, she did get to go on her European adventure, but only to find out that when it comes to a honeymoon, three's a crowd. The two weeks of enjoying local cuisine, sightseeing tours, and lazily exploring the cobblestoned streets of Italy she had planned were ruined by an unplanned fetus the size of a raspberry. While Bruce sipped on Prosecco and Aperitivo, gorged himself on oven-fired pizzas, creamy risotto, and hearty pasta dishes, Ann struggled to keep dry bread and mineral water down. Their romantic gondola ride ended abruptly after she nearly capsized the boat while heaving over the side, the gondolier fighting to maintain control, shouting Italian expletives at them as she regurgitated lemon gelato into the canal. Unsurprisingly, she struggled to connect with the life growing inside her.

Nonetheless, she did everything the doctor suggested. She picked out decorations for the nursery and even marked the calendar with a heart around October 12. As the baby grew, stretching her taut abdomen into an unrecognizable bulge—translucent and veined—she played the part, stroking her belly adoringly, pretending she wasn't bothered when Bruce started kissing her stomach more often than her lips.

She couldn't have prepared for the paralyzing trepidation that consumed those nine months. She, who had always been a carefree spirit, self-assured and confident, was suddenly overcome with angst, and no matter how many times she reread *What to Expect When You're Expecting*, she couldn't shake the sinking feeling that this baby was an unreconcilable mistake. She felt as though the alien growing inside her had not only hijacked her body, but also her mind, and she no longer recognized herself. Despite buying a closet full of cute maternity clothes, stocking the nursery with plush bunnies, and attending Lamaze classes, she still couldn't see past her anxiety—couldn't manage to get excited about the baby's arrival.

The final blow came at the obstetrician's office when she had a meltdown on the scale. It settled on a number thirty-eight pounds heavier than she'd ever seen it, and while Bruce was happy to lie to her, the scale didn't. The doctor tried to placate her—told her it was normal to feel blue, normal for a woman's body to go through changes, normal to feel uncomfortable in her own skin—but she saw the way his eyebrows shot up when she stepped on that scale. She politely accepted the antidepressant prescription he offered, but opted instead to go on a strict diet and restart smoking.

Subsisting on a daily SlimFast and celery sticks, she passed her days chain-smoking on the couch. Her husband wasn't one to argue; he didn't question her story about the doctor recommending she start smoking again to bring her blood pressure down.

She, like millions of others, was captivated by the O.J. Simpson trial. In the summer of 1994, she'd sat on the edge of the coffee table, watching police cars and media helicopters trail the white Bronco. As the coverage ramped up, her interest in the case became an all-consuming obsession. CNN, Dateline, ABC: everyone had an opinion—though, of course, she was becoming something of an expert, and had no doubt he was guilty. The baby's name came to her one afternoon as she flipped through news broadcasts: Nicole. It was her first feeling of interconnection to the life inside her.

On October 3, 1995—nine days before her due date—as 150 million watched the O.J. Simpson verdict, Ann panted through contraction after contraction, praying her husband would make it back from Alberta in time for the baby's birth.

"Why does this baby have to come today?" she screamed between contractions.

"Don't worry, dear, he'll get here in time," her mother-in-law said.

Just after midnight—less than two hours after Bruce ran into the labour room, frantically scanning to see if he was too late—the doctor lifted the slimy infant from between Ann's legs.

"It's a boy!"

As Bruce kissed her forehead, she collapsed in exhaustion, tears streaming down her face. The baby was lifted onto her chest, his tiny fingers clawing at her breast. She remembers looking at the foreign creature, searching his squished face, his oblong head, his puffy eyes, for any feature that would link her to the child in her arms; it didn't look like her, it didn't look like Bruce, and it wasn't her little Nicole. As the baby greedily latched on to her, sharp fingernails pinching her tender skin, Ann let herself cry.

"I know," Bruce said, wiping a tear from his own cheek. "Isn't he just beautiful?"

Ann didn't have the heart to tell him that hers were tears of disappointment. It turned out to be the first of many disappointments in their son's life.

———

Ann pushes herself up, the metal legs scraping along the floor, the chair bumping up against the cabinets behind her. Bruce stirs briefly before settling back to sleep. She can't stand to look at Evann like this anymore, can't stand to see him lying there, pockmarked skin and protruding bones, covered in a towel that barely qualifies as a loincloth. She can't stand the feeling of that nurse's beady eyes watching her through the window. Someone is always watching them through that fucking window. That particular nurse is getting on Ann's nerves. She's been sitting at that little desk for two straight days, and there's something in the way she maintains eye contact whenever she speaks, her thick round glasses magnifying her pale blue eyes, that makes Ann squirm. It's as if that nurse can sense the darkness inside her, and is trying to access a portal into her soul. Ann can see right through her tactics: the friendly persona, the way she introduces herself every time she enters the room—as if they're too stupid to remember her goddamn name from one hour to the next—the way she speaks to Evann, tells him she's going to turn him this way or that, even though they all know perfectly well that by all indications, the body lying there is nothing more than a shell. Ann has read enough novels and watched enough *Dr. Phil* to understand what this "friendly" woman is trying to do: First, she'll establish herself as a friend—make them feel comfortable enough to forget that she's scrutinizing every word they share, watching their body language through her little window—and then the real work will begin. Soon, the staff will start digging into the past, start picking at old wounds, looking for a key piece of information that might confirm their suspicions that

Ann has failed as a mother. After all, her son is dead, and the blame always falls on the mother.

Ann pokes her head out through the sliding door. "Is there a reason you have him exposed for the entire world to see?"

"Sorry?"

"Is there a reason you insist on leaving him uncovered like that? Really? Can't you cover him up? So we don't have to sit there and look at our dead son's genitals. I mean, Jesus Christ, don't you people think he deserves a bit of decency? Because he's a junkie, he's not worthy of a goddamn blanket?"

She pulls the door closed behind her, not wanting to wake Bruce. The nurse shifts uncomfortably in her chair. Ann crosses her arms. She's pleased to see her squirm, pleased to have taken back her power. It's been almost three days since she received the phone call from the doctor, and for the first time since, she feels solid on her feet.

"Of course not. His body is no longer able to regulate his temperature, so I've left him uncovered to help keep his fever down. I'm so sorry. I hope I haven't done something that's made you think I care less about your son because of his circumstances, because I certainly don't feel that way." She rises from her chair, resting her hand on Ann's shoulder. Ann raises her eyebrows, and the nurse lets her hand drop. Looking into her eyes, Ann can see the young woman—Kaitlin, as she's so frequently reminded them—is holding back tears. "I don't often share this, but I know what it's like to love someone through addiction. My dad is addicted to cocaine. Last I heard he was living out of his car. And believe me, I know there are healthcare workers who have nothing nice to say about people living with addictions, but I promise you, I will treat your family and your son with the same respect I would want for my own family."

Ann supposes she should feel for this girl, who probably isn't much older than Evann, but she's had enough of her theatrical compassion. There is no way anyone in the healthcare field can feel anything but disdain for the addicts clogging up the system, and her very presence is only muddying the waters for Bruce, who can't seem to grasp that his son isn't going to wake up. Either Evann is dead, or he's alive, and since every sign is pointing to him being dead, Ann can't see why Kaitlin insists on brushing his teeth and turning him side to side every two hours, spot on the goddamn hour. It's confusing her husband, and it's pissing her off.

"Well, I'm very sorry to hear that. But frankly, I don't think that's an appropriate thing to be sharing with a mother who is in the midst of losing her child. Is there a charge nurse around? A manager? I'd like to speak to someone about my son's care."

41

NICOLE

She goes back and forth all day before finally deciding to visit. Her parents left the decision to her, but the very act of giving her the choice has made her think that maybe she isn't strong enough to handle it. Her mom is clearly against it, but that's probably because she's worried Nicole will say something she can't take back. She plays through the scenarios, tries to imagine her brother attached to tubes and machines like she's seen on *Grey's*, and eventually curiosity gets the best of her. He looked rough the last time she saw him. How much worse can he be?

———

It turns out it's not his appearance that bothers her. It's the smell. The acidic, throat-burning, unrelenting, inescapable stench that fills every corner of the stuffy hospital room. That smell is what finally gets to her.

The visit starts off fine, even though her dad has gone full Mr. Rogers. With her hoodie zipped over her nose, she studies her brother —the droplets of condensation clinging to the tube sticking out of his mouth, the thick pasty saliva stuck to his lips, the clay-coloured sludge draining from an origin she thankfully can't see. None of it bothers her.

On some level, she knows that she should probably feel bad; if anyone had the opportunity to do more for him, it was her. But then she remembers what he'd done, all the horrible things her mom had told her.

"You know," her dad says, coming up behind her, "your brother has loved you from the time you were in your mom's stomach."

Nicole gives him a guarded smile. Something about the way he holds his face in an unnaturally wide grin, his eyes filled with tears, sends a shiver down her spine. She pulls her sleeves over her hands, wraps her arms tight across her thin waist. She's heard this story before, but given the circumstances—given that her father looks like he's about to have a mental breakdown—she lets him tell it again.

"He was so excited while she was pregnant. Wanted to know everything about how the baby got in there and how the baby would get out—which, I have to say, made for some hilarious and awkward discussions with our three-year-old," he says, laughing. "You remember, Ann?"

"Oh God," her mom says. "Do you remember your sister explaining it to him? I mean... we didn't want to lie to him, but we also didn't really know how much to explain, so we told him the baby grew from an egg in my belly, and that she would come out through a zipper. But your Auntie Barb told him everything! So we're standing in line at the grocery store one day and this elderly lady says, 'Well, young man, it looks like you're about to become a big brother!' and Evann stands up straight—all proud—and goes, 'My mom grows eggs in her belly and when she and my daddy do sex, which is allowed 'cause they're big enough and so it's okay for mommies and daddies, the egg makes a baby and when the baby is ready it'll come out of Mommy's vagina.' I honestly thought the poor lady was going to have a stroke right there in the store! And what could I say? He wasn't wrong. If there were camera phones in those days, we'd have gone viral!"

Nicole smiles nervously. Tears stream down her dad's cheeks as her mom finishes her dramatic rendition of toddler Evann schooling Granny in the supermarket, complete with the extra loud, extra huge inhale Evann took before blurting the entire spiel in one breath.

She's not used to seeing her parents interact like this under the best of circumstances, let alone in a hospital room with their son's rotting corpse stinking up the joint. Her mom briefed her on the drive over, warned her that her dad is still in denial, and asked Nicole to be patient with him. He really can't be blamed, she said; he didn't know the truth about Evann.

After what feels like hours of her dad rambling on about what a good brother Evann is, how much he loves his baby sister, how close they were when they were little, Nicole stands abruptly. "I think I need to go," she says. She can feel the blood draining from her head, the room starting to spin.

"Okay, honey. Why don't you sit down for a minute. You're looking a bit pale." She slumps back into the chair. Her dad crouches down in front of her. "Just take a few deep breaths."

Nicole turns to her mom, wide-eyed. *He doesn't actually think that's going to help, does he? Doesn't he notice the smell of shit in the air?* Her mom raises her eyebrows and shrugs as she always does when she can't say what they're both thinking.

"You know what, Bruce, I'm just going to take her home. She's had enough."

"She's fine. She just needs to catch her breath," he says, turning back to Nicole. "Have you had anything to eat today? Maybe you just need some juice or something? Your blood sugar might be a bit low."

No, she hasn't had anything to eat. She never eats breakfast. Or lunch. Is he really that clueless? Has he actually not noticed the three and a half pounds she's worked so hard to lose? The nights she eats broccoli and chicken while they have pizza? Thank God she can count on her mom; without her, she'd have no one to tell her when she's getting "fluffy" around the midsection. A few pounds here and there can ruin a dance career, but what would he know about that? He shows up for recitals—and that's about it. Tight-jawed, she looks to her mom for support. *Does he honestly think that breathing more of this toxic air is going to make me feel better?* She's starting to see what her mom meant. Her father really does live in his own little world.

42

BRUCE

AFTER A RESTLESS NIGHT OF TOSSING AND TURNING, BRUCE SETS up the coffee pot and leaves Ann a note before tiptoeing out of the house. Pulling on his wool jacket—the red plaid faded and stained from years of use—he feels a tug at his neck. He untangles the gold lure from a loose thread, trying to remember if Evann's necklace had been there, in among the tubes and lines and wires. He had two pendants custom-made—one for each of them—for Evann's thirteenth birthday. Back in those days, things had been simple between them. Just the two of them, camping and fishing whenever they could get away, enjoying each other's silent company. Every time he feels that lure against his skin, he thinks about the good times they had together. Then he remembers the day his relationship with his son changed forever.

———

It started as an amazing day out on the Cowichan. The sun was warm against their backs as the river, cold and clear, flowed around their waders. They'd found themselves a little honey hole; hardly even had time to set their lines before they'd have another bite. Evann got lucky—bagged a beautiful brown trout, damn near two-footer—which they gutted and grilled over the fire. It was the kind of day fish tales were made of, but that isn't why Bruce remembers it.

"So. Your mom tells me you want to quit karate," he said as he cracked open another beer. "What's that all about?"

"I don't like it."

"That's just 'cause you haven't got to the good stuff yet," he said, smiling. "Wait 'til you're breaking boards with your fists. Then you'll be hooked."

"Never gonna happen. Pretty sure you need at least a brown belt before you can even think about that," Evann said, raising his eyebrows. "Besides, those guys are posers. They only do it to make you think they're tough, and I don't care about any of that. I hate going. I never even wanted to do it in the first place." He looked into his lap. Bruce watched him bend the tab on his Sprite can back and forth.

"That's not what your mom said." He leaned forward on his knees, but his son wouldn't meet his gaze.

"Big surprise," Evann said, rolling his eyes. The can made a *ting* as the tab broke off in his hand. He used it to scratch at the log beside him. "Mom only makes me go 'cause it's close to Nicole's dance studio. That's all she really cares about—Nicole and her stupid ballet."

"Ev. You know that's not true, buddy."

"Yeah it is." Evann looked Bruce straight in the eye. "She signed me up for it so I'd be out of the way. She got tired of me tagging along to dance stuff. She won't even take me on Thursdays because it doesn't line up with Nicole's schedule. She gets Sam's mom to pick me up."

Bruce swallowed the lump in his throat. Evann threw the tab in the fire, watched as it turned red hot.

"I don't get why she won't just let me stay home by myself," he said. "It's not like I can't take care of myself. I've been doing it since I was a kid."

"Is that so?" Bruce asked sarcastically. "Your mom has been home with you every day of your life, but you've been taking care of yourself?"

Evann's cheeks flushed. They both stared into the flames. The fire crackled and popped, filling the silence between them. It was Evann who'd taught him that it wasn't the fire making the crackling sounds, but the wood itself. Where his seven-year-old had learned that the wood heating up caused the cellulose inside the log to turn into a gas, which then got trapped but continued to expand until eventually it burst and made the sound, was beyond him. He'd been camping his entire life and had never put two and two together before Evann explained it: more moisture, more crackling.

Evann finally spoke. "I don't wanna burst your bubble, Dad," he said quietly, "but she isn't who you think she is."

"What's that supposed to mean?" Bruce could feel his blood pressure climbing. His son—who usually considered his every word carefully—was barrelling headlong toward crossing a line.

"It means she's not the perfect mother she pretends to be," he said. Bruce hadn't wanted to see it then, but looking back he knows how uncomfortable Evann was. His son had gone out on a limb, trusting his dad would be there to catch him before he hit the ground. "Do you know that some of my earliest memories are getting myself up and pouring myself a bowl of cereal while she slept in? I was supposed to keep myself busy, not wake her up unless there was an emergency. Like, before Nicole was born, so I would've been, what— three or four? That's fucked up."

Bruce's vision started to narrow. He'd seen it with his own two eyes, the way his wife made the kids breakfast, packed their little lunch kits. The way she'd pull Evann into her lap to read a story with him. "Come on. You don't actually expect me to believe that, do you? Your mother gave up everything to be home for you two. She waits on you kids hand and foot."

"Why is it so hard for you to believe that she's different when you're around?"

"Watch it, pal."

"No, Dad. I'm sorry. I know you don't want to hear it, but I need to get this off my chest. Nobody ever listens to me. I told you, like, last year, that I hated karate. Before I was even signed up I told Mom I didn't want to do it, but she did it anyway. You said I had to finish one round, which I did, and then she signed me up *again*—even though I told her I didn't like it. So then I stuck it out through another class, still hate it, and I'm still not allowed to quit! I've been asking *forever* to do drawing lessons, or at least be allowed to stay home so I can practice by myself, but she won't let me! She never wants me to be happy! She only cares about her precious little ballerina."

"That's enough, Evann. She's your mother. She loves you both, and she's doing her best. Give her the goddamn respect she deserves."

Evann looked into his lap. "You're never even home, so how could you know what she's really like?"

"Excuse me?"

He lifted his head, looked Bruce square in the face. "I said, you're never even home," he said, tears in his eyes. "Of course you don't see what a bitch she is."

In the fifteen years he'd been a father, Bruce had never, *ever*, even considered hurting one of his children, but before he could stop himself, he had his son pinned on his back in the dirt. "Don't you ever speak about your mother that way, you disrespectful jackass," he said through clenched teeth.

He'd never seen that expression on his son's face, but he now knows what it had been: betrayal. His son never looked at him without hurt in his eyes again.

———

248

Bruce is just finishing his fourth cup of the barely palatable hospital coffee by the time Ann arrives, a large double-double and a breakfast sandwich in hand.

He pulls off the lid, inhaling the familiar aroma of Tim Hortons coffee. "How's Nicole? She was already in bed when I got home last night."

"Fine."

"Just fine?"

Ann shrugs. "I don't know what you want me to say, Bruce. I told you I didn't think it was a good idea for her to see him like this, but you pushed her."

They finish eating in silence. Bruce pulls his chair over to sit beside Evann.

"I meant to ask," he says, "do you have Ev's necklace? I asked the nurse, but she didn't know anything about it. She said it's pretty common for jewellery to be sent home with family, though."

"Nope. Haven't seen it," Ann says, not looking up from her iPad. "Wouldn't be surprised if he pawned it."

Bruce slowly lifts his head from the side rail, reaching for the pendant around his neck. His hand is damp with his son's sweat. "He wouldn't do that, Ann. We both know it meant a lot to him."

"Yeah, well, I think it's pretty clear neither of us really knew him, did we?"

It lands like a punch in the gut. There are still so many questions unanswered. So many they might never get the chance to ask.

"I wanted to talk to the doctor about that, actually. Is it possible there was some mix-up with the blood work? I mean, fentanyl? Heroin? Really? We just saw him in October and he was fine. It doesn't make sense."

"Jesus, Bruce. Look at him. He might as well have *junkie* tattooed across his forehead."

That one knocks the wind out of him. "Did you notice anything off the last time we saw him?"

"No, Bruce." She meets his eyes. "I didn't notice anything. Don't you think I'd've said something if I was worried about him?" Returning to her screen, she mutters to herself, "Not that you'd listen, even if I had."

She isn't wrong. He'd grown tired of her constant complaints about Evann over the years. Once Bruce felt self-assured that their son wasn't destined to be a mass murderer or a puppy killer, he'd more or less taken to ignoring Ann's criticism.

Ann sets her iPad down. "Ask them whatever you want, Bruce, but it's not going to change anything. I mean, he's obviously made some really bad decisions over the past few years. I'd like to say I didn't see this coming, but we both know that I tried to tell you that sending him off to university was a mistake."

"We're not doing this again." They'd never formally discussed it —some things were better left unsaid—but they'd come to an understanding, settled into a sort of "divide and conquer" approach to parenting. He hadn't seen the harm; it was perfectly natural for a mother to be closer to her daughter, and a father to be closer to his son, so why fight nature? Now he sees the other side of it. To the victor go the spoils, and hearing her say it confirms his suspicion that his wife has added a stroke against him in the parenting tally. The worst part is that he knows he deserves it. It was his job to be there for Evann—a job that he's failed at miserably.

Considering what might've been if he hadn't been so damn stubborn—if he'd been there when his son needed him most—is enough to send bile bubbling into the back of his throat. His wife is like a lit match—always has been—and he knows that as long as he doesn't provide the kindling, she'll burn herself out sooner or later. But he's hardly slept, and his patience is running thin. She can be so reckless with her words, yet conveniently, she never chooses to throw anything in his face when he's handing her the keys to a new SUV or paying off another astronomical credit card bill without question. That's their deal; he keeps his high-paying job in the oil field to allow her the freedom to focus on raising their kids. He's more or less given her carte blanche when it comes to the kids, but there have been a few instances where he had to push back.

Although Evann has proven himself to be a talented artist—undeniably so—Ann didn't think he should pursue it as a career. She was perfectly clear in her opinion that the world didn't need another Starbucks barista with a useless arts degree. After trying all her tricks to change Evann's mind, she aimed to get Bruce on her side, saying that Evann had never stuck with anything meaningful in his entire life and that university would be no different. As she saw it, their son was too immature, too irresponsible, a loner who would have trouble making friends in a new city. Bruce listened patiently while she executed her smear campaign, but ultimately he'd pulled rank: they'd set aside money for their children's educations, and since he was the one to earn that money, he decided their children were free to use the funds in pursuit of whatever career they chose. As far as he was concerned, there wasn't much difference between Evann getting an arts degree and Nicole going off to a dance academy. They finally compromised, telling Evann that once his education fund was spent, there would be no more withdrawals from The Bank of Mom and Dad. And Bruce had stuck to that promise, although now he's left to wonder if things might've been different if he hadn't.

"Did you see that?" Bruce jumps to his feet. "He moved. His eyelids moved. He tried to open his eyes. Evann? Ev? Ev! Can you hear me?" His heart hammers in his chest. He saw it, he's certain. His son is trying to communicate with them, trying to open his eyes. "Evann!" he shouts, grabbing him by the shoulders. "Ev! Open your eyes, buddy! We're here." The ventilator blares as Bruce shakes Evann by the shoulders, droplets spraying on his son's face as the machine blows *phhh, phhh, phhh.*

"It's all right," the nurse says on her way in to silence the machine. "The tubing just came apart."

"No! He moved! I saw his eyelids move! He's waking up!"

A second nurse and a respiratory therapist stand ready in the doorway. The ECG tracing spikes violently as Bruce continues to shake Evann, begging him to open his eyes. Thick saliva slides down the corner of Evann's mouth as his head sways back and forth against his chest.

A crowd forms around the doorway, peeking in through the window, drawn by the commotion, the incessant alarming of the heart monitor.

"Bruce, honey. Why don't you move out of the way so that she can reattach the tubing?" Ann says, gently tugging on his shirt.

"Mr. Cartwright, I just need to get in there, okay. I need to reattach him to the ventilator."

"Listen to me," Bruce says. "I saw it! He started to open his eyes."

"We heard you, Bruce," Ann says, "but you need to calm down, all right? Let these people do their jobs."

The respiratory therapist connects a bag to the end of the breathing tube. He squeezes and releases, resuming the rhythmic rise and fall of Evann's chest.

"Please. Ann, please," Bruce pleads, tears streaming down his cheeks. "Please just get them to check."

Ann grabs him by the front of the shirt. "Bruce," she says firmly. "Get a grip. Get out of the goddamn way so these people can take care of our son."

43

ANN

The two of them sit in the crowded family room, uncomfortably crammed onto a love seat, facing Dr. Linden and the dishevelled social worker—the latter of whom has been getting on Ann's nerves since she first introduced herself. Ann has never understood how some women can care so little about their appearance, and wonders if this woman—Sandy, according to her name tag—had even bothered to look in a mirror before coming to work, her wild curls a blend of natural greys and whites, haphazardly clipped out of her face. She's the mother with the son in ICU, and even she manages to paint on a little mascara and lipstick before leaving the house.

Beside her, Bruce sits with unnaturally straight posture, his hands folded in his lap like a schoolboy. She can tell by his subtle squint, the slight delay in reopening his eyes with each blink, that the Ativan she slipped out of her purse and under his tongue has taken the edge off. As usually happens when they're forced to co-inhabit small spaces, Ann feels a pull toward Bruce, the couch sagging beneath his considerable weight, leaving her pinned against the armrest on one side and uncomfortably off-kilter on the other. For the amount of taxes they pay, she would've thought the hospital might provide some comfortable furniture.

They listen while the doctor lays out the facts: Their son was found pulseless as a result of a toxic drug overdose. After waiting to be sure that there are no residual drugs in his system, they've run a battery of tests, which have conclusively determined that Evann is brain dead. Ann has seen enough medical dramas to know what that means, but Bruce insists on hearing it from the horse's mouth, staring blankly as the doctor explains that there is no possible way Evann tried to open his eyes earlier. The tests have proven that there is no longer any blood flow to his brain. The drugs Evann took slowed down his breathing, eventually causing his heart to stop. That lack of oxygen caused his brain to swell so significantly that it had nowhere to go but down through the base of his skull. It's called herniation, and it means that without the ventilator breathing for him, Evann will die in a matter of minutes. He will never take another breath on his own.

She attempts to adjust herself into a more comfortable position, tucking one leg over the other, trying to create distance from the heat radiating off her husband, which is making her sweat. She subtly digs her elbow into his side, hoping he'll take the hint to move over a bit. The room is closing in around her. Ann leans forward, resting her head on a white-knuckled fist, pressing the claws of her solitaire into her temple. She struggles to maintain control of her breathing as she fights back wave after wave of nausea. The room falls silent, and for the first time Ann notices the ticking of the analogue clock echoing through the small space. The delicate skin of her temple begins to burn under the pressure of her ring. Evann has a faint scar above his left eyebrow from it—though it isn't visible now among all the blemished spots where he's picked his skin raw. It hadn't been her intention to cut him, but in fairness, he should've known better than to lie to her; he'd had plenty of chances to learn that she would catch him every time. It was just a harmless little backhand, but the sharp diamond scraped along his forehead and cut him. She can still see his look of shock as he brought his mittened hand to his face, though she hadn't immediately understood why; by five years old he was well aware that his actions had consequences. "Stop being dramatic. I barely touched you," she said, not realizing she'd drawn blood until later when she washed his mitts.

Ann is lost in thought when Dr. Linden clears his throat.

"At this point, there is nothing further we can offer your son." He takes a deep breath, scanning back and forth between Ann and Bruce. "Before we talk about the next steps, do either of you have any questions about what I've just explained?"

Bruce's usual baritone is hardly more than a whisper. "Are you sure there hasn't been some sort of mix-up with the blood work?" The doctor frowns, and Bruce continues, "I understand what you're saying—Evann's heart stopped, and that starved his brain of oxygen— but as far as we know, he's never even tried drugs. Couldn't there be some other explanation for why his heart stopped? This is just so out of character for him."

Ann sighs, struggling to breathe beneath the palpable weight of Bruce's grief. It's no secret that she and Evann have always had a tenuous relationship. Bruce has always been closer to their son—she's never denied that—so she's used to him viewing Evann through rose-coloured glasses. He missed so much when the kids were little, and she suspects that Bruce has always felt the need to overcompensate for the time he was away at work, which would explain why he'd always been so lenient with his son, so willing to overlook his many shortcomings. But this is over the top. It doesn't take an MD to see that Evann is most definitely a junkie.

Evann was lazy and unmotivated, reclusive and standoffish, and —as they've recently learned—a skilled and cunning liar. There is only so much a mother can do to correct those attributes; some traits are more nature than nurture. As hard as she's tried over the years, her husband has been unwilling to face reality, even when it's slapping him in the face.

Ann can see that Dr. Linden is choosing his response carefully.

"Unfortunately not," he says after a long pause. "While it's true that we are seeing *some* cases of recreational users inadvertently taking drugs laced with fentanyl, when we look at Evann's health records, we can see that he was started on OST, opioid substitution therapy—methadone, in his case—fairly recently. I understand that this is quite a shock to you both, but Evann wouldn't have qualified for that program unless he met the criteria. And building an opioid dependency that requires methadone certainly doesn't happen overnight."

"Correct me if I'm wrong," Ann says, cutting in, "but it's sounding an awful lot like you think we should've magically known that our son—who, as far as we knew, was working on a bachelor of arts degree—was actually a junkie."

Wide-eyed, Dr. Linden turns to Sandy. The social worker winces. "That's certainly not the case, Mrs. Cartwright. Your son had an addiction. A substance use disorder, to be specific. Substance abuse is very complex, and finger pointing—the shoulda, coulda, woulda—will tear you apart. From everything Bruce has told me, Evann was a remarkable person, and the fact that he struggled with addiction issues doesn't negate that." She forces her mouth into a thin smile, brushing a wayward curl from her face. "That said, I would encourage you to reconsider your choice of language. Labels only perpetuate the stigma, which is part of the reason people choose to use in hiding, rather than out in the open where they might get help."

"Mmhmm," Ann says, pursing her lips.

"I can't speak to Evann's state of mind, but there are a lot of reasons someone might not want to admit they are struggling," the doctor adds. "Maybe they're ashamed, fearful. Maybe they don't feel they have anyone to reach out to. Many people self-medicate, using drugs to cope with past traumas, mental health issues, that sort of thing. What we do know is that Evann did take some steps to turn his life around. His records show that he was resuscitated after an overdose earlier this month, right before he checked himself into detox. It looks like he was on the waitlist for a subsidized treatment bed."

"But I don't understand why he wouldn't come to us," Bruce says.

"We could've helped him, could've paid for him to go to rehab, or get back on his feet. Whatever he needed." He slowly pushes himself up from the couch, moving to stand by the door. His enormous hand rests on the door casing as he stares at the wall.

The doctor continues, explaining that it's unclear why Evann decided to return to the Island but there was likely an issue with having his methadone prescription transferred. Apparently, that's not unusual—not many physicians are comfortable prescribing OST— and with no better option, Evann's physiological dependence likely led him back to street drugs. Dr. Linden says it's quite common for addicts to overdose after a period of sobriety, miscalculating their dose based on their new, lower tolerance.

Ann listens passively, not terribly interested in what the doctor has to say. She's already heard everything she needs to know. Now she wants to know what the next step is in putting this nightmare behind them. She follows the social worker's gaze over to Bruce. With his head rested against his forearm, he looks as though he's relying on his grip on the door header to hold him upright. "Can I get you a glass of water or something, Bruce?" the social worker asks. "Should we take a few moments before continuing?"

"Oh, yeah, don't worry about him," Ann says. "He does that sometimes. It's his way of coping, which is a perfect example of why having a doting mother isn't as positive as you'd think. He never had to learn to toughen up. His mommy was always there to make things better for him." Ann rolls her eyes. Under her breath, she adds, "You'd think that might've changed by the time he hit his fifties." If Bruce hears what either of the women has said, he doesn't react. Dr. Linden looks nervously between Bruce and the social worker.

"Bruce!" Ann says. His head snaps up, the trance broken. "The doctor is trying to speak to us."

———

They shuffle back to Evann's room in silence. The doctor laid it all on the table, gave them all the options, and told them to take their time in deciding.

Bruce leans over the side rail, letting his head rest on Evann's chest. "Jesus," he says finally. "I know it's what he'd want, but I just don't know if I can do it."

Ann rubs his back. "I know, hon. I know this is hard. But you heard what the social worker said. We don't have to make the choice. He already made it. He registered to be an organ donor."

"But he's our baby, Ann. Of course we're going to say yes—of course our son would want to give this gift, and we would never go against his wishes—but the idea of his heart—this heart—beating in someone else's chest..."

Ann pulls him to standing, burying her face in his flannel shirt. His musty smell is familiar, a pleasant reprieve from Evann's nauseating body odour.

"I know. So let's take it one step at a time. We'll meet with the transplant coordinator. Fill out the consent—see what she has to say." Reaching her arms around him, she wonders how long it's been since she's been able to give her husband a proper hug, aware of the extra fifty or sixty pounds separating them. Considering how hard she's worked to stay trim over the years, Bruce could've at least laid off the Quarter Pounders. Maybe this will be a wake-up call—for all of them —a reminder that longevity isn't guaranteed, that their time together is finite. If they can just get through this, they can have a fresh start, just the three of them. She exhales a heavy sigh. "We can let them do the extra tests—let them see if his heart is strong, if his lungs are okay, let them do the blood work. We can go from there." Knowing what Evann has put his body through, she doubts they'll even want his organs.

"Yeah, fine." Bruce pulls away from her. He slides his chair alongside the bed, resting his hand on Evann's.

"In the meantime, we should start thinking about what we're

going to tell people. Your parents and sister have been messaging me non-stop. I can't hold them off by myself forever."

"Then let them come."

"Bruce, honey. I know this is hard, but you can't be serious. You saw what happened with Nicole. Your parents are in their eighties. The last thing they need is this kind of stress." She can't see his face, can't get a read on him. Her husband is a man of few words, but usually she has some idea as to what he's leaving unsaid. She's never known him to be so emotional, so irrational, so unpredictable. His silence is making her uneasy. "Yeah, no. I don't think they should come. It would be too much for your parents, and there's no way I can handle your sister right now. She's intolerable under the best of circumstances. We can call them tonight and update them—give them the gist of what's going on—but then I think we just put out a Facebook post. Something about how Evann has had an accident, that he's suffered a serious brain injury, that we're not accepting visitors at this time but we appreciate their thoughts and prayers, blah, blah, blah."

She's pushed too far, and she sees it as soon as the words leave her mouth. The muscles in Bruce's jaw clench beneath his stubbled face. He leans back in the chair, balancing it on two legs as he interlaces his fingers. He stretches his arms forward until his knuckles crack. The knot in Ann's stomach tightens.

"Enough," Bruce says, hauling himself out of the chair. "Just —enough."

Under the heat of his glare, the room begins to spin. She's losing control. She's stepped over the line, and she knows it, but admitting it isn't in her nature. Her options now are fight or flight. Before she has the chance to make her move, Bruce kisses his son's moist forehead, grabs his jacket, and stalks out, the sliding door slamming shut behind him.

44

NICOLE

HER MOM KNOWS TO GIVE HER SPACE.

She always seems to know what Nicole needs, even when Nicole herself doesn't. Looking out over the street where Evann taught her to ride a two-wheeler, she watches the fog from her breath advance and retreat on the window. She remembers the bike Evann helped pick out for her fourth birthday—pink, with streamers on the handle-bars, so tall she could barely touch the ground with her tippy-toes. She remembers strapping on her helmet, dreaming of being able to cruise the cul-de-sac with the big kids, but she doesn't ever remember being scared. She'd trusted that her big brother was there, that he wouldn't let go until she was ready, and he hadn't. While the other kids toddled along on their training wheels, Nicole climbed the ranks, pedalling her legs faster and faster, her white-blonde curls blowing in the wind.

Outside, the street is quiet. The big kids have grown up and moved out. The little kids are preoccupied with sports or school or Instagram, their rusty Civics and hand-me-down Jettas leaking oil in front of abandoned basketball hoops. It's unseasonably cold for June, a cloud cover blanketing the city, threatening rain but unable to produce—unable to release the heavy burden; fitting weather for the girl who has so many reasons to cry, but no tears to shed.

His first call had shocked her. As soon as he said her name, she knew there was something wrong. There was something in his voice, something she wasn't quite able to put her finger on, but it triggered the same gut feeling she had last October. In a matter of minutes, she knew that she had been wrong not to say something about the pills she'd found in his backpack at Thanksgiving. At the time, she hadn't known exactly what they were, though she did know that the mismatched medications weren't Naproxen. The fact that her brother didn't even stir as she snooped through his stuff should've been an obvious clue that he was in trouble.

It's not as if she didn't consider talking to him about it because she did—for days afterwards. But every time she thought about texting him, she imagined her mom's voice: *He's a big boy. He can take care of himself.*

So instead, she ignored her gut and did her best to forget all about it.

He'd never asked her for anything before, and she didn't understand why he called her, how she could possibly help him with whatever trouble he'd gotten himself into. He said he didn't want to get into it over the phone, but that he'd tried to call their dad and it hadn't gone well. Evann didn't think their mom would help, which was fair; there'd never been any debate about which of them was Mom's favourite, and even less so about what she thought of Evann's choices. In their mom's eyes, his childish fantasy of supporting himself by drawing and colouring was not only a delusion, but a senseless waste of their money.

Not wanting to pressure her into anything, he simply asked her to think about it. They exchanged I love you's at the end of that first call. She promised not to say anything to their parents, but of course, she told her mom.

Her stomach growls, begging for something—anything—other than celery and green tea. Her parents left money for takeout since they're spending pretty much all day at the hospital. Her mouth waters at the idea of biting into a slice of cheese pizza, but she lifts her shirt and pinches the flesh hanging over her leggings, a disgusting reminder that the last thing she needs is to gorge like a pig. She's already had to miss dance class twice this week, and she's up to 102.4 pounds. Girls like her can't afford to let their weight creep up.

Maybe she hadn't thought it through all the way before talking to her mom. She didn't really consider how she might react, telling her about the call with Evann in the same way she told her everything else. Her mom is her best friend. She's the one who held Nicole while she cried through her first breakup, took her shopping for thong underwear when the other girls made fun of her granny panties, let her get her belly button pierced even after her dad said no. But when Nicole told her that Evann was in trouble—that he was in over his head, that he needed help to get back on his feet—she slammed her open hand down on the dining table, sending the dog skittering out from under her feet.

Nicole should've predicted Evann wouldn't get an easy pass; he never had. But that didn't stop her from pushing. Haven't they all made mistakes? Didn't he deserve a chance to get clean? A chance to make things right? She begged and pleaded, screamed and sobbed, trying to get her mom to give in; trying to convince her that helping Evann was the right thing.

She carried on, late into the night, before finally, she broke through. But as soon as her mom opened the lid on Pandora's box, Nicole wished she could slam it shut.

She'd thought she wanted to know—needed to know—why her mom was being so cold, so stubborn, so unforgiving. But once she learned what she'd been trying to protect her from, Nicole understood, even if—at first—it didn't make any sense. She spent sleepless nights and anxiety-ridden days officiating a game of tug-of-war in her mind. On one side, she had no memories of Evann ever doing anything to hurt her, let alone anything inappropriate; but on the other side, her mom had given her word, and she's the person Nicole trusts more than anyone else in the world.

Her mom had made her promise not to say anything to her dad, admitting that she'd never disclosed the full extent of Evann's issues to their father. With no one else to turn to, Nicole spent many days racking her mind, reliving their childhood together, trying to reconcile the new facts with the brother she remembered: quiet and introverted, maybe a little strange, but also kind and generous and protective. In every memory, she loved to spend time with him, watching him draw, always wanting to tag along with him—and he let her. He never complained, never told her to get lost, never so much as gave her a wedgie. As far as big brothers went, she thought she'd been lucky. But had she just been too young—too naive—to see it?

Obviously, they grew apart over the years, but Nicole figured that was just normal for siblings, not that there was a more sinister explanation. And it's not like they hated each other. Over Thanksgiving, he came home just to watch her performance. He gave her a beautiful hand-drawn portrait of a ballerina in first arabesque; they'd even made plans to go for pizza together. But that was before she found out what he'd done.

She has none of her own memories from the things her mom described—no recollection of the turmoil it caused, the therapy she'd had to attend—but the longer she thought about it, the more she sat with the idea, the more real it felt. She'd even seen the evidence: Evann had been treated by a psychologist. It hurt her mom—she could see it did—to retraumatize her, to speak about things they'd spent so long trying to forget.

Nicole had started to question everything.

Maybe her brother had crossed a line. Maybe she was a victim.

The only way to know for sure had been to confront him.

45

BRUCE

HE JAMS THE KEY IN THE IGNITION AND FORCES THE TRUCK into drive. Without thinking, he finds himself once again making the trek through the forest, down the steep staircase, and onto the secluded beach. It takes a long time before the hammering in his chest settles. Her auburn hair might come from a box, but his wife certainly has the temperament of a redhead. Usually he isn't bothered by her shouting, her insults, the nights she makes him sleep on the couch, but he's starting to see everything he's given up at his wife's behest; all the missed family dinners, the clear divide between brother and sister, father and mother, mother and son, father and daughter. Father and son. He's gotten so used to being walked on—to following Ann's lead, seeking Ann's permission, looking to Ann for direction about how to look, how to act, how to feel—that he's allowed himself to forget what's important. His family is broken, and he's been complicit in its breaking.

She never has been able to relate to their firstborn, seeing his desire for solitude as a character flaw to be changed, rather than an innate personality trait. What she can't seem to understand is that, when given the space, Evann has—or *had*, the realization of which sucks the air from his lungs—lots to say. He just hadn't always said it in a language she cared to understand. What he had to say came through in his artwork: in the way he would transform a blank page into a stunningly detailed pencil drawing; in the way he could point a camera at a perfectly ordinary object and capture something extraordinary. It's not that he couldn't speak; of course he could—and did. It's just that in contrast to Ann—who can be carefree and reckless with her words—their son had chosen to speak only when he had something worth saying. When he didn't, he was perfectly content to remain silent.

The sky is turning a crimson blend of pinks and oranges. The energy in the ocean is different today; unlike the last time, when it was calm and complacent—the frothy water delicately sprinting up the sand—today there's an intensity to the waves as they crash against the shore. A large flock of seagulls circles low over the water, hovering in the wind, a phenomenon Evann taught him about on one of their many fishing trips. The kid was an encyclopedia of interesting facts—an observer, taking in his surroundings, studying the obscure workings of the world, stashing those seemingly insignificant details away in his bottomless memory. According to Evann, a day or so before a big storm, gulls fly in a circular pattern low over the ocean, which allows them to recalibrate their barometers. Then they'll retreat to the safety of the shore to wait it out. The night sky is clear—not a cloud in sight—but Bruce is willing to bet anything a storm is incoming. He's never known his son to tell him something that didn't turn out to be true. That is—until it all turned out to be a lie. As he watches the foaming tendrils make their advance up the beach, he decides. He'll tell Ann what he's done. It won't change anything, but at least it will be off his conscience.

———

He takes his time getting back to the hospital, understanding that when he re-enters the room, they'll start with a fresh slate, as they always do. Any perceived transgressions will be forgiven, though certainly not forgotten. There is no statute of limitations on any of his past offences; old skeletons in shallow graves, waiting to be resurrected at her convenience. But for now, they will move on as if she hadn't said such ugly, heartless things, as if he hadn't heard what she said about him, what she said about Evann. It's as if his wife has a reset button; it doesn't matter how upset she gets, when she decides it's time to move on, it's time to move on. There will be no acknowledgement, no discussion, and certainly no apologies.

If he's lucky, she'll already have gone home to drown herself in a bottle of wine as she so often does when life gets too real. If he's really lucky, she'll feel bad, and while it won't get him an apology, it might at least buy him a bit of leniency when he tells her about his call with Evann.

He catches her just as she's leaving, crossing the lobby with her head down, typing something into her phone. His jaw drops when he sees her. She nearly walks into him before noticing him standing there.

"Oop! Hi, honey. Sorry, I was just letting Nicole know I'm on my way home." She reaches up to kiss him on the cheek.

"Did you get a haircut while I was away?"

"Oh," she says, touching her hair. "Yeah, I did. Cindy had a last-minute cancellation. What do you think?"

He's been trained to notice—and compliment—her haircuts, regardless of his real opinion, but he can't bring himself to play her game now. They both know she doesn't care what he thinks.

"You—" he chooses his words carefully. "You actually went to get a haircut. While our son is in the ICU?"

"Yes, Bruce. My roots had grown out. They looked awful. I couldn't put it off any longer." She looks him up and down. "And you don't expect me to sit there all goddamn day, do you? I needed some time for myself, which—I assume—is where you've been."

Bruce shakes his head. It's all about appearances for her. It always has been.

"We're not really going to do this here, are we?" Ann says. "I don't know why it's such a big deal to you. It's not like Evann knows the difference."

He runs his hand through his thinning hair. After more than twenty years together, he still can't understand how she can be so callous, so crass; how she can talk about their son dying so flippantly while he's lying in a bed upstairs, his broken heart still beating in his chest. He takes a deep breath, resolving—once again—to be the bigger person.

"Look," he says, "I need to talk to you about something."

46

ANN

"Why did you not feel the need to tell me about this before?" Ann wipes the moisture from her upper lip. She can feel anger rising from deep within her gut, threatening to overtake her. It doesn't happen often, but she's been known to see red, and when that happens, there's no stopping the vicious things that might come out of her mouth. This shouldn't bother her so much. It's not about the money; it never has been. They have plenty, and Bruce makes plenty. It isn't about the money; it's that her husband has gone behind her back, has lied to her, has once again chosen his son over his wife.

"Because I knew you'd fight me on it," he says simply.

"So when we agreed that once the education fund was spent, that was it, you actually had no intention of holding him to that?"

"No. I had every intention of holding him to that, and that's exactly what I did. That's what I'm trying to tell you, if you'd just let me finish." Bruce looks into his lap.

Ann pours herself another glass of wine as her husband makes his confession: He co-signed for a credit card that Evann then maxed out —on a cash withdrawal, no less—and hadn't made any payments on. It's not actually as serious as he initially made it sound, but there's no harm in letting Bruce squirm a little. At the end of the day, it's definitely going to cost them, but at least she'll never have to worry about Evann pulling a stunt like this again in the future.

"Wait," Ann says, suddenly connecting the dots. "So you're saying that you talked to Evann about this? Recently? What, exactly, did he have to say for himself?"

"Not much. He called me—just so happened to be the day I got the letter from the credit card company, threatening to take me to collections and told me he was in some trouble." Bruce runs his hands over his face. "I didn't give him much chance to explain. I sorta jumped down his throat about it."

Ann takes a slow sip from her glass. "And... When was this conversation?"

The colour drains from Bruce's face.

Busted, Ann thinks.

"Are you telling me that our son called you—from *detox*, after *overdosing*, I would imagine—and the only thing you talked about was a *fucking* credit card?"

She doesn't like how smug it makes her feel. He isn't like her—he's soft—and she knows he'll spend the rest of his life wondering what might've been if he'd let his son speak. In any other circumstances, she'd have led a round of applause for his tough-love approach; she honestly hadn't thought he had it in him.

"I'm so sorry, Ann," he says, reaching for her hands. "I didn't know. I just... I didn't know."

She looks into her husband's eyes, studies his face, dark bags heavy beneath his eyes, his salt-and-pepper stubble growing into a scruffy beard. He's aging before her eyes.

"You can't blame yourself, Bruce. Evann made shitty choices, and sometimes shitty choices have shitty consequences."

———

Ann slides down until her shoulders are covered, lavender-scented bubbles tickling her chin. Bruce has gone back to the hospital, presumably to beg their unconscious son for forgiveness, so she opened another bottle of Merlot and drew herself a bath. What a whirlwind this week has turned out to be. And here she'd been thinking she was the only one with a secret to keep.

She'd told Bruce she forgives him, and she means it. He has always been a fantastic father, so much so that—once upon a time— Ann was jealous of the easy bond between him and Evann; Evann, who was uncertain and introverted in her presence, yet comfortable and sure with Bruce. Her husband had been so gracious with her, so reassuring. He understood that she'd only ever had an example of how not to parent, knew it would take her a while to hone her maternal instincts. "Kids don't come with an instruction manual," he used to say. He was right. Evann certainly didn't. Nicole didn't need one.

Fortunately, her second was an easy child, because her first demanded every ounce of her patience. He was clingy, reaching for her constantly, and throwing a fit if she left him for even a moment. Never had she imagined that time on the toilet would be her only alone-time, and even then, once he was old enough to crawl, he sat at the door and wailed. Eventually she figured out that if she left him in the Jolly Jumper in the spare bedroom upstairs, with the shower running and the bath fan whirring, she could escape his incessant screeching and enjoy some peace and quiet. She felt a pang of guilt when she retrieved him the first time, a look of betrayal on his red tear-stained face, snot soaking the front of his jumper. But the next time was easier, and the time after that, she saw through his manipulative tactics. Of course he'd scream and cry if it got him her undivided attention; that was exactly what he wanted. If she left him long enough, eventually he'd scream himself to sleep. She never had that trouble with Nicole, who was a quiet, curious baby. She never fussed when she was left alone and didn't whine to be picked up. Whereas

Nicole would fall asleep wherever Ann put her, Evann spent many of his naps passed out in the Jolly Jumper.

Her phone dings, a text from Nicole: *"Goodnight Mama Bear! Stay strong. Luv u soooo much!"*

Ann's eyes well with tears. What a blessing her daughter has been in her life. That little girl stole her Mama's heart from the day she was born, but as she's grown up, she's become Ann's saving grace, her constant source of support, and her best friend. That day—the day she did what had to be done to protect her precious daughter—she'd whispered into her daughter's tear-soaked hair: "How different life would've been if you'd come along first." And knowing everything she knows now—all the stress he would cause, all the money he would cost, all the pain their family would suffer—she still fucking means it.

47

NICOLE

THREE WEEKS EARLIER

He hadn't left a number where she could call him, so she had to wait for him to make the move. That left plenty of time for her to play with the frayed edges—to pull at loose threads, unravelling everything she thought she'd known—exposing an ugly accusation that had started to look an awful lot like the truth.

When her phone rang late one evening, the caller ID displaying UNKNOWN CALLER, Nicole ran downstairs.

"It's him," she said, trying to catch her breath.

"Be strong, baby girl," her mom said, kissing her cheek. "You got this."

They sat across from each other at the dining table, the phone on speaker between them. Ann rolled her eyes as Evann made small talk, asking how dance was going, how their parents were, whether they'd done anything special to celebrate Mrs. Potter's birthday.

Get on with it, Ann mouthed silently.

Nicole tipped her head back impatiently.

"Did you, uh—" Evann stopped, hesitating.

"Did I, uh—" she mimicked.

"Did you get a chance to think about what we talked about?"

"You know what, Ev, I did. In fact, I had a chance to think about a lot of things."

She and her mom had talked at length about what she should say, about how her brother might react. She laid out the allegations, just as they'd practiced, unsurprised that he denied everything. They took turns rolling their eyes as Evann stuttered his way through his defence.

"I'm not sure what to tell you, Evann. There's proof. Literal evidence that Mom and Dad had to take you to see a psychologist. I mean, how the fuck do you explain that?"

"Where are you even getting this stuff? Jesus, Nic. Please, just listen to me, okay? You're not actually buying this bullshit, are you? I saw a psychologist because I was having nightmares, pissing all over the house, not because I'm some sort of fucking pervert. Jesus Christ. I can't believe you actually think that."

"I don't *think* that. I *remember* it," she said. "There's a difference."

Her mom squeezed her hand.

"Are you telling me that in the past week—right after I tell you how much I need you—you suddenly have a bunch of memories of me, what—touching you or some shit? Do you actually think Mom and Dad would've let that happen? I mean, fuck. Mom would've loved to have had a reason to have me sent away to some group home." Nicole held her head in her hands, listening to her brother weep. "She fucking did this, didn't she? She fucking did this." She could hear the agony in his voice, could barely make out what he was saying between his sobbing.

Ann scribbled on a napkin. She tapped her finger over what she'd written: *Pathological liar.*

Nicole nodded weakly.

Ann pulled it back, adding, *Stay strong, baby girl xo.*

"Listen, please," Evann said. "I'm trying to figure out how to get home, okay. They're putting me on a waitlist for treatment beds on the Island, and when I get there—once I've got a few weeks under my belt—we're going to talk this out, okay? I swear to God, Nic, I love you more than anything. I would never—have never—done anything to hurt you. Jesus Christ, I can't believe she'd do this. Why would she do this to us?"

Her mom reached across the table and ended the call. "That's enough."

Nicole stared vacantly while her mom pulled her to her feet. She was distantly aware that she was being led to the couch, pulled into her mother's lap like she was a little girl again. Against her mom's chest, she let herself cry, trying to let the sound of her mom's heartbeat, her soft *shh, shh, shh,* drown out the voice of doubt screaming in her mind.

"I did my best, baby girl. I tried to help him, I really did. But you have to be strong. Do you hear me? You have to stay away from him. He's too unpredictable, too unstable. We don't know what he might do. So you have to stay strong. It's just you and me, baby girl. We need to stay strong."

48

BRUCE

As the double doors swing open, Bruce locks eyes with the sweet young nurse—the one who had taken care of Evann in the early days. He tries to remember what she said her name is, embarrassed that he's forgotten after she was so good about reminding him every time she entered the room.

"Hello, again. It's too bad we don't have you as Evann's nurse again. I don't mean—. What I mean to say is that of course everyone here has been wonderful. But you seem to have a special gift, and it's nice to see a familiar face," he says, smiling. "We really appreciate you taking care of our boy."

"Oh—Uh, thank you. That's very kind of you," she says. She smiles politely, yet even in the dim light he can see her cheeks turning red.

Perhaps she's just tired at the end of a night shift, but he gets the impression he's making her uncomfortable. Maybe only the most senior nurses are assigned to patients like Evann. There has been a noticeable uptick in tasks for the poor staff to complete since they signed the consent forms: blood work and IV bags and fiddling with knobs, "road trips" for this and that scan. It has become nearly constant. Not wanting to put the girl on the spot, he wishes her a good night and heads for Evann's room.

He's no longer going home, sleeping on a cot the nurses dragged into Evann's room. Regardless of what Ann might think, he isn't simple, nor is he delusional. He understands that his constant presence makes no difference to their son, but he can't bring himself to leave Evann alone in this sterile room. At least, that's what he tries to believe.

In reality, he's avoiding the house because he can hardly look at Ann without breaking down. All these emotions are so raw, so unfamiliar. He's spent a lifetime swallowing back tears, acting like he's never anxious or scared or hurt. He thought he'd feel better once everything was out in the open, but now he sees the pity in Ann's eyes, and that makes him feel more pathetic than keeping the secret had. She says she forgives him, and for the first time in a long time, he actually believes her, which is what makes it worse—so much worse. He'd done something awful—made an unforgivable error in judgment, one that has cost their child his life—and she's given him a free pass. But he knows deep in his heart that were the roles reversed, he would resent his wife until his last day on this earth.

Bruce settles into his chair and watches the respiratory therapist draw blood from the line in Evann's wrist. In another life, maybe he'd have done something like that for a living; something that made a positive, measurable difference to real people, instead of sacrificing time with his family to extract dead dinosaurs from the ground, only to make rich men richer. He's ashamed to admit that until a week ago, he believed public servants were a bunch of overpaid crybabies. Now, having seen everything these people do—how hard they work, how skilled they are, how overworked and undervalued they really are— he knows they're invaluable.

"There's a fresh supply of Tims at the desk," he says. He'll be forever indebted to the men and women who have taken care of his family; no amount of doughnuts and coffee will ever suffice to express his gratitude, but the staff seem to appreciate it, and it's all Bruce has to offer.

He adjusts himself so he can't see the clock. They'll be taking Evann to the OR in less than fifteen hours, but he can't think about that yet. He wants to enjoy his last day with his boy. He lowers the side rail like the nurses taught him, rests his elbows on Evann's bed. If he allows his imagination to run a bit, he can forget about the tubes and lines—can imagine Evann is just sleeping.

When the kids were little, he used to slip into their rooms while they were sleeping. It started when they were tiny—small enough to sleep in cribs—but he continued the tradition even as they got older. Sometimes he'd lie on the floor and listen to their breathing, other times he'd sit with them and gently brush the hair from their faces. It was in those peaceful moments of stillness that he had a chance to really see his kids, to take notice of the subtle changes in their features from one hitch to the next. They changed so quickly back then, and he'd missed so much of it. First words, first steps, first days of school. First visit from the tooth fairy, first report cards, first dance recital. Bruce missed so many of Evann's firsts, but he'll be here with his son right up until his last.

When Ann wanders in several hours later, he makes his announcement: he's called his parents. His sister is picking them up and bringing them to the hospital. Evann will have his family by his side in his final day.

"I know what you're thinking, Ann, and I've thought a lot about it, okay—so please, just hear me out. You are absolutely right. The fact that Evann overdosed doesn't change anything. And it is no one else's business. But we're about to lose our son, and that is unbearable. No parent should have to experience this, and pushing our family away isn't going to make this pain any easier. It'll just drive a wedge between us and the people who love us."

Ann opens her mouth but closes it without speaking. Bruce pulls her into a tight embrace.

"I know Nicole doesn't want to be here, and that's fine, but I want the rest of our family here. They love us, and they love Evann." He sniffs loudly, brushing tears from his cheeks with the sleeve of his Stanfields. "And... Evann left us a little present, so in a way, everyone will be here after all."

Ann turns around slowly. One of the nurses had found Evann's sketchbook tucked in a belongings bag in the cupboard and suggested that Bruce hang a few of his pieces for the staff to see. Most of the illustrations were incomplete, but near the back, were two beautiful illustrations: one of their beloved Mrs. Potter—the piece Bruce had seen him working on over Thanksgiving—and a portrait of Nicole, an exact replica of the photo on the mantel, dated June 2016.

"It's really something, isn't it," Bruce says, wrapping his arms around her shoulders. "He really did have an extraordinary ability to take any old pencil and a blank sheet of paper, and to create something incredible, didn't he?"

49

ANN

She steps forward, stands face to face with their daughter. Her chest is still, a held breath trapped for one... two... three long seconds.

She's never seen anything like it. It's an image she's seen so many times that she's stopped seeing it, but he'd captured every detail. She'd been so mad at him for taking her new camera that day—until she checked the memory card a few months later and found just one photo: an action shot of Nicole riding her bike, her open-mouthed smile framed by the wispy blonde hair peeking out from under her helmet. There's something different in the way Evann has portrayed it here; she can almost hear Nicole's squeal, can see the unbridled joy in her daughter's young eyes.

Her legs wobble beneath her. She feels like she might be sick, like she might faint. She's manufactured so many reasons to hate her son —most of which she can no longer remember. Those she can remember no longer seem justified.

It had seemed so black and white; she was just trying to protect her daughter. She'd convinced herself that meant keeping Evann away, and it was a price she'd been willing to pay.

Of course she'd suspected that Evann was in trouble long before Nicole came to her. What mother wouldn't see the bags under his eyes, the weight loss, the irregular sleep pattern? What woman wouldn't notice a diamond missing from her side table? But there had been so many reasons not to do anything about it.

For starters, who in their right mind would ever willingly admit that their kid is a junkie? Not only would it be humiliating, it would also be ridiculous to expect anything other than judgment from their friends and family. It's not as though they would receive compassion —not for an ailment their son had brought on himself. No one made him do drugs. He played with fire, and he got burnt.

More than anything, she'd worried what impact it would have on Nicole. It's one thing to grow up in the same house with a weird older brother, but imagine if her friends—her dance academy—had known that her brother was one of those whacked-out bums littering the streets—leeching off the system. Admitting Evann had a problem would only risk Nicole's future, and Ann hadn't been willing to let that happen. She did what she had to do to protect her family—to protect her daughter.

But had she taken it too far? She never intended to drive a wedge between the kids—just to get Nicole to back off, to let Evann go about his life, whatever the consequences might be. The idea started as a seedling, but before she could step back, could take stock of what it might grow into, it spread out of control. She weaved such an intricate tale—a tangle of fact and fiction, confusing her own childhood and Nicole's, her brother from her son—that she no longer has a firm grasp on the truth.

Ann staggers over to Evann's bed, takes hold of his hand, and falls to her knees. Bruce pulls the door closed behind him, leaves her alone.

Alone to make her amends. To apologize to the boy who never had a chance, the boy whose tragic story began the day he was born to the wrong mother. To beg her dead son for the forgiveness he'll never get the opportunity to grant.

50

NICOLE

Nicole strokes the dog's ears as she snores, her heavy head in her lap. Mrs. Potter isn't really supposed to be up on the couch, but what does it matter now? She stares at her cellphone, one minute sliding into the next. Her parents are at the hospital, and that means that every second that passes is a second closer to the end of her brother's life.

They didn't ask her if she wanted to be there. They probably assumed she didn't have the stomach for it; probably thought she'd have another freakout.

But that's only because they don't know she can handle it.

They don't know what she's capable of—what she's done to protect her family.

They don't know that she was there the last time.

She's already watched her brother die once.

———

There wasn't a cloud in the sky the day she met Evann in the park, the sun warm against her bare arms. She slipped off her flip-flops, closed her eyes, and let her toes sink into the freshly cut lawn, breathing in the smells of spring as she ran through her choreography in her head. *Step, kick, ball change, pivot, turn, chasse, step, leap...*

Deep in her visualization, his voice startled her. Had she not heard him first, she wouldn't have recognized the gaunt-faced man in the thick hoodie as her brother. In hindsight, she probably should've left right then, but she'd already gone to the trouble, and she figured it would be a small price to pay to get him to leave her alone.

She should've known he couldn't be trusted with that amount of money. She really, *really* should've known. And perhaps she did. Perhaps that's why she met him in the first place, why she answered his desperate call. Whether out of selfishness or pity, it doesn't matter now.

———

She didn't expect it would happen that fast. Goodbyes not yet exchanged before he pulled out his phone. A frenzied text sent. An instant response received. A reticent excuse. He had somewhere to be. They shared a rigid embrace with the inappropriateness and unfamiliarity of strangers. He whispered into her hair, but she pretended not to hear. "I know what you think of me, but I swear to God, Nic, none of it's true. You've gotta believe me." She pushed him away, unable to stand the smell of unwashed skin any longer.

Unable to fight the impulse to *know*, she trailed him.

She watched as he greedily stashed the money away. With all he had left strapped to his back, he made his way through the park to the vacant swing set. A chance encounter—entirely on purpose—with a well-dressed man, his attire far too juvenile for his apparent age.

Her heart raced. Her breath caught in her chest. Time slowed as she watched.

Money exchanged, the merchandise handed over with expert discretion.

A short walk up to the lookout point, the sun creeping toward the horizon.

Time passed slowly. She began to wonder if she'd miscalculated him, misunderstood his motivations, his intentions. He spent a long time looking out at the ocean, fussing in his bag, flipping through old sketches before he finally emptied that tiny package—spent it in his nose.

She held her breath as he nodded off, the rise and fall of his chest slowing. Slowing. Slowing.

A life there. And then gone.

She didn't mean to. Or, rather, not to. Perhaps she should've done something. Jumped into action. Played the hero.

But she didn't. She stood there—frozen in place.

Perhaps it's better this way.

Caught in a tornado of conflicting emotions—disgust, relief, sorrow, pity—she rushed away, whispering her secret into the soft breeze, words never to be spoken again.

The dog startles awake when Nicole's alarm sounds at precisely eight o'clock. They'll be taking him into the operating room now, preparing to cut him open. Twenty years of life amounting to nothing more than a series of organs to be recycled.

Goodbye, brother.

A NOTE

This book is a work of fiction. I am not an expert in addictions medicine or policy, and I encourage you to seek out information around these issues from people who have dedicated their careers to this field. There are many, but I've learned an incredible amount from the works of Dr. Gabor Maté and Benjamin Perrin, in particular.

I'd like to share a bit about the inspiration behind Evann's story. In 2017 through 2019, I was working as a Registered Nurse in an Intensive Care Unit. Our ICU was seeing a steady stream of patients after toxic drug overdoses—everyone from casual weekend partiers, to street-entrenched individuals with long-standing addiction issues. Sometimes, we were seeing the same people readmitted after subsequent resuscitations. I was burnt-out, and surrounded by other professionals fighting compassion fatigue. While the vast majority of my colleagues were outwardly professional, there were those who still held antiquated beliefs, still used harmful terms like "junkie", and continued to discuss drug use in terms of choice rather than dependence.

Meanwhile—and unbeknownst to all but my closest friends—my

father was battling his own addiction. At the time, I didn't understand how the man I'd looked up to—the man who had coached me in hockey, the man who had worked his entire life to provide for his family, only to have it all slip away—could be the same man living in his car, battling first a cocaine, then a methamphetamine, habit. I picked up Dr. Gabor Maté's book, *In the Realm of Hungry Ghosts: Close Encounters with Addiction*, and to be frank, it changed my perspective on addiction. What I came to learn was that my dad—like so many others—was self-medicating to cope in the only way he knew how.

My dad was fortunate. The stars aligned and a publicly-funded treatment bed opened at a time when he was willing to accept help. On September 13, 2023, he celebrated five years of sobriety. Tragically, Evann's story—like so many others—does not have a happy ending. In April 2016, a Public Health Emergency was declared in British Columbia. Since then, over 12000 individuals have died from toxic drug overdoses in my home province. The statistics are staggering, but numbers are easy to ignore. I hope that as tough conversations around decriminalization and safe supply continue, you think of the people like Evann—each with a story to tell—and consider not how policy change might impact you, but how it might be life saving for them.

If you or someone you know is struggling with substance use or mental health issues, please reach out.
Centre for Addiction and Mental Health (Canada)
Substance Abuse and Mental Health Services Association (USA)

Suggested readings:

In the Realm of Hungry Ghosts: Close Encounters with Addiction by Dr. Gabor Maté

Overdose: Heartbreak and Hope in Canada's Opioid Crisis by Benjamin Perrin

Fighting for Space by Travis Lupick

Empire of Pain: The Secret History of the Sackler Dynasty by Patrick Radden Keefe

ACKNOWLEDGMENTS

I'd still be sitting around in my housecoat dreaming about what it would be like to write a novel, if not for the endless love and support of my husband, Josh. Thanks to his encouragement and the countless hours he spent talking through my jumbled ideas, I was finally able to put Evann's story on paper. In my housecoat.

Not everyone can fact-check drug use and street life nuances with their dad, but I'm thankful I can. Thankful my dad lived to tell the tale, and thankful that he's since dedicated his life to helping others experiencing addiction.

I'm eternally indebted to the group of incredibly talented and generous people who I'm lucky enough to call my friends:

Josh, who keeps me fed and caffeinated, makes sure I put real clothes on every once in a while, and has read the manuscript more times than any spouse should have to.

My beta-readers: Mike, Simone, Saundra, Ruth, Randi, Ashley, Madelaine, Riley, and Christina. Their generosity and feedback encouraged me to keep going.

My very humble—and outstandingly talented—friend, Mike, who deciphered my scribbles and a few inspiration photos, and illustrated the stunning cover for *Less Than*. He, along with Simone and Josh, patiently participated in many Doughnut & Design Meetings while I struggled to explain my vision. Check out his other work @michaelbernierart on Instagram.

My extraordinary proof-readers—Sara, Alex, and Joanne—who answered my frantic call and graciously dropped everything to read the entire manuscript in the two days before my deadline.

My ever-patient friend, Kevin, who is always ready to help with tech—(user error)—issues, and Randi, who is forever willing to offer her keen design eye.

My other friends, family, and co-workers—too many to name—who have shared so much enthusiasm for this project, and have been there to cheer me on along the way.

A special thank you to Daniel, who went above and beyond his role as audiobook narrator, bringing the characters to life with his years of experience working in the Downtown Eastside.

Finally, thank you to my editor, Heather Sangster, who tirelessly poured through the manuscript, caught every loose thread, and helped polish *Less Than* into something I'm proud to be sharing with you.

ABOUT THE AUTHOR

Alyssa holds a Bachelor of Science in Nursing Degree from Vancouver Island University, and has worked as a Registered Nurse for over a decade. She and her high school sweetheart are avid travellers, currently living in the beautiful Okanagan Valley.

Less Than is her debut novel.

For more information, visit adlongbooks.ca

Manufactured by Amazon.ca
Acheson, AB

11355221R00173